Don't miss these other exciting titles by bestselling author

Vickie McKeehan

The Pelican Pointe Series
PROMISE COVE
HIDDEN MOON BAY
DANCING TIDES
LIGHTHOUSE REEF
STARLIGHT DUNES
LAST CHANCE HARBOR
SEA GLASS COTTAGE
LAVENDER BEACH
SANDCASTLES UNDER THE CHRISTMAS MOON
BENEATH WINTER SAND
KEEPING CAPE SUMMER (2018)

The Evil Secrets Trilogy
JUST EVIL Book One
DEEPER EVIL Book Two
ENDING EVIL Book Three
EVIL SECRETS TRILOGY BOXED SET

The Skye Cree Novels
THE BONES OF OTHERS
THE BONES WILL TELL
THE BOX OF BONES
HIS GARDEN OF BONES
TRUTH IN THE BONES
SEA OF BONES (2018)

The Indigo Brothers Trilogy
INDIGO FIRE
INDIGO HEAT
INDIGO JUSTICE
INDIGO BROTHERS TRILOGY BOXED SET

Coyote Wells Mysteries
MYSTIC FALLS
SHADOW CANYON
SPIRIT LAKE (2018)

His Garden of Bones

A Skye Cree Novel

VICKIE McKEEHAN

beachdevils
PRESS

His Garden of Bones
A Skye Cree Novel

Published by Beachdevils Press
Copyright © 2015 Vickie McKeehan

His Garden of Bones
A Skye Cree Novel
Copyright © 2015 Vickie McKeehan

This book is a work of fiction. The characters, incidents, and dialogue are drawn from the author's imagination and are not to be construed as real. Any resemblance to actual events or persons, living or dead, is entirely coincidental.

Published by
beachdevils
PRESS

ISBN-10: 0692426043
ISBN-13: 978-0692426043
Printed in the USA
Cover design by Vanessa Mendozzi
Wolf designed by Jess Johnson
All Titles Available at Amazon

Visit the author at:
www.vickiemckeehan.com
www.facebook.com/VickieMcKeehan
http://vickiemckeehan.wordpress.com/
www.twitter.com/VickieMcKeehan

ACKNOWLEDGMENTS
For Gene,
the only one who encouraged me
to follow my dream

Into the darkness they go,
the wise and the lovely.

Edna St. Vincent Millay

His Garden of Bones

A Skye Cree Novel

VICKIE McKEEHAN

beachdevils
PRESS

Prologue

Fifteen years earlier
Pocatello, Idaho

An Easter cold snap had moved through the Snake River Plain the previous night, blanketing the area with two feet of snow. Though the storm had dumped a generous helping of the white stuff all over the playground, by mid-morning kids in the Fairwood section of the city had come out to take advantage of what was probably the last snowfall of the season.

On this Saturday just before the holiday the children donned their winter gear—wool caps, mittens, scarves, and warm coats. Noisy laughter filled the park as the rambunctious youngsters fought over swings, climbed on jungle gyms, and slid down slides—all except for Dillard Barstow.

Dillard sat off to one side by himself. The tall, lanky teen studied the other kids while sketching on the pad he took everywhere with him. He watched as the kids paired off into groups. Some played a game of tag while others tossed a football back and forth. He'd always been reluctant to join in with the classmates he'd known since kindergarten. None of the activity interested the skinny boy who was a little too tall for his age anyway. Despite his height, he'd never been athletic and because of that fact he made sure he steered clear of the jocks. Truth be told, Dillard steered clear of most people. He tried to avoid going home where his father often called him a wuss and gave him grief. As bad as his father was, his mother was much worse. She liked to bully everyone around her. Dillard seemed to be her favorite target.

Maybe that's why the boy chose the path of least resistance. Dillard would simply evade any situation that might end up in a confrontation. There was no need to go looking for trouble when he could find plenty of it at home.

To his credit, the shy, troubled fourteen-year-old was known among his teachers for his smarts and artistic talent. No one in town would likely put Dillard Barstow in the category of ball-busting bruiser.

Today, he stationed himself near the sandbox where he could keep an eye on pretty Camilla Prentiss, the dark-haired girl with hair so black it gave off an almost purple glow. He loved all that hair and how soft it looked.

She'd brought her little brother along to play in the dirt while she leaned back against a tree to read one of the Harry Potter books he'd seen her check out at the library. Several months back she'd caught his attention because she lived two streets over from him on Maplewood. The lovely Camilla had been on his radar ever since.

This morning he didn't mind the little boy so much as long as he got to see the girl of his dreams. At eleven, Camilla was three years younger than he was. Despite their age difference, there was something about the way she carried herself that made him realize they were destined to be together. He liked to watch her from a distance. Getting to know her wasn't an option. He dared not approach her for fear of rejection. He was far too timid to engage in an actual conversation. But he couldn't deny the crush he had on her. He'd heard other kids at school, girls mostly, use that word when they really liked someone. Girls often talked about their "crushes" during lunch or before school or they snickered about it on the bus.

But it was a different story with eight-grade boys, like him. Sometimes in gym class the guys used much stronger language. Even in the boys' bathrooms, Dillard had overheard crude remarks when the others didn't know he was listening. That's when it had happened. That's when he realized what he'd like to do to Camilla.

He didn't need to talk to her. For the past six months he'd been keeping track of everywhere she went and everything she did by following her around the neighborhood whenever he got the chance. That's how he knew everything there was to know about Camilla Prentiss.

There'd been the time last summer when he'd stationed himself outside her bedroom window while she slept. He'd stayed there for hours and hours and been lucky enough to see her get up to go to the bathroom. His stakeout had lasted until four-thirty that morning. That perfect time right before the sun came up when he'd had to leave to get ready to go to church.

From that day forward, he'd trailed after her on her trips to the mall, then again each time she walked to the store for her mother. He knew for a fact that just recently she'd started babysitting on a limited basis for the Grainger family. The Graingers lived a block over on Cedar Ridge and whenever Mr. and Mrs. Grainger went out to dinner on Saturday nights, Camilla looked after the couple's baby daughter. He knew because he'd kept a vigil outside the living room window. Once, he'd almost gotten caught when the Graingers had returned earlier than planned. Since their meal out had lasted no more than ninety minutes, he hadn't had the time to work up his courage to act, to do what he wanted to do with Camilla.

That's why tonight would be special. He'd see to it.

For weeks now, he'd felt the change occurring inside him. He'd recognized the signs building. His urges had grown stronger and stronger. If his control slipped, he knew there would be no turning back. Up to now, it had taken a tremendous amount of effort to lock away his burning fury. But with each tick of the clock, he felt himself losing ground, losing another inch on the tether that held him back from opening that door. He saw a sliver of blinding light and knew full well he had no choice but to break through the barrier to get to the other side.

He glanced over at the other kids to see if anyone had noticed him. As usual, no one had. For much of his life Dillard Barstow had been an invisible entity. So far, he'd been lucky. No one had caught on to the seething rage inside.

Dillard was fed up with it all. Tonight he would release all those feelings he'd kept under wraps for so long. Tonight would be his inaugural run.

After an hour or so, he watched Camilla gather up her little brother and walk off down the street, heading back to her house.

For now, he made himself sit like a statue to keep from going after her. Now wouldn't work. Following her might tip his hand. Broad daylight wasn't the best time to act. The little brother would surely get in the way and need to be dealt with. So he would wait for her to walk over to her babysitting job at the Graingers'.

Tonight he'd let loose his inner demons. His heart beat faster just thinking about it.

Glancing down at the Timex on his wrist, he counted the hours until Camilla would leave her house. He'd have to bide his time till then. In the meantime, there were a hundred things he needed to do to get ready. He would go over his plan until he left nothing to chance.

That afternoon, he prepared right up to suppertime when he packed a satchel and snuck out of his house at six-thirty on the dot. Since his parents were headed to a planned event at church and would be there until ten that night, he had more than ample time to spend with Camilla.

It took him seven minutes to walk over to Cedar Ridge. Once he reached the Graingers' single-story home, the first thing he noticed was that the couple's car wasn't parked in the driveway. Panic set in. How long had the Graingers been gone? If they usually stayed out for an hour and a half—as his frequent late-night skulking in the shadows said they did—the clock had already started ticking.

Damn his mother for making him clean his room. If he'd been able to leave earlier he would've been here to note the exact time they'd backed out of the driveway. Now he wasn't exactly certain how long he had to get inside.

Taking several deep breaths to settle down, he needed to get his mind back on the prize. He had to get a grip—with his first kill he was bound to make a few mistakes.

Okay, so Camilla was already inside alone with the baby. But since the Graingers ate a meal with lightning speed, he had to work fast. He'd have to step up his plan of action because they'd be coming back soon enough.

That kind of thinking had him moving his ass around to the back of the house. He peered through the window of the baby's room, the window he'd already broken the lock on, two nights before. The little girl wasn't in her crib yet. He couldn't see or hear anyone around, so he lifted the frame of the glass and scuttled over the ledge, dropping onto the floor. Without a sound, he scurried on all fours into the closet before Camilla caught him—and slid the mirrored door almost closed.

Impatient, he waited, watching through the slice of an opening he'd left.

His wait lasted so long he thought about crawling back out through the window. But then he heard footsteps coming down the hallway toward him and hoped it wasn't the Graingers.

Through the crack, he saw Camilla come into the room to tuck the sleeping child into bed. He watched as Camilla pulled the blanket over the baby. The moment she turned to go, he burst out of his hiding place, jumping her from behind. Camilla twisted and fought but he managed to cover her mouth with his hand and tackle her to the floor. Straddling her, he tried to keep one hand over her mouth while she bucked and struggled. Afraid of losing the upper hand, he reached for the first thing that had weight to it—a small wooden rocking horse. He brought it down over Camilla's skull. The force of the blow knocked her out. But he knew it wouldn't last for long.

Knowing he needed to hurry, he pulled Camilla down the hallway into the living room and continued dragging her across to the kitchen. He threw back the door and pulled her out onto the back patio. He left her there on the concrete long enough to go retrieve the bag he'd left under the windowsill.

When he noticed Camilla was coming to, he took out the roll of duct tape, yanked off a strip and stuck it across her mouth so she couldn't scream. He dug out the rope, used it to wrap around her wrists.

Camilla started crying. But he'd prepared for that. Annoyed with her, he grabbed the flashlight he'd brought and used it to hit her on the head again. He jerked the groggy, injured girl to her feet and forced her to walk across the yard.

If he didn't want to get caught, they had to get moving and fast. Using the massive oak trees as cover, he tugged her along behind him. The two slogged through wet leaves and mud left over from the nasty weather the night before.

Because he had a particular destination in mind, he took off through the verdant forest of conifers using the zig-zag pattern he'd practiced many times before. Using the beam from the flashlight, he had no problem finding his way in the dark to the hiking trail behind the subdivision. The path would eventually lead to the isolated, rugged terrain at the foot of Bonneville Peak.

The darkness slowed down their progress but not enough for him to stop short of his destination.

He stuck to the plan.

Soon the fast-moving current of the river caught his attention as it churned with the new rainwater from yesterday's storm. The sound of the stream told him they were almost there. The summer he'd turned twelve, he'd discovered one of the best places to retreat, a small natural cavern in the side of a rock formation. Secluded, the cave made for a perfect hideout.

Camilla put up a fuss when they had to cross the brook, but he slapped her to get her moving again. From there he pinpointed the exact spot where the embankment sloped upward. Dragging Camilla up the steep hill, he looked for where the landscape leveled off, searching for the place in the cliff that formed the opening. He felt along the uneven rough wall until his hand hit air. He shoved Camilla inside the cold damp cave and watched as she stumbled. The girl went down on both knees.

That monster he'd carried inside him for so long roared through him like a raging beast. Before he knew what was happening he struck her in the head with his flashlight. Her body dropped to the cold, hard ground.

To his surprise the first trickle of blood seduced him in a way he hadn't expected. Wanting more, he hit her in the head again and then rolled her over so he could see her face, her eyes. He pounced on the top of her chest, yanked off the strip of duct tape from around her mouth so he could touch his lips to hers. Clumsily he tried to kiss her. But when she turned her head away from him, he punished her by poking his finger into one of her eye sockets. The girl struggled and tried to get away, but with her hands tied with rope she had difficulty making any real progress.

Dillard, larger and motivated, caught up with her and used his body to keep her pinned down.

While the circle of light glowed from his flashlight, while shadows skipped on the cave wall, he let his fingers do the rest as they wrapped around the girl's throat. He held on—tight, tighter, refusing to let go of little Camilla.

It seemed like it took all his strength to squeeze hard enough until she stopped fighting him.

When he realized she'd grown still, he reached around her body and brought her up against his chest. As he watched Camilla take her final gasp of air, he vowed to find her a special place, a place that only he would ever know about.

With one hand, he stroked her hair, his fingers becoming bloody from the gaping damage he'd done to her head. He realized then he'd never forget the silky texture of all that raven black hair or the fragrance from the scented shampoo she'd used earlier.

He sniffed the air again, found the smell of blood and death intoxicating, far more so than he'd fantasized about. He closed his eyes, but not against the reeking stench. He chose instead to suck in the deep breaths of the floral scent he imagined. The aroma of Camilla, the whiff of the flowers he envisioned would stick with him always. It would remind him of fragrant purple blossoms, like sweet perfume. He tightened his grip on the strands of Camilla's raven locks so that he could bring her closer. Awkwardly he planted a kiss on her lips, as they turned colder and bluer. He moved his hand across one breast just beginning to pop out, finding it harder than he'd thought.

Rocking back and forth, his mind captured every nuance of the moment. Maybe because he knew that from this night forward he would forever measure success by his precious little Camilla. He would treasure every minute, replay every part over and over again for later. He sat back taking in the delectable shade of her hair. She was like a delicate bud, a fragile blossom he would shape into his own. He would plant Camilla in a garden of his very own, the one he would create, create just for his raven-haired beauty.

As he looked around his sanctuary, the walls of the cave suddenly began to close in around him. But he took comfort in the fact that he was no longer alone. He'd never be alone again, not with Camilla here next to him.

Because Camilla he would keep with him forever.

Chapter One

Three weeks before Christmas
Seattle, Washington

Tall and lean, Skye Cree walked between towering high-rises that speared the night sky like giant peaks of steel. Along the dark streets she made her way west toward the harbor. The gentle waves of Puget Sound lapped against the docks as she stepped onto the pier to look out on what she considered her turf.

Night, and all it held, encompassed the woman who wore black from head to toe—a turtleneck and snug pants under a long leather coat, high-top combat boots on her feet, and a watch cap tucked over her raven hair. The attire meant she was dressed to move. Her athletic skill, practiced and refined from the age of eighteen, meant she could defend herself in a fight, and often did.

With a weariness that came from an all-day hunt, she climbed to the highest point of the jetty and looked back at the skyline then out to sea. She scanned the massive expanse of coastal water.

Her flawless Native American looks blended with the darkness around her except for one distinctive feature, a trait she'd inherited from her mother. Her violet eyes were usually the first thing anyone noticed. Their deep purple color radiated out into the black of night allowing her to home in on any movement close by.

From her spot above the wharf, she had a great view of the bay but more important the row of lofts and warehouses where trouble tended to find its way inside. With low-hanging clouds overhead, she studied a heavier than usual fog rolling in, the mist so dense at times it twisted and turned like a thick tangle of knotted rope.

She tried to block out the noisy boat traffic in the bay but with ships, ferries, and tankers from all over the world vying for shipping lanes, but it was almost impossible.

As if on cue, the captain of a passing ship laid down on the horn, blasting the air three times signaling it neared one of the buoys in the channel. The sound echoed back on shore loud and clear, enough that Kiya, Skye's Nez Perce spirit guide, growled into the foggy night. The snarl from the wolf set off Atka, the companionable malamute puppy that yipped in response.

Skye snapped her fingers to shush the din so that she could hear farther down the row of abandoned warehouses. For the last half hour, Kiya and Atka had been on the scent of…something. The canines had tracked what Skye hoped was the fourteen-year-old girl who'd gone missing that afternoon from the local mall. Gwen DeLargo hadn't been seen since noon that day, when the teen had met up with her running buddies from school, only to disappear after a trip to the restroom shortly after lunch. Gwen's friends had notified Security.

While detective Harry Drummond and his cronies concentrated on surveillance cameras, Skye had hit the streets. Backed by the Artemis Foundation, the hunter had rallied her own set of friends and family to get the word out, to get flyers printed and distributed in record time.

Skye lifted her head, breathed in several puffs of chilly air before taking in the sounds of urban living—the bus coming to a stop at the corner, the commuter train pulling into the station to the east, no doubt the last one of the night. She caught sight of the hot dog vendor packing up his cart at the corner of Madison and Western, the steam still rising from the trailer.

At that moment, the sound of a car engine caused her eyes to dart southward. She sharpened her gaze to the lone man slamming the doors as he got out of a white paneled van. Under any other set of circumstances that was no big deal. But a white van had been seen speeding away from the parking lot at the mall around the same time Gwen had disappeared.

Skye centered her focus on the forty-something man, who stood about five-nine. There was something about the sneaky way he jumped out of the front seat and looked around to make sure he was alone—almost as though he had something to hide.

She watched as the man slid open the side doors, reached his arm inside, pulled out a roll of carpet padding and dumped it on the ground before turning back to grab something else from the back.

Even though it was an odd time of night to be catching up on installing carpet, Skye decided the guy fit the neighborhood. The older, rundown area wasn't that different from other sections of town trying to remodel and upgrade the buildings. And God knew this part of town could use a little sprucing up.

She heard herself let out a heavy sigh. It wasn't exactly relief, more like frustration. Pivoting on her heels to head the other way, she signaled to the animals to follow. But when both canines stubbornly kept eyeing the van, she turned back to stare at what captured their attention. It was in that split second that she noticed he brought out a huge comforter and tossed it over his shoulder. Skye could've sworn she saw the blanket wiggle. Whatever was in there, or rather whoever, seemed to be squirming to get out.

Skye's mouth went dry. After an all-day search for Gwen, could it be this simple?

She automatically reached for her nightstick and went flying down the path to the concrete viaduct below, Kiya and Atka on her heels. The wolf and malamute soon took the lead, covering the distance faster than she could. Soon all three were able to burst out of the greenbelt and onto the pavement and into the man's line of vision. The confrontation startled the carpet layer who tightened his hold on the bundle he held.

"Who are you?" the guy asked. "Where the hell did you come from?"

"The more important question is what's in your blanket? Why would it be moving like someone's struggling to get free? And why are you doing your best to conceal what's in there?"

About that time, Skye heard a muffled groan coming from the dirty, stained comforter.

"Now see, that's weird. Your haul shouldn't be moaning. So let's make this simple. Just set the bedding down on the ground and step back."

"Who do you think you are? Dirty Harry? Who's gonna make me? You? I don't think so."

"Really? You're planning to push this when my feet are killing me? Okay, but that makes you more than a pervert. It makes you an idiot."

Challenged, the man dropped the bedding and reached toward his waistband. Skye saw the glint of a pistol. Before he could take hold of the weapon, she whirled and brought her boot down on top of his foot. She rammed one elbow into his gut, threw her forearm backward and put a fist into his nose. She angled into a turn, brought her knee up to his crotch.

While he doubled over in pain, Skye whacked him over the head with her nightstick. He dropped like a rock.

She bent down and snatched up the weapon, a twenty-two caliber Smith & Wesson he'd stuffed down his pants. For safekeeping, she slipped the small handgun into the top of her boot.

In four long strides, Kiya stood over the man's chest, ready to rip out his throat.

"Good girl," Skye told the wolf. "Atka, come on, girl, get over here and latch onto his pants leg for me and don't let go." The malamute didn't have to be told twice, clamping a set of sharp teeth into the man's jeans narrowly missing his skin.

Skye stroked her fingers through canine fur while noting the overriding fear in the man's eyes. Even the blood coming from his busted nose wasn't enough to garner any sympathy. "What do you suppose we have here? What type of sick beast is this?"

Bleeding and winded, the man groused, "I didn't do a thing. Get these filthy dogs off me. They're the beasts, dirty, filthy, smelly animals! Get 'em off me!"

Looking down on the man they'd been after all day, Skye studied the suspect, decided to put a great big ding in his bravado. "Her name's Kiya. In case you haven't noticed, Kiya's a wolf and will rip out your throat quicker than you can take your next breath."

Just as she'd hoped, his face went whiter. She reached out, took the man's chin in her hand to turn his head from side to side. "My, my, what are all these scratches doing all over your face? I know I didn't put those there. Let's see if we can find out who did."

He slapped her hand away and said, "I got a cat at home."

"Sure you do. Keep an eye on this sick excuse for a human being, will you, Kiya? He tries to bolt, you have my permission to take a bite out of his jugular."

The wolf obediently sunk a pair of incisors into the first layer of the guy's skin at the neck.

When the bundle in the blanket on the ground began to groan louder, Skye walked over and knelt down to peel the layers back on the comforter. She uncovered a dazed and frightened teenage girl with brown hair and huge glassy brown eyes. No surprise that the description fit her missing teenager.

"Hey there. Gwen DeLargo, right? A lot of people have been looking for you."

"They have? Help me," the girl sputtered out, struggling to raise her hand high enough so she could point a finger in the direction of her kidnapper. "He did things to me. Help me. Please."

The girl's glassy eyes and slurred speech indicated the teen had been drugged. Listening to those all-important first words from a victim, Skye knew she needed to sear them to memory for later—the legalities ever-present on her mind to get a conviction and make it stick.

Skye removed her cell phone, punched in a number she had on speed dial and began trying to comfort the young girl while she waited for an answer on the other end. "Rest easy, he'll pay for what he did. Count on it."

When her friend and cohort picked up, Skye relayed their location to detective Harry Drummond. "I've found Gwen DeLargo and the bastard who took her. Get here fast with the paramedics else I'll have to get her to the ER on my own."

"I'm on my way. Don't do anything you'll regret later," Harry warned.

Skye shot a look over in Kiya's direction. The wolf, with the help of the malamute, had been vigilant at keeping the suspect on his best behavior. So far.

"Where's the fun in that?" Skye asked dryly. But even with the jab, she added, "I've done this before, Harry. I know the drill by now."

"Good. Then I'm on my way."

After disconnecting the call, Skye looked over at the frightened teen. "Help's coming."

"It's already here. Thank you. You know who I am?"

"Sure. Your picture's been all over the news all day."

"It has? How did you find me?"

"I have my sneaky, covert ways," Skye said with amusement, doing her best to get the girl to relax, which she knew was damned near impossible after the scum-sucker had put her through an all-day ordeal.

"Does it have anything to do with that white wolf over there?"

Skye lifted a brow in surprise. "You can see the white wolf? I'm impressed. Not everyone does."

"I see the wolf, I see the dog, too. Unless I'm seeing double."

"Nope. There's two. They work as a team. Kiya's the leader of the pack and the one that found you. Atka is still just a puppy and pretty much follows wherever Kiya goes, although she does have great instincts."

"Kiya's beautiful. Her eyes are like violet. They match yours. You both have gorgeous eyes. I love wolves."

Skye sent the confused girl a wide smile. "Funny about that, I do too."

But just as Skye thought everything was going well, Gwen rolled herself in a ball and began to sob. Skye wrapped the teen up, rocked her back and forth, and listened while Gwen went into a rambling recount of her day.

"I just wanted to go shopping for a new outfit that I could wear to a party I was going to this weekend. I just wanted to spend the day with my friends. Now look at me. I'm bloody and sore and I feel just awful."

"I know, honey. The monsters out there have a way of finding you when you're most vulnerable, alone, and off-guard. He singled you out among a sea of people. You did nothing wrong. It wasn't your fault. You need to believe that. Before you know it, things will be back to normal. In a few hours you'll see your family. I promise. Everything will work out. Your life will get back to normal and you'll be fine."

"No, it won't."

"Sure it will. Don't let this cause you to feel like it's the end of the world. It isn't. You survived."

"Thanks to you." Gwen took a shaky breath. "Don't leave me though, okay? Please."

"I'm right here. I'll ride with you to the hospital if that's what you want."

"What about the wolf?"

"Kiya? She knows her way home."

"And Atka?"

"Like I said, Atka will follow Kiya wherever the wolf decides to go." As sirens blared from down the street, getting closer, Skye added, "Hear that? That's my cue to get over there and relieve Kiya from her guard dog duty."

"He raped me," Gwen announced.

Skye squeezed Gwen's shoulders tighter and held on. "I figured that out. Talking about it sometimes helps. Once you get to the hospital, the police will ask you a bunch of questions. After that, there will be someone there asking you if you want counseling. Take them up on it. Your family will be so worried about you, they'll make every effort possible to help you any way they can. And remember, everyone handles this kind of thing differently. Me? I prefer taking names and kicking ass."

Understanding finally appeared in Gwen's puffy eyes. "This happened to you?"

"It did. I was much younger than you are now. Not only did I survive I got stronger every day."

"Oh my God, really? You aren't just making this up to make me feel better, are you?"

"Would I be out here wandering the streets in the middle of the night looking for you if I was just making it up?"

"I guess not. You saved me."

"I'll kick his ass again if you want me to," Skye offered with a wink. She lifted Gwen's chin so she could look into the girl's eyes. "Or just say the word and I'll hold him down while you give him something to whine about while he's waiting for his bail hearing. It'll be fun. I'll tell the cops he provoked us," she added with a smile to lighten the somber mood.

But when Skye saw the fear come into the teen's eyes at the words "bail hearing," she tabled the snarky veneer and opted for solace instead. "Don't worry. The judge will keep this loser in jail and deny his bail. He's headed for a cozy cell in County."

"Are you sure about that?"

"Positive. Look, I need to get over to this guy now and make sure he doesn't try to take off before he makes a move on Kiya and I have to watch my wolf tear him to shreds. Not a bad idea but I promised to give up excessive force. Besides, I'll keep him as far away from you as I can while I'm making sure he doesn't get his throat ripped out. How's that?"

"I don't want you to leave me but I don't want him to get away either." When Skye let her go, the girl quickly huddled into another ball.

But by that time an ambulance rolled up and then a squad car followed. Harry Drummond's city-issued, unmarked SUV pulled to a stop behind the police cruiser.

"Ain't that just like the cops?" Skye kidded. "You sit here and wait for one, and then they all show up at once."

Skye felt Gwen tense up as Harry dragged the suspect up off the pavement and put him in cuffs. The paramedics swarmed and with some reluctance, Skye handed Gwen over to their care. "I'll be right over here while they take a look at you."

"Ride with me to the hospital, okay?"

"You bet."

Skye left Gwen temporarily to meet up with Harry on the sidewalk. "How's it going?"

"Better now. Nice work. His driver's license says his name is Mark Brantley. He keeps going on and on about a white wolf practically sitting on his chest and attacking his jugular."

Skye rolled her eyes, flicked a glance at the spot where Brantley stood. "I don't see a pool of blood or a wolf, do you? The only canine here is Atka and she's obviously a dog. Besides, you know how these criminal types are so delusional that they make stuff up when they get nabbed. It's actually very scary. You should do something about that."

Harry chuckled, tossing Brantley a look of disdain. "Yeah. Right. Just so you know, I got a call right after yours. A jogger found the body of another young woman tonight, dumped in an alleyway behind a retail shop in University Village. I'm afraid this one's a real bad guy, Skye."

"They're all really bad guys, Harry. How young is this victim? Does she fall into the age group of the others?"

"Don't know yet. I'm reserving judgment until I see for myself."

"Isn't U-Village a little too trendy and upscale for the guy who cut up those other two victims? Damn, I was having such a great night, too. Sounds like he might be trying to get your attention."

"Or yours."

That had her mouth creasing into a frown. "Could be. What is that, the third one this month? As I recall, the others were found near The Jungle. You sure this is the same guy? Why use The Jungle twice but switch to a highly visible mall now?"

"You know as well as I do these assholes often change things up. Maybe tonight The Jungle was too crowded. Or maybe he wanted something more high profile. We'll know soon enough. But I'd say based on the description of the cut marks, it's the same killer. And get this, the RCMP in Vancouver, British Columbia, report they have another three missing girls there. That info came in this afternoon when we sent out the BOLO on Gwen."

"Damn. And we're still playing defense trying to figure out where he kept Carrie Montague and Taylor Dinsmore for two years before they both showed up dead last week."

"With breast implants cut out."

"Yeah, that detail's been bothering me. Neither girl had implants when she went missing. That had to happen during their confinement. What kind of plastic surgeon does augmentation on fifteen-year-olds anyway?"

"Some guy who takes the money and sleeps just fine at night because he doesn't give a damn about ethics."

"But even a reputable doc needs parental consent for plastic surgery performed on anyone under the age of eighteen. If I remember correctly from the files, Carrie and Taylor were only fifteen when they went missing."

Harry sent her a knowing look. "That's right. Not only that, but we're dealing with someone who gave them belly rings, tongue studs, and tattoos they didn't have when they disappeared."

"Which might indicate that we're dealing with a sex trafficker who sold them to a buyer. In turn, the buyer used them during the years they were gone, kept them in captivity, and then discarded them when he got tired of whatever they were doing to aggravate him. The bastard obviously wanted his girls to sport bigger boobs. What I can't figure out is why insist they get the implants in the first place and then cut them out? It doesn't make sense."

"Carrie and Taylor went missing a week apart. And then two years go by before they turn up dead a week apart. It's odd."

"Odd is an understatement. It makes no sense," Skye repeated.

"But then what about this business ever does? When you figure it out, be sure to let me know. As soon as I get this piece of shit that took Gwen booked and caged, I'm heading straight to U-Village. Meet me there."

Skye's shoulders drooped with fatigue. She'd been picturing her king-size bed back at home and how much she wanted to get to know it better. "And you're telling me this why? I have a bad feeling I already know."

"I want you there to see the crime scene firsthand this time around instead of just studying the photos."

Reluctantly she conceded it was true. "It's always better to see the real thing instead of photographs after the fact. Sure, I'll do it, but I promised Gwen I'd go with her to—"

"Then you should stay with her. While I'm doing the paperwork on Brantley, you spend some time with Gwen. Make her feel as comfortable as possible until her family gets to Harborview. Then we'll meet up at the crime scene. Here's the location." Harry held out his phone with the map already displayed onscreen.

Skye peered over, keyed in the info into her own phone for later. "Why not? With Josh out of town I've got nothing better to do than walk the streets at night and stay up twenty-four/seven without getting my beauty sleep."

Harry smiled again. "Josh must hate missing all this fun. When's the hubby due back anyway?"

"End of the week. These gamer conventions are a pain sometimes. This one's in New York, downtown Manhattan at the ritzy Belmont."

"Has the fact that you're married to an oversized kid escaped you?"

"Hardly."

"Isn't his new game featuring the hot, female, crime-fighting warrior debuting for real at this swanky event?"

Skye stifled a chuckle and rolled her eyes. "Yeah, for some reason it's his pride and joy. You and Elizabeth are coming to our Christmas party, right?"

"Wouldn't miss it. The wife's already bought a fancy dress. You know I'm giving up my badge for good at the end of the month. The thirty-first is officially my last day."

"So you've been saying for the last two years. If it's for real this time think of the party as a retirement bash. What will you do with all that time on your hands? Have you thought of that?"

"Sleep late, eat regular meals, maybe exercise. The wife's been bugging me about getting on the treadmill again. Maybe I'll try to eliminate the stress in my life."

This time, Skye laughed out loud. "Yeah. Right. Maybe in your dreams. Something tells me you have a very skewed view of retirement. I don't see you sitting around collecting a pension."

"I'm tired, Skye, fed up with the job."

"I hear ya. Oh look, the paramedics are loading Gwen up. I gotta go. See you in a couple hours."

Almost two hours later, Skye walked out of the ER and headed for her Subaru. Kiya and Atka were waiting for her next to the car.

She gave Kiya a stern look and said, "Nice trick, but you guys were supposed to go home. I'll be fine."

Kiya responded by nudging Skye's hand while Atka simply began licking all ten fingers. "Food and treats are at home, guys. Go home." When both animals refused to budge, Skye added, "Okay, okay, you're both trying to tell me something. I get it. But I'm headed to a secure area where cops will be everywhere. There's no point overreacting and worrying about me for no reason."

Her cell phone dinged. The readout let her know it was Josh. She shook her head at the timing certain it wasn't a coincidence—another worrywart to deal with. At times his innate connection to Kiya could be eerie at most, exasperating at the very least. But then what did she expect after his life-changing transformation? After putting him in harm's way, she couldn't really complain about his link to Kiya.

On the other end of the line Josh warned his wife as if he'd been eavesdropping on her debate with Kiya and

Atka. "Hey beautiful, listen to the mutts. They're usually right."

"It's maddening to know you heard that conversation from three thousand miles away."

"I wouldn't go that far but I worry. Besides, I find it incredibly sexy. Now if I could only see what you're wearing. I'm working on that. Although I have this tendency to picture you naked."

She burst out laughing, the tension of the day falling away. "I can't not go to the crime scene, Josh. Harry wants me to check it out for myself, give him my take. I said I'd do it. I can't back out now."

"You've got to be exhausted after searching all day for the DeLargo girl. The abduction made the Seattle newscast, which I make a habit of checking any time I go out of town. Finding Gwen, your rescue story, it already hit the Internet."

"How do they do that, upload the story so fast? If you read about it then you know I took care of the guy by myself. I'm just glad it's over and Gwen's alive. The upside is that finding Gwen made her parents elated with relief."

"You handled the guy like I would have. Look, I miss you. I should've let Todd try his hand at a presentation and stayed put in Seattle."

"Yeah. Right. I can see Todd standing up on stage in front of nine hundred people doing just that. Not. You did the right thing to go and take care of Ander All Games."

"Maybe I'll come home early and we can celebrate the phenomenal success of the new game. It is, you know, incredibly successful."

"With you at the helm of course it is. But don't leave your fun on my account. I'm fine despite what Kiya and Atka are trying to tell you from a distance. I can always call Travis, even though he does have a new woman in his life."

"Your father is seeing someone? When did that happen? Have you met her yet?"

"He is, and no, I haven't met her yet but we're invited to the ranch on Sunday. I suspect she'll be there. Her name's Chenoa Starr."

"Pretty name."

"Really? You think so? You don't think it sounds like it belongs to a stripper?"

"Maybe a little. How'd they meet? Travis never goes anywhere much unless it concerns business, you, or his horses."

"Bingo. Chenoa bought one of his mares. I think he's smitten, Josh. For the past week, he never shuts up about the woman."

"Ah. Don't worry. We'll meet her, grill her for any ulterior motives and then decide if we like her enough to let her near Travis."

She laughed again, beginning to miss him even more. "I guess I had this hope in the back of my mind that one day he'd hook up with Lena Bowers."

"Lena? I know she's been like a mom to you since you came to Seattle. I'm sorry. I guess we don't always get what we want."

"I know. I love you. I gotta go."

"I love you, too. I'll say it again… Listen to the mutts. They must be picking up on something. I'm able to do the same all the way from here. They're wary of the situation for a reason."

"Stop worrying about me. It has to be five a.m. there in New York. You might think of yourself as part wolf but you still require sleep like a human before the big demo in the morning."

"I always worry about you regardless of where I am."

"I know. I love you, Josh Ander."

"I love you too, Skye Cree. Take care. I'll see you on Friday."

Skye hung up with a heavy heart. No doubt about it, she missed Josh. To Kiya and Atka, she pointed a finger and said, "Okay, you're both allowed to come with me but only if you stop sending out an SOS to Josh. And Atka stays in the car. She's still too much of a puppy and jumpy to be allowed near evidence that needs bagging and tagging."

She pushed the key into the door lock and muttered to Kiya, "And keeping you penned up is a total waste of time, impossible to do. But I don't want you out wandering around, got it?"

Typically, the wolf ignored her.

Skye beat Harry to University Village by ten minutes. The fashionable, upscale mall near the University of Washington made for a strange place to dump a body—especially for the potential serial killer they thought was on the loose. The crime scene techs and the coroner must have thought so too because they were still hard at work taking measurements and photos when Skye walked up to the area roped off by yellow tape.

The area was different than what Harry had described to her earlier. For one, the place wasn't an alleyway at all but rather a small stretch of undeveloped right of way, a short twenty yards from the front door of the nearest shop.

Unlit, but adjacent to the parking lot, the locale might play into their guy's previous disposal method. If this was the same dude, he'd left his two previous victims in a wild, bramble-filled dump ground bordered by I-5 and Beacon Hill known as The Jungle.

She wasn't ready yet to accept that he might've made the jump to a retail shopping outlet. That is, until she spotted the handy hedge that could easily hide his unloading a body out of his car.

Skye ducked under the tape and took up a stance near a band of shrubs high enough to block out what was happening on the other side. She made her way around bog and huckleberry, even caught strands of her hair in a tall vine of some kind. After getting her hair out of the mess, she got close enough to the woman's naked body to realize the young victim hadn't been killed here. Keeping her distance to six feet, she guessed the woman's age at probably no older than twenty.

The victim's ashen face had been left battered and bruised, her throat marred by deep purple crevices, her naked body mutilated.

She was still studying the face while fighting a wave of nausea when Harry interrupted her train of thought.

"Most of the shops around here closed up at nine o'clock, some even earlier at eight. We're lucky the jogger decided to go for a run when he did. Otherwise the body would've been out here longer. By the time he happened along, the parking lot had pretty much cleared out."

She took a couple steps closer to the body, swallowed hard as she tried to count the stab wounds. She gave up after ten. But it was the condition of her breasts that sickened Skye the most. Both had been mutilated beyond reason.

"What you're saying is that the body hadn't been here for that long, another hurried drop and dump. Is this the runner's regular route?" Skye wondered aloud.

Harry went over the notes from the first cop who'd arrived on the scene. "Yep. Jogger works third shift and says he routinely runs along here three times a week before clocking in at his job at midnight. He made the 911 call at three minutes after ten. What are you thinking?"

"That our killer didn't have a lot of time to select the best dump site. He went with whatever was handy. Tonight it happened to be near the local shopping center and a jogger happened along soon after." Skye caught the attention of the medical examiner, Roger Bayliss.

She sidled up to the fifty-six-year-old man known far and wide to be a grumpy old man. "How long do you think she's been dead?"

Roger Bayliss gave her an unsympathetic look without bothering to answer.

Knowing she wasn't exactly dealing with a people-person, she huffed out, "Okay, I'll play. Best guess, maybe under six hours."

"Do you see an autopsy table here?" Bayliss snapped. "Maybe if I didn't have to stop and answer stupid questions every time something pops into a cop's head, or yours, I could get a little work done in the field. In case you haven't realized it yet, it's three in the morning."

Unruffled at the doctor's surly attitude, Skye leveled her voice as she pointed out, "Look, I've been on my feet all day looking for Gwen DeLargo. You know her, right? The girl abducted from another mall some twelve-plus hours ago. I found her tonight with a sleazy pervert who'd spent hours raping her. Harry dragged me here when what I really wanted to do was go home and crash. So before you get your panties in a twist, I'd like to be able to gain something for my efforts. Knowing when she died would help. Maybe because the family of this woman deserves a clue what happened to their daughter, or sister, or…"

"Knock off the sob story, Cree," Bayliss retorted in a huff. "I get it. You were close when you estimated six. I'd say this one's probably been dead no longer than eight hours tops. After he stabbed her multiple times, she lived through that ordeal before he removed her breast implants. I can tell you she probably bled to death from the mutilation—somewhere else. That's my assessment in a nutshell."

Another wave of nausea hit Skye at the idea the young woman had been alive while the killer had cut out her implants. She shot a look over at Harry. "Okay, so it fits with the other two. That connects the three victims to one killer."

"Yeah, plus it's something we held back from the media," Harry added with a nod. "Reporters don't know about the mutilation and removal of the breast implants and I'd like to keep it that way."

"That's fine by me," Skye muttered under her breath. "Both Carrie Montague and Taylor Dinsmore went missing when they were fifteen. Both families gave DNA in hopes of a future match. Both girls were listed at the foundation."

"And? Our guy must have cut out the implants because he knew they could be used to ID his victims."

Skye wasn't so sure. She chewed her lip while still trying to figure out the puzzle. "Why go to the trouble of putting them in and then brutally hack them out? As I recall Bayliss didn't even need the implants for ID purposes with Carrie and Taylor because he used dental records along with the DNA the families provided. So why cut out implants the killer obviously wanted them to have?"

"Because he's a sick bastard," Harry muttered.

"That goes without saying. But there has to be more to it than that, another reason we haven't figured out yet." Clearly stumped, Skye suddenly snapped her fingers as a realization dawned. She took two steps back toward the body and stared. "That's it, I knew this girl looked familiar. That's Lisa Williams. She went missing four years ago on a trip to the lake with a group of friends. She was sixteen at the time. I have her photograph still tacked up on the wall at the Artemis Foundation."

Bayliss overheard the claim. "Come on. You can't be serious? There's no possible way you could make an ID to her face when it's ashen and lifeless like it is now."

Harry was just as skeptical. "Skye, are you certain you remember the face? Lisa had to have changed quite a bit from a teenager to a young woman."

Skye nodded even though the purple streaks in the victim's hair did cause a chink to form, although it wasn't enough to dissuade her. "Sure, Lisa's looks have changed during those key years. But her mother made sure I had

Lisa's sophomore picture from high school tacked up on my board alongside the age-progressed photo Mrs. Williams had done. I've stared at both images over the years to recognize that face. Still don't believe me? Then how about this? Lisa had the same jet-black hair *and* a very distinctive almond shape to her eyes. Then there's the unusual slope of her nose. This victim has all three characteristics. See? Try to look beyond the dye-job." Skye stepped even closer to point out the features in question. "I'm telling you this hacked up mess belongs to the missing Lisa Williams."

Bayliss stared at Harry. "I hate to admit it, but Cree sometimes gets it right. There are times when she does know her stuff."

Harry's mouth tightened. "So girls who disappeared from the area years earlier are now turning up dead, getting dumped like trash now after having their breasts made bigger? Why?"

"Cut out, the girls no longer have the implants because he cut them out. Changed his mind maybe? I don't know. The girls grew into women, women who were no longer attractive to the pervert for some reason. One thing's for certain. He didn't want these girls around any longer and did something about it. It's like he wanted us to find them by putting them in a high traffic area. The homeless uses The Jungle all the time. They come and go there like campers. Our killer put them there knowing they'd be found."

Harry pursed his lips as though he'd taken a sip of sour milk. "Not getting enough attention to suit his ego so he does something about that, too."

"I'd say so." To get into the right frame of mind, Skye squatted on her heels and spotted movement along the row of hedges. Knowing instantly it had to be Kiya because she'd left Atka secured in the car, she felt relieved to catch sight of the wolf roaming in and out, tracking a scent. It didn't take long for Kiya to pick up a trail.

Skye headed in that direction, following the wolf, covering almost the entire length of the right of way. She didn't realize Harry was hot on her heels until she stopped a few feet away from her spirit guide.

"What is it?" Harry asked.

"I'm not sure what but something's off here." Drawing in several deep calming breaths, she pulled back branches on the perfectly trimmed underbrush. After taking a few more steps into the muck, that's when she spotted it. "Unbelievable."

"What?"

"Some kind of flower left here."

Harry studied the row of boxwood. "Is that all? I didn't even know this plant bloomed this time of year."

"No, I mean someone left us a beautiful black flower on the ground. I don't know what kind... Wait, I think it might be a dahlia. Yeah, I'm pretty sure it's known as a black dahlia. And look, there's a partial shoe print in the soft ground next to it." She took out her phone to capture the image of the flower on her cell before moving over to inspect the print.

"That doesn't make sense, Skye. This couldn't belong to our killer, not this far from where he dumped the body out of his car, a car he obviously pulled into the empty parking lot to avoid detection. Why would he go out of his way to walk here *behind* this bank of shrubs and leave us a flower?"

"Good question, but he came down here for a reason," Skye said, taking off further into the growth of bushes. "Oh my God. Get the crime scene people over here."

"What now? Why?"

Skye let out an audible sigh. "He gave us a gift by dropping one of the breast implants. There, see the blood trail. Geez, I don't understand what he was doing over here either. Think about it. It would've been difficult at best for anyone to look for anything this far from the body, if not for..." She'd almost admitted it was Kiya's discovery that got them this far. Needing to focus better, she began to question the absurdity of leaving the implant here at this location. There had to be a reason. And one glimpse at Harry had her picking up on his disbelieving look before he yelled instructions to the tech team.

"I'm not sure how you find these kinds of things," Harry noted. "But don't ever stop."

"I'm pretty sure he wanted us to find this. It's too convenient otherwise—first the flower and the shoe print and then the implant. It's either that or he's all of a sudden gotten very sloppy. My guess is it's like you said before. The killer didn't get enough press with the first two, so he upped the risk factor to get more."

She thought of Jason Berkenshaw and how he'd done the same thing by sending her a box of bones. It had been his undoing. But his victims had gone through pain and suffering. Even though she was still clad in a heavy leather coat the idea of what these women had to endure brought a chill from head to toe. At that same moment she felt something else run through her system, a sense they were being watched.

When the wolf looked southward, lifting a regal head in that direction, Skye paid attention to every nuance, every sound from the crime crew behind them. During times like these she had to focus. Getting through this surreal scene was now her goal.

"Could he be watching us right now?" Skye proffered aloud.

Harry's hand immediately went to the sidearm at his waist.

Skye narrowed her eyes to check out the parking lot a second time, trying to come up with a quick tally of police vehicles and names to go with some of the unmarked cars just in case. If their killer was hiding in plain sight anywhere nearby, it was a great dodge—for now anyway.

When Kiya trotted off farther south, Skye followed, keenly aware that certain eyes were on her and the wolf.

When Harry started to shadow her footsteps, Skye shook her head and mumbled, "Stay here. Make sure the techs take a mold of that partial we found. You never know when the smallest thing might lead us to our killer."

Chapter Two

Two hundred yards away he sat perched on the rooftop of the Methodist church watching through a pair of high-powered binoculars while the detectives milled about below. He'd left the body in the most obvious place on purpose.

It was pure irony sitting on top of a chapel. Towering above the scene might give him a great perspective but he'd never once in his adult life recognized religion, certainly not the doctrine he'd been born into. His parents had done their best to raise him in the strict Mormon dogma. From day one, though, not much about it had stuck.

Back then he'd been scrawny Dillard Barstow, invisible to the world. As a small boy his mere name had been cause enough for the neighborhood kids to bully him. At school, the name-calling often got out of hand. He'd often wondered what kind of stupid parents named their kid Dillard anyway. How on earth could a man be expected to go through life with a name like that?

The answer was simple. A man couldn't. So once he'd left Idaho for college, he'd done something about it. At the first opportunity, he'd paid the required fee to the court and changed the name his parents had given him at birth.

He sat back and tried to relax but still kept an eye on the activity at the mall parking lot. The misty, cold night air caused another memory to flash in his head—back to the night, similar to this one, when Dillard had taken his first sip of vodka. He'd been thirteen. His parents had left him alone to attend one of their ever-boring church events. That night, he snuck out of the house to his cave where he'd stashed several bottles of Smirnoff, the booze he'd swiped on one of his trips to the next town over, the trips he frequently made alone when he was supposed to be at church camp, or at school. But that night, he'd gotten so blind, stinking drunk on the stuff he hadn't been able to stand up. It had taken him twelve hours to sober up enough to make his way back home. That recollection made him smile. But how he'd been punished for breaking his curfew did not. His father had taken a belt to him and beaten him black and blue.

From that, he'd learned that anything obsessive he did had best be kept to himself. The experience taught him a valuable lesson. In that troublesome path through life when making decisions—secretive versus honesty—secretive won out every time.

Now the full-grown man went by a different tag and had a wide array of interests.

One of them happened to be horticulture and plants, especially flowers—dahlias were his favorite. He'd come to his passion for botany at a very early age. Some people had made fun of him for it, mainly his parents.

None of that mattered now.

These days no one told him what to do or how to do it. He indulged in the finest food and alcohol available on his budget, fancied buying first-rate seeds and soil for his garden, lived in the best house his income afforded, and frequented the rare five-star restaurants he treated himself to on special occasions. Although he did his best to keep everything to reasonable moderation, he did have a few weaknesses. He consumed espresso like a fiend, smoked the occasional cigar when the mood hit, and enjoyed all that young females offered.

But that was a secret best kept close to his vest.

So instead of following in the footsteps of his parents, he'd embraced what his maternal grandmother had done her very best to teach him—her love of Mother Earth. From his visits with her he'd learned the most important aspects of his life, things he still carried with him today.

He'd inherited his grandmother's green thumb, a talent he'd taken to the small town of Corvallis while attending Oregon State. During four years in pursuit of a horticultural degree, his classmates had considered him nerdy and strange. But during his grad school days his professors thought of him as nothing short of a botanical genius, a regular herb doctor, a whiz with plants. They'd marveled at what he could do with roots and bulbs. But it was his ability to cultivate cannabis that made him a highly sought-after man on campus and always flush with ready cash. His gardening skills didn't, however, make him popular with women.

It was just as well. He'd always been a loner. And sooner or later his proclivities tended to come to light at odd times no matter what he did to hide them.

When he spotted Skye Cree making her way onto the scene and hobnobbing with cops, her arrival caused his anger to spike. Man was the hunter, the warrior, not the woman, never the woman. The woman cared for the home and the children. He'd learned that much from his mother. She didn't go out and mingle in a man's world. She certainly didn't take on fighting crime the way Skye Cree did or try to make herself an all-important Seattle icon. The woman seemed to crave making headlines. In his mind, the whole attempt made her an aberration, particularly an insult to her Native heritage.

Through the lenses of the field glasses, he focused on the female in question, dressed all in black, dressed much as he had for his outing tonight. For now though, he dismissed her athletic physique and zeroed in on her spirit guide. The wolf had sniffed out the implant he'd cleverly dropped just the way he'd hoped.

He chuckled at his inventiveness. Now the authorities would no doubt consider him sloppy and careless, a theatrical production he didn't intend to waste.

He'd been anything but reckless tonight, or last week, or the week before that. Normally he didn't resort to using a knife. After all, he wasn't a butcher. He much preferred to get the job done with his own bare hands. There was too much satisfaction in that to opt for a weapon. But when the situation called for staging, when you were looking to get a reaction, the best way was to create a brutal crime scene, the bloodier the better. The cops leaned toward a narrow focus if you didn't toss multiple victims at them. Add in all that blood and it would get him the desired results. He didn't think twice about anyone catching him. What concerned him was losing control of the situation.

Skye Cree didn't need to know that three victims barely scratched the surface. The way he approached the situation, the cops should be thanking him. He'd given them a gift and returned three women back to where they'd started out. Why couldn't they appreciate his generosity?

From now on he intended to eliminate the people in the underground he did business with. He'd steer clear of his old clients, especially those who defiled the flowers he sold them—like the women he'd given back.

How ridiculous was it to add unnatural elements to something so naturally beautiful? Adding tacky tattoos and augmentation to an already perfect blossom seemed ridiculous to him. Discoloring the skin or distorting perfectly proportioned boobs into something hideous wasn't worth taking a shitload of money anymore. He should have realized before now there were people who failed to appreciate the magnificence of the human body. Mother Nature didn't make mistakes.

Going forward, he'd have to find a way to close up shop. He'd end his online presence—mostly. He'd stay in the chatrooms, of course, those he used to attract the most naïve. At this stage of his life, he could afford to take a pass on the profit. Besides, there were risks involved now. No way did he intend to get caught by some loose-lipped, low-level pervert who couldn't keep his trap shut. Knowing the idiots didn't appreciate what they'd been given made him realize he was wasting precious resources for very little gain.

He'd never minded them returning the merchandise. That wasn't the problem. He'd made a name for himself in the underground trade by having the most generous return policy. After all, he could easily find another buyer for any girl he'd taken back. But not when their appearance had been altered in such a way as to devalue their worth. To unload damaged goods like that, it took dealing with a lower class of people, people like hard-core drug dealers or street pimps who wanted to make a fast buck. He'd learned a long time ago those types couldn't be trusted.

Since he couldn't afford to put time and money into the caring and feeding of the merchandise for an indefinite period of time, he'd have to put an end to the tradition. Taking them back would no longer be an option. He was done putting up with customers who took advantage of that perk.

Through the binoculars, he saw that the wolf had taken the bait and done a superb job of finding what he'd purposefully left for the fools. If not, Cree and her Nez Perce instincts would have fallen flat. In the future, surely he wouldn't need to go that far and cut out body parts each time to get a reaction—unless of course, the genius hunter Skye Cree couldn't find her way out of a paper sack. Then he would do what had to be done.

Maybe his own spirit guide would take care of the wolf for him. He turned to the panther, black and sleek, that nuzzled his knee. Dillard ran his hand along the animal's body and smiled. "You'll level the playing field for me if it comes to that, won't you, my friend?"

Dillard spoke in the language of his grandmother's native Greek tongue when it came to his history, his roots. His grandmother's people believed the panther stood for reawakening, a sign to begin anew. It was his panther, Oreias that had given him the power to become what he was now. Oreias had given him a new meaning to life.

While the Cree woman used her spirit guide to find the bad guys, Dillard used his as his power source. Orieas was as much a part of himself as his right arm, and as such, deserved the lofty title.

"It's only fair, my friend that we go up against the hunter's wolf, don't you think?"

As a reply the panther purred into his master's hand.

"In our world we know something about betrayal by family, don't we? We come from a proud people who took down a king."

The fierce panther butted his head into Dillard's big palm.

"It isn't that I think she'll catch me. No, not that. But she and her wolf are certainly on the hunt. We have to counter that, prepare for it. If those two get close, if they find anything at all, they'll have to do it on our terms. If we eliminate her wolf spirit, she'll have to deal with us using her own merits, her own skills, and we both know she doesn't have squat."

Since Camilla, so very long ago, he'd refined his methods and taken advantage of his talents, which had eventually led to his discovery. He could make a shitload of money in the sex trade. It hadn't take long to find out how lucrative it could be, especially when there were men out there willing to pay a hefty fee to own a young girl—men who didn't have the gumption to go out and do what he did—men who didn't have the skill set or the guts to fulfill orders the way he could. That's why he charged them dearly for his services. That's why any request for specific types of females cost extra.

Relying on his Internet search skills he'd been able to connect with masses of people—a reminder that he didn't always get to keep every prize he landed for himself. He refused to sell his best stock. The best he kept for himself.

His nine-to-five job was just that. It wasn't exactly rewarding but more like a paycheck. That's why he'd had to diversify years ago to pay for his lifestyle. Keeping up appearances meant something.

But those days had come to a close. With Carrie, Taylor and Lisa gone from his house, he could start anew. Everyone deserved a fresh start. Obviously, he needed new blood, new power, new everything. Maybe if he widened his hunting grounds beyond Seattle and Vancouver, it would bring about better selections.

If he scoured the area to the north, he might happen upon someone who looked like the Cree woman with her same striking features, her same eyes—the very characteristics he'd been drawn to initially. It was all the incentive he needed to continue the hunt.

Over the past ten years, he'd made plenty of trips across the border into Canada, explored all that British Columbia had to offer. He could say without hesitation, the Pacific Northwest held a lot of promise. But it was winter. Cold, snowy weather had never suited him all that much. If he needed to see snow and ice, he'd simply head back to where it had all started. And if he braved the frigid weather, he might as well land back on familiar turf.

Or maybe he would revisit his old college haunt, go back to Corvallis, Oregon, and relive the glory of his time spent there.

He itched to take a road trip. It'd be just the thing to pick up his spirits. It might make him forget how playing with fire, or in this case, Skye Cree, could get him caught. Playing tag was a sign that he needed to stay on guard, be more cautious.

"That's why it's so important to give up my extracurricular activities, keep my interests closer to home.

Keeping my gardens tidier, weed-free, and without flaws is the goal."

He scrubbed the panther's ears again with his big hands. "The two of us have always made a good team. Your predatory instincts were handed down to me through my ancestors for a reason. Remember how my parents acted when I told them I had a spirit guide? Remember that? They thought I was crazy and refused to believe me. They might've laughed behind my back then but they aren't laughing now, are they?"

Dillard continued to talk to himself like that, sitting atop the roof of the church until the sun came up. Watching Skye Cree head to her car, he made a pact. If the woman thought so highly of her hunting skills and came for him, he would be ready.

It was inevitable that one day soon they were destined to meet face to face. His fate rested on the opportunity of a lifetime. He didn't intend to waste it. Maybe it was because his adversary bore such a striking resemblance to his little Camilla that she fascinated him so. The Cree woman was a little older than he was used to hunting. But it didn't negate the fact that she'd be a prize asset, a lovely addition to his purple field of dahlias.

"Imagine that, my friend. Imagine if we could add Skye Cree to our garden. Imagine having a woman like that with us and keeping her forever. Either way, she'll soon learn a thing or two about what she was truly meant to do."

Chapter Three

The moment Skye burst through the front door at home—a few minutes after eight a.m.—she started toeing off boots and shedding her clothes. Drained, she tossed her jacket on the bench in the hallway and watched the dog and the wolf in their exuberance both skid on the hardwood floors.

She went in search of orange juice, hoping to put an end to a craving she'd had since Harborview. Heading for the kitchen, she followed the animals to the fridge. After pouring a bowl of chow for Atka, she pulled out the plastic jug, drank straight from the bottle. Even though she could've used several over-easy eggs and a couple slices of bacon, she passed on the temptation, too tired to bother with food. As she slugged down more juice, she was just grateful to be back home.

Home was an old country farmhouse on Bainbridge Island, thirty minutes west of Seattle across Puget Sound. The house had been built in 1909 amid green rolling hills complete with pretty gabled windows and a wraparound porch to die for. The private stretch of beach and the spectacular view across the water were each a bonus.

The renovated four bedrooms and three bathrooms were no doubt a lot of space for two people. But Kiya and Atka helped fill part of the void with doggy noises and doggy merriment, not to mention the doggy trouble they got into on a daily basis. The canines often used the cherry orchard out back and its rows and rows of trees to dig and explore. That tendency to dig had forced her to fence off the part of the backyard she'd dedicated for planting and growing a vegetable garden.

After months of settling in, Skye had yet to really flex her homemaker muscles. Sure, she took her turn throwing together breakfast, same with cooking evening meals. She often switched off chores with Josh to maintain that balance necessary to achieving happy and successful coupledom. But when it came to anything beyond that, she had trouble keeping the hydrangeas, sweet fern, and pepperbush that grew in abundance around the house from dying due to neglect.

There hadn't been a whole lot of time to do any of the things she'd planned to do. Which meant no major garden yet. She'd wait for spring for that. Hopefully she'd be able to carve out some time to plant at least a few rows of lettuce. Too many missing kids to look for, too many bad guys to hunt down, to really spend valuable time digging in the dirt. Because of her schedule, she rarely took a day off even on weekends.

As she studied the view from the back door she realized that needed to change. Looking out over jutting coastline and rocky outcrops, she knew the past twenty-four-hour ordeal had taken its toll—she was almost too tired to think, even too tired to jump in the shower.

And she missed Josh.

The house seemed almost too quiet without him. He should be here waiting for her. Because each time she came back home to this personal sanctuary—the pastoral countryside, its rolling slopes and sand dunes, the little shallow pond, and the cathedral of trees at the rear—it never failed to make her feel as though she'd been given a special gift.

Josh had been the one to point out the area's unique mix of Native American and European history that had given her such a sense of belonging here, that feeling she'd missed since losing her parents. It was more than that, of course. She'd fallen in love with a man who hadn't tried to change her, who had accepted her and all the quirks she brought with her.

As she climbed the stairs to the master bedroom, Kiya and Atka bounding up ahead of her, she looked forward to what she hoped was at least five hours of uninterrupted sleep.

Once she got undressed she crawled beneath the covers, bone weary. Settling in between the sheets, Skye Cree knew she was one of the lucky ones. Every single day she took stock of what she had. Her father, Travis Nakota, said it was because her ordeal at such a young age caused her to appreciate all the little things in life a lot more.

She had no doubt that was true.

Before drifting off completely she thought of Josh and how great it would be when he got back home. She wasn't sure when it had happened but she'd forgotten how to sleep alone. All she knew now was she didn't like it very much.

Oh, she knew she wasn't completely alone, not with Kiya and Atka snuggling up beside her in bed. Instinct had her running a hand over Josh's side of the bed. But even with missing that lump of security she'd grown so accustomed to, the lure of sleep had her closing her eyes. Her last thought was of Josh, right before she heard flutes in the distance starting low and then rising. But exhaustion finally took over and blacked out any other thoughts or sounds.

While Skye slept, Kiya grew uneasy. The wolf raised her head before unfurling to pace back and forth at the foot of the bed. Kiya's prowling roused Atka. The malamute got up to investigate and roam the room with the wolf.

Vigilant, both animals stood at the window united in one, like-minded goal —to protect their master.

Across the country, it was almost eleven o'clock inside the main convention center in midtown Manhattan. Ander All Games held center court with its debut of the brand-new game, *Princess Kilda*, featuring a red-headed warrior goddess constantly put in perilous situations but able to fight her way out of whatever danger came her way.

A throng of gamers had squeezed around the display to get a better look at the battle raging between Josh and Todd Graham. The images on the eighty-inch, flat-screen TV illustrated all *Princess Kilda*'s clever features—plenty of chases that required good reflexes, fight scenes that took teamwork between online partners, bad guys to fight to the death, and brilliant 3D graphics that incorporated magic lasers.

The feedback so far had been positive. Already the buzz on the Internet had exceeded their expectations along with record sales.

But during the demo Josh had trouble concentrating. His mind was back in Seattle. Something was off. He kept seeing someone lurking around the house. Without a vivid description of an assailant, the recurring images left him distracted and frustrated. Not being able to put a finger exactly on the problem troubled him. But when your wife was a crime-fighting warrior in real life, his mind had a tendency to think the worst. Over the past couple years he'd gotten used to worrying about her safety. But this nagging feeling he had in his gut was different. It made him recognize that he needed to get back home.

When he ended up getting Kilda trapped and surrounded by her enemies, he realized someone else needed to step in and fill his shoes. At the break in action, Josh handed off the controller to Tate Brock, the man he still thought of as a brother-in-law.

Josh slapped Tate on the back and met the younger man's eyes. "I'm done here. But do me a favor. Try not to choke."

"Are you kidding? I love this game. So do all my friends. I can't believe it's based on Skye."

Josh looked out on the sea of enthusiastic faces in the crowd, gamers who were enjoying the show. "Yeah, well, I wish she'd been as thrilled about it as everyone else."

"Give her time. When the sales go through the roof, she'll enjoy knowing how she was the inspiration for it all."

Josh shook his head. "If only." With that, he made his way out of the convention hall just as Todd Graham caught up with him.

Josh could tell his second in command was annoyed with him for the abrupt departure. Todd had Asperger's and rarely made public appearances anywhere. The two had known each other since middle school, which meant Josh knew how difficult it had been getting Todd to come down to the exhibit hall in the first place, let alone join in the action. Usually Todd avoided people, all people. Gaming conventions had been off limits in the past. That's one of the reasons Josh immediately began to apologize. "Look, I'm sorry but I have to head back home."

"Home? Now? We just kicked things off. What gives? You've been acting weird ever since you got here. And acting weirder than me, makes me…worry."

"Who took your place back at the demo table? Somebody has to keep their mind on the prize while I'm gone."

"Leo. He's the best one to give Tate a run for his money. Look, is it Skye you're still worried about?"

"You know it is. She's in trouble. I can feel it. Whether she admits it or not, she's in danger. I can't sit here in New York…"

"Then catch the next flight back to Seattle. With your mind someplace else, you're no good to us like this anyway. If it's real, the danger, that is, let us know. You'll need backup."

Josh slapped Todd on the back. "Thanks. I hoped you'd understand."

"Since I'm not married anymore, I don't really…understand. But if Skye's in over her head you need to be there."

"Exactly. I'll see all of you when you guys get back to Seattle."

Skye woke that afternoon to a misty drizzle. Her stomach rumbled and made her realize she wasn't just hungry, but ravenous. And her brain craved coffee.

Tossing back the covers, she threw on a fresh pair of jeans and a sweater and looked around the room for Kiya and Atka. Both canines seemed antsy. They paced back and forth in front of the bank of windows looking out into the vast backyard.

"What do you guys see out there? Come on, let's go downstairs and rustle up some grub. I'll let you out to pee."

But as soon as she reached the kitchen, Atka and Kiya went on alert. Both went wild growling and barking, setting off a din of fierce noise, all directed at the backyard.

On instinct, Skye followed their line of vision to the glass door and beyond. That's when she spotted the vase.

Placed prominently on the outdoor teak table, it was hard to miss. She knew immediately that the buds were an exact match to the flower Kiya had found earlier in the field at the mall.

Puzzled, Skye moved to the glass, but not before she went to the counter and pulled out the biggest knife from the butcher block. Keeping the weapon clutched in her hand, she scanned the lawn all the way out to the ornamental pond. Even though she didn't see any movement, she wasn't comfortable enough to open the back door. Instead she stood there staring at the arrangement—a dozen or so deep purple dahlias standing straight and tall in a crystal clear container. Raindrops had gathered on the tips of the petals and told Skye the vase had been there for several hours.

Even though the canines were itching to get outside, Skye wasn't eager to let them. Not yet.

Damn it, this was her home. How dare someone try to scare her on her own property and think, by doing this, they'd bring danger to her doorstep.

It was then she decided to rein in her suspicions, get a grip on her fear. What if it was simply a coincidence and Josh had sent them? At the moment, she wished like hell she believed in coincidences. Maybe the florist in town had dropped them off. What if the flowers had been delivered while she napped? Maybe when no one answered the door they'd brought them around back to the patio. There, a simple explanation.

Maybe.

She took out her cell phone and hit Josh's contact info. But his cell rang once and went straight to voicemail. Probably on the floor of the convention center right this minute, she decided as she ended the call.

To hell with it.

With the knife still in her hand, she opened the door and watched as Kiya darted straight to the table to sniff around its base, Atka doing her best to do the same. Skye let them check things out before she stepped onto the concrete. It didn't take long before the animals took off to follow the scent toward the woods. The fact that Kiya and Atka had gone in that direction instead of circling around the house to the front door caused her florist theory to evaporate.

Skimming the yard, Skye's eyes darted back and forth. She quickly located the little card sticking up out of the bouquet. Snatching it up, she slipped it out of its miniature envelope, read the message. *Hope these flowers grown from my own garden brighten your dreary day.*

Okay, so no threat exactly, more like an implied 'shove it in your face' act. So they weren't from Josh, or from any florist in town, but from the same sick bastard who'd cut up three young women.

She called to Kiya and Atka and dashed back into the kitchen, leaving the floral arrangement where it sat and flipping the lock on the door behind her.

She went to the wall phone to place a call to Harry then decided to text him instead.

Got flowers from our killer.

She had to wait ten minutes for a response.

How the hell did he know where you lived? Don't touch them or go near them until I get there.

She didn't have the heart to tell him that ship had already sailed so she simply texted the word "okay" and left it at that. Better to tell him in person she'd already handled the card.

If her head ached for a caffeine fix before, it morphed into migraine status now. Trying her best to keep her emotions intact, she strolled to the coffee machine, got busy with the ordinary task of brewing a cup.

While she waited for the machine to do its work, she fed the animals, then cracked eggs for an omelet. She dragged out veggies—scallions and spinach—and used the cutting board and the sharp knife to dice and slice. She whipped up the mixture before dumping it into a skillet. Letting it simmer until it was ready to fold over, she slid the eggs onto a plate.

While she devoured her way through the entire dish, she booted up her laptop to research "black" flowers. She discovered they weren't black at all, but rather vibrant purple in color and only appeared black depending on the variety of flower. When gardeners got the urge to experiment with the color black, they did it with plenty of dogged determination. Sometimes it took years to roll out a black rose, a lily, a tulip, or a hollyhock. During her search she found a picture of an orchid so dark in color it looked like a bat with whiskers. It seemed throughout the gardening world black flowers were considered "the death flower."

Skye would have to agree. Coupled with the fact the killer sent a dahlia, a black one at that, it meant the guy had gotten his macabre missive across in spades.

At the sound of a car pulling into the driveway, Kiya and Atka raced toward the living room. She bounded up out of the chair to follow them into the front room. Thinking she'd be there to greet Harry, she was shocked to see Josh's car rolling up the driveway. She heard the garage door open and went on alert. How had the killer managed to commandeer Josh's Fusion out of airport parking?

Whoa. She took a deep, calming breath, knowing full well she needed to get a better handle on things, namely her imagination. It was working double time. She scrubbed a hand over her face. Of course it had to be Josh sitting behind the wheel and driving his own vehicle. As the car made its way into the garage, she sent a text to Josh's phone. *Where are you exactly?*

A few seconds later, the door to the laundry room opened and she heard a familiar voice say, "Hey, honey, I'm home."

The canines went wild. Skye sprinted through the kitchen and saw Josh's grin first, then his arms full of luggage and shopping bags. Without waiting for him to free up his hands, she jumped into his body, causing him to lose his hold on the stuff he carried. The force knocked him back a step. She wrapped him up and began to plant kisses on his face.

Kiya and Atka were almost as exuberant with their wet snouts and tongues.

"Are you trying to scare me? Why didn't you call and let me know you were coming home early?" Skye ranted in between kisses.

"I should definitely go out of town more often. I wanted to surprise you. Looks like I did. Plus, I knew what you'd say. You'd tell me not to bother. But it looks like you're happier to see me than I thought you'd be."

Looking into his calm, silver-gray eyes she took hold of his chin. "Of course I'm happy to see you. Why wouldn't I be? I'm so glad you're home. What's all this stuff?"

"I picked up a few souvenirs." He dug in one of the sacks and brought out a twelve-inch replica of the Statue of Liberty made out of pewter.

The cheap knockoff made her laugh. "I'd say the street vendor outside the Marriott saw you coming."

"That's what Leo said."

She held up the statue, tested the weight. "At least it isn't plastic. We'll give it a treasured spot on the mantle."

The doorbell rang. "That'll be Harry, I hope," she said as she darted off to answer it. "Come on, you'll want to hear this."

"What's Harry doing here? This is about that crime scene, isn't it?" Josh shouted to Skye's back. To get his answer, he followed her into the other room.

As soon as Harry walked through the door Atka pounced. Surprised to see Josh at home, Harry tried to ward off the energetic puppy while at the same time holding out his hand in greeting to Josh.

"Hey, aren't you supposed to be in New York?"

"Came home to surprise my wife. What are you doing here?" Josh asked, taking hold of Atka's collar and pulling the dog away from the detective.

"How'd you get the news so fast that we have another serial killer on the loose? What do you think about the guy sending Skye flowers while she took a nap?"

Josh sent his wife a hard look. "You might've mentioned the serial killer this morning when we talked."

"Oh, come on, you had a hunch there was something going on that's why you came back early." She lifted a shoulder and took his hand in hers. "There's no need to be mad at me. I didn't level with you because—"

"She didn't want you to worry," Harry finished.

"I admit the flowers did freak me out a little."

Josh angled his head to plant a kiss on Skye's forehead. "We'll discuss your willingness to level with me later. Where are they, the flowers?"

"Here's the note that came with them," Skye acknowledged, handing it to Josh. That's when it occurred to her. "How come Atka didn't have a fit when the guy brought these into the backyard? That dog normally kicks up a fuss when she spots the mailman. Look how she attacked Harry. Why didn't she bark and wake me up?"

"I was about to point that out. Maybe she did but you were so exhausted you didn't hear a thing." Josh read the brief one-line message and shook his head. "It isn't exactly a declaration of war, is it?"

While they debated the tone of the note, Harry watched them pass it back and forth, and grumbled, "How many times do I have to tell you not to touch that damn thing? You both should know better. It's evidence."

"Sorry. Too late," she admitted, leading the way into the kitchen. "It's probably okay because a guy like this isn't going to make stupid mistakes by leaving his DNA or prints on anything."

"Yeah, I'm sure he's a genius, a serial killer just thought you needed cheering up and decided to do something about it. He took a lot of risks by coming here to our home," Josh remarked, his comments laced with irritation. "Let's see this flower arrangement."

"There. On the patio table outside."

Josh opened the door and got his first look at the black dahlias. He turned back to Skye. "I hate to point this out to you but the Black Dahlia got chopped up into pieces and someone left the body parts in a field. You ask me, I think this guy's meaning is crystal clear. How did he know you were helping Harry this soon into the case anyway?"

She went into the details about what she'd found at the shopping center and the condition of Lisa's remains. She reminded him about the Montague and Dinsmore cases and the particulars of those two victims. "That means you're pretty much up to speed now, except that I did get this vibe from the crime scene this morning that maybe the killer watched us the entire time we were there in the parking lot."

Harry's eyebrows popped up. "You didn't mention that."

"Now you know how I feel," Josh quipped. But the humor faded when he let the facts of each case sink in. Even the hard edge he'd developed over the past two years slipped slightly at knowing how the young women must've suffered. "Just when you think you've seen sick and twisted, someone else comes along and tops the list. Cutting out their breast implants is a cruel, sadistic bent. Add to that, he not only sees you at the crime scene but now he knows where you live."

Josh started to pace, the wolf instincts inside beginning to kick in. He wandered the room to help him sort out his thoughts. "Let's see how fast we can catch this perverted bastard."

"Agreed, even though the holidays are approaching fast. Our killer could go out of town or go cold. Either way, we have our work cut out for us." Skye squinted at Harry. "You know we'll have to go through the database at the foundation to see if there are other victims out there that fit the pattern, maybe girls who've fallen through the cracks."

"I believe I'd remember any reports where a victim had her breast implants removed," Harry pointed out. "And so would Roger Bayliss. The coroner might be difficult to deal with, but he's as thorough as they come. Bayliss keeps up with what's happening in other jurisdictions, always has. Besides, there were no serial numbers on that implant we found to trace back to a surgeon."

Skye's brow creased. "Really? That's odd. Why not? That has to be significant."

Harry stopped short. "Maybe because it was three in the morning that fact didn't resonate with me like it should have. If I'd been thinking clearer, I'd have asked Bayliss about it then. Buy hey, that's one more reason I'm getting too old for this job."

She patted Harry's back in a sympathetic gesture. "No need to beat yourself up. I was pretty wiped myself. We know it now and that's what matters."

"Isn't that against medical regulations? Using implants without serial numbers?" Josh asked.

"You bet. Those numbers are there to keep track of them in the event of problems, leaks, that sort of thing, so doctors have a way of making patients aware of the issues."

Picking up the issue, Josh tossed out a few facts. "Implants are treated just like other medical devices—cardiac defibrillators, pacemakers, shunts, rods and screws used in spinal surgeries. They all have serial numbers."

"Maybe Lisa's were from a foreign manufacturer. No serial numbers means they're running under the radar."

Josh frowned and shook his head. "Even foreign manufacturers maintain reputable standards, or should. Maybe we should focus on the ones that don't." He looked long and hard at Harry. "Let's go back to something you mentioned earlier. You found no other notifications from other law enforcement agencies or jurisdictions about this type victim anywhere else nearby, correct?"

"That's what I'm saying."

"Then why these three? What's unique about them? That's the question," Josh reasoned as he continued to roam the room. "What was special about Montague, Dinsmore, and Williams? Did they have the same hair coloring? Same color eyes? Do each of these women fit a type?"

Skye shook her head. "They were dissimilar in looks. Montague was more like a dishwater blonde, Dinsmore a variation of a redhead, and Williams had black hair with purple streaks in it. You know, the way some women dye their hair in bright shades to set themselves apart from the norm. The day Lisa went missing, however, she exhibited what could only be considered a much more conservative style than what I saw this morning."

Josh jingled the loose change in his pockets and pondered what that meant. "Okay, so he doesn't look for a 'type' per se. He concentrates on opportunity and availability. After hiding these three victims for years, he brings them out in the open, casts them off where he's sure they'll be found. Why? What do we know about each victim? Harry?"

"I emailed Skye the files with the particulars two weeks ago. She should have them in her inbox."

"I can do better than that. I emailed them to myself and printed them out." Skye crossed over to a desk in the corner of the kitchen, a workstation she used for such things when she was at home, and retrieved several manila folders from the drawer. She flipped through the folders gathering data. "According to their autopsies, all three were Caucasian. Carrie Montague was five-six, weighed one-twenty. Taylor Dinsmore five-three, weighed ninety pounds. Lisa Williams, five-five, weighed one-fourteen. No traits in common except for race and gender—different hair colors, different heights. So I'd say you're right, Josh. No pattern as to type."

About that time Harry's cell phone rang. The detective listened to what was obviously the medical examiner calling. Harry repeated the conversation word for word for the benefit of Skye and Josh. "Bayliss says there were no traces of semen on Lisa Williams. But she did show signs she went through childbirth, and not recently. Maybe eighteen months ago. That's a guess. Wherever Lisa was held during the four years she was gone, she gave birth there."

"That's a sad and disturbing thought."

As soon as Harry hung up, the discussion between Josh and Skye took off in that direction.

"Could that have been his purpose? He wanted offspring and that's why the other girls were discarded because they didn't comply?"

Skye wasn't ready to buy into that. "You mean because Carrie and Taylor didn't get pregnant? That theory doesn't work for me. Namely because they all three ended up tossed out like garbage. So what's the incentive? Lisa gives birth but she meets the same fate as the other two. No, that just doesn't play. These three girls were originally abducted by a sexual predator, who also happens to be a trafficker. Then they're turned around and sold to the highest bidder. These girls were destined for whatever perverse life for the specific purpose of filling said pervert's urges. My guess is that for whatever reason these three girls were cast off, maybe even returned."

"Returned? That's a new one," Josh said.

"That almost sounds a little too fantastical," Harry added.

"Not so new and not so fantastical when you stop and think about it. The girls are destined to be used for whatever perversion it happens to be, then they're returned to the seller for whatever reason. Maybe the buyer grows tired of their whining, or no longer likes the way they look, or maybe they become ill." Skye held up a hand. "Not saying Carrie, Taylor or Lisa got sick and that's what triggered their disposal. Just thinking out loud here. Anyway, when the seller gets his hands back on the merchandise, he either makes the decision to keep them around for resell while making more profit on his original investment, or he chooses to end the cycle. For some reason, this killer opted to waive the flow of cash and torture these three in an almost identical manner to the bitter end."

Josh stopped pacing as if he'd just thought of something. "You remember mentioning the profiler, Emmett Cannavale?"

"Sure, we were looking for Jason Berkenshaw at the time. We could still make a point of reaching out to him. He frequents Seattle because he has family ties in the area."

"Cannavale's specialty happens to be sexual sadists. I picked up his book last summer, read the thing cover to cover. Doesn't make me an expert by any means, but Cannavale does say that these particular types are known for their meticulous planning before a crime. Based on that, I'd say the guy we're looking for is leading us down the path he wants us to follow. Why else would he deliver the flowers personally right to our back door?"

"Another level of psychological fear and manipulation without all the pain," Skye said in agreement. "Not a bad strategy on his part. He lets me know from the get-go he knows I'm involved in the case. I get rattled because he knows where I live, it gives him the edge."

Harry scratched his head. "It still doesn't tell us much about our killer."

"I'm afraid you'll have to wait for a height and weight description," Josh kidded. Then he turned serious. "Count on me installing security cameras around this place by the end of the week. I could kick myself for not doing it before now."

"Never underestimate the seedier side of life," Harry said with a grim expression. "If you have a box handy I'd like to take those flowers back with me to the lab. They might be able to determine where they came from."

"Let's hope so. Then you'll want the card too just in case," Skye offered. "You think he'll come back out here again?"

"I have no idea. But we'll be better prepared next time he does," Josh promised.

Chapter Four

As soon as Harry left, Josh reached out to stroke Skye's hair, then yanked her into his chest. Impatience had his hands roaming down her body. When his lips crushed over hers it set the mood. They both went under, a sense of urgency floating between them.

"I flew all the way back early and I want my homecoming present," he mumbled as he moved to nibble her earlobe.

His eagerness tugged at her heart knowing there'd been a time when she couldn't tease about such things. "Since when did you become so demanding?"

"Since I haven't had my hands on you in almost a week." He captured her around the waist, began to nibble her ear while taking her by the hand, leading her upstairs.

The drizzle had cleared and slivers of afternoon sunlight drifted through the bedroom windows in a buoyant display of wintry triumph.

The room's tasteful décor—mahogany and lace—came together to usher in a big dose of lived-in comfort. Unlike the furniture at the loft, they'd selected pieces that gave the farmhouse its homey feel, that sense of "crawl in between the sheets and stay awhile." The design was a reminder they'd blended old with new, modern with traditional and made it all come together to offer the perfect laidback sanctuary away from the hustle of the city.

Josh hit the remote for the stereo. Bono's voice sailed out in a soulful rendition of *I Can't Help Falling in Love With You.*

"I missed you," he declared before covering her mouth in an eager kiss.

Warmth ratcheted up. This is what she'd missed.

"I didn't even have time to spruce up for you. I still have the street smell on me from before. If you'd called to let me know…"

The wolf inside him sniffed at her throat and hair. "There's no way you could smell any better to me than you do right this minute. You give off an aura that says home to me."

Love and pleasure brimmed from the inside out. She grabbed at his pants, began the process of getting him out of them. Clothing peeled over hips and along arms as tops and bottoms flew to the floor.

In a show of haste and hunger, he fastened his mouth to hers. They circled to the bed, naked bodies filled with heat and want.

With a seductive bent she strained against him while his hands roamed over smooth skin. Little fires ignited, moved through every cell like bolts of electricity. When he ran the tip of his tongue over one breast, then took it into his mouth, she all but floated in flight.

As the tune changed to Bach, as the first trumpets blared in unison, as violin strings soared, his fingers glided lower, seeking the moist heat.

His touch brought sensations shivering through her, slamming together in a rippling force of pleasure.

He tasted, savored, and gave more. In answer, she arched up, twisted and bucked till she took him into her. Locked together, they sailed through spirals going up and up toward that one lofty goal. Layer by satiny layer, the little tremors built until finally leveling off to aftershocks. They glided over feathery clouds, dropped down to earth again as sunlight washed over the bed.

Naked bodies still entwined, they lay winded and sweaty.

He buried his face in her hair until he could move. Once he rolled off, they lay nestled in each other's arms. Wrapped up, she ran a hand across his bare chest. "It feels right having you back home."

Josh burst out a laugh and kissed her forehead. "I sure hope so." He grabbed hold of her chin, met her eyes. "If I didn't know you better I'd think you actually missed me this trip."

"What's that supposed to mean? I confess that this big house seemed too quiet while you were gone, too empty without you here to bug me, and what do I get in return? A hard time about it just because..."

He covered her mouth for a long kiss putting a stop to the objection. When he pulled back, he looked into her eyes. "Mind telling me why this trip was so different than all the others?"

She puffed out a breath. "I don't know, it just...maybe my unease increased when Harry brought me in on the first two victims and now the third. I've seen some terrible things over the years but...the mutilation to those bodies was beyond anything I'd encountered before. Then..."

"He shows up here. I get it."

She burrowed closer into his body. "In the old days I would've found a way to deal with this kind of brutality by myself."

"There's no need for that now."

"Maybe so, but it takes a self-realization to get there, to come as far as I have. I've grown accustomed to having you to lean on and now when you're gone..."

"I feel the same way when I'm on the road." He pressed his lips to her forehead in a tender gesture. "I'm starving. Why don't we order from that French place in town that delivers?"

"The new place? Sure. Beats the cheesy chicken nachos I had planned to throw together in a pinch."

Josh crawled out of bed to call in the food.

Forty-five minutes later they were feasting on pork tenderloin and an assortment of fresh veggies as they sprawled in front of the TV.

While the lighthearted comedy *Love Actually*—a movie they'd seen many times before—droned in the background, they talked about the old motel they'd bought and were in the middle of revamping. At the project's completion it would provide individual studio apartments to homeless families.

"Right now I have to crack the whip on the most recent contractor I hired and fire his ass for not showing up to the job site while I was in New York."

"At all? What is that, the third contractor since we started this remodel? We don't seem to be able to find anyone who knows what they're doing or wants to stick it out for the duration."

"I'm disappointed to say the least."

"Why did you hire him in the first place?"

"Tate recommended this guy personally."

In a playful gesture, she reached over and mussed up his hair. "You're such a loyal guy to family. It's such a good thing you do to keep Annabelle's brother in your life. I love that about you. Tate practically worships you."

"I wouldn't say that. But he was just a kid when Annabelle and I got together, just a kid when I married his sister."

"So let me guess, when Tate recommended this contractor you didn't have the heart to say no to either of them."

"That's about right. His name's Hank Fielding. Hank worked hard for ten days or so, ripped out the guts of some of the rooms but then when I went out of town, for some reason he stopped showing up. No phone call, no email, no notice."

"Hmm, here's a thought. Why not see if Travis could recommend someone reliable? We plan on seeing him on

Sunday, right? He knows a slew of people. If nothing else, he'll be able to point us toward a reliable company that specializes in getting the job done right."

"I guess that's what I'm afraid of, I'll find someone who'll want us to tear the entire place down and rebuild from scratch."

"Would that be so terrible? The building itself needs work, the foundation is crumbling, the interior is in shambles, the plumbing shot. Maybe the best thing is to tear it down and start from the ground up. The contractors we've hired so far seem to work for a week or two then go onto another project of their choosing. What have they gotten done other than cause your blood pressure to jump and get you frustrated?"

"Point taken. Okay, I'll solicit a little advice from Travis and see what happens. But that doesn't change the fact I still have to can the current contractor. I sent him an email."

"Want me to do it?"

"Fire the guy? You? Really?"

"You don't think I can do it?"

"Sure. It's just… Why would you want to? This guy's a bit of a strange bird."

"What's that mean? Is he dangerous? Unsavory? How strange?"

"No, not dangerous. At least I didn't pick up on anything like that. Tate said Hank was a gamer, said the guy picks up extra money now and then doing construction. I thought I'd do a nice thing, you know. I took everything at face value. But after Hank stopped showing up, I'm sitting in my hotel room and I decided to check out his references."

"Uh-oh."

"Yeah. I discovered Hank's company is a complete sham online. His entire Internet presence is a fabrication. He does have a contractor's license but no recent real experience to speak of."

Skye didn't like the sound of that and made a face. "So Tate doesn't know that his so-called friend basically conned both of you about who he is and what he does for a living. That's a major red flag."

"Yeah, it's one reason I'm steamed about the whole thing. I'm tired of hiring contractors who lie and don't deliver."

"Okay, so what if we both confront him together? If you want to take the lead, I'll be there to have your back. Why not send him an email? You may not even get a reply. Maybe he's already moved on to a better-paying gig."

"Sounds like a plan. Do you plan to go out tonight?"

"No. I was out all day yesterday and part of last night. I'm taking your suggestion and doing more delegating at the foundation, patrolling more during the day. Although the trend shows the scum seems to crawl out at night."

"It just seems that way."

"I suppose so."

They were just finishing up dinner when the kitchen phone rang. It was Harry. Skye put the phone on speaker so Josh could listen in.

"Just so you know, not surprisingly, the lab didn't find a single print on the container holding the flowers."

"So the guy wasn't sloppy," Josh said.

Skye chewed her lip. "Typical. I'd go door to door and quiz the neighbors to see if they saw a delivery but the nearest house isn't all that close. We're fairly remote out here."

"All the more reason to take precautions," Harry warned.

"Which reminds me to call a security company," Josh said, moving to his cell phone on the kitchen counter.

Chapter Five

The two-story Western Firebird motel sat vacant in the old section of downtown Seattle, right off the I-5 corridor.

Realtors were shocked to learn anyone would actually throw money into an abandoned building that hadn't really thrived since the eighties.

From its grand opening four decades earlier, the motel had once provided an appealing spot for vacationing families looking for an inexpensive place to bring the kids. The marketing targeted out-of-towners from Canada or Spokane or as far away as Colorado. Back then you couldn't beat the location. You could see the sights and all Seattle had to offer within walking distance. You could eat at several ethnic restaurants, get breakfast at three in the morning, or catch a movie without shelling out cash for a cab.

But by the nineties business dried up. Most of the family activity in the area dwindled and was replaced by urban decay. Drug dealers moved in, bringing violence and nightly shootings. During part of that time, the area was a killing ground for serial killer Gary Ridgway, who was fond of picking up young girls for sex along the route from downtown to the airport and beyond to Tacoma.

When the last owner died in 1992, the relatives decided to close the doors for good, which meant the ancient sign—in the shape of a giant bird—had stood unlit for more than twenty years. The overhang sagged and needed major reinforcement, windows were boarded up, and the asphalt parking lot had pits and holes the size of craters. The cracked swimming pool hadn't seen sparkling water in decades, and was now nothing more than a catchall for blowing debris and dirty rainwater.

Its rundown condition was no doubt the reason Josh and Skye had scored the property at a dirt-cheap price. They wanted to use it to put a dent in the homeless population—a worthwhile project but one that had, so far, proved a pain in the ass to get off the ground.

This morning they stood outside next to the crumbling sign, a fine mist falling, and watched an older model Dodge Caravan with peeling paint pull into the lot. No doubt the vehicle belonged to Hank Fielding, the contractor they intended to let go. Josh had emailed him two nights before to set up the meeting. The man's firing wasn't exactly something they looked forward to doing.

Josh spotted the driver—the man he'd hired only two weeks earlier—and a woman with long brown hair sitting in the passenger seat cuddling a baby on her lap.

A tall, thin man in his early twenties got out from behind the wheel and immediately began to apologize.

"I know what you're thinking. That I'm no good at my job and you're gonna can me. But before you make it official, if you'll just listen for a minute and give me a chance to explain."

Josh exchanged looks with Skye, their sympathies merging into a holding pattern.

It was Josh who said, "Okay, let's hear your excuse although you should know I've already found out the business you listed on your resume is totally phony, a figment of your own imagination, so don't even try to fake me out again."

Hank ran an unsteady hand through his longish hair. "What would you do if you had a family and couldn't find work? It's true I invented myself because I was desperate to find a job and I couldn't. I didn't know what else to do but come up with a fake company so I could try to find work, maybe latch on to a job in construction. I didn't make it to the site the last few days because the baby got sick Monday night and now my wife has the same thing. I spent the day before yesterday waiting in line at the free clinic for them both to see a doctor. The doctor thinks it's the flu. So he prescribed some decongestant and cough medicine and someone had to take care of the baby when my wife got sick."

To Josh the more Hank talked, the more convincing his story sounded. But Josh needed to clear up a few things. "You could've called to let someone know what was going on. You've only been on the job a short time. As contractor you were in charge, yet you haven't even hired a crew yet, which I found odd at the time."

"That's just it, there's more. I couldn't pay my cell phone bill the last few months and they cut me off. Without it, I couldn't call anyone. I jumped right in on this job. I ripped out cabinets and tile in nine of the rooms in the ten days I worked. That's pretty good on my own. There's no phone here at the motel so I didn't get a chance to call for any laborers. But while I was on the clock I worked hard. Check the rooms for yourself."

Josh already had and was impressed by what he'd accomplished in a short amount of time. He listened as the guy went on in a desperate attempt to save his job.

"The only way I saw your email was because I went to the library to use one of their computers. As soon as I read it, I knew I had to get my butt over here and explain."

In Skye's mind that didn't fully detail why he couldn't use a pay phone and make the call to say things were unraveling. But staring at the female and infant waiting for him in the car, there was no doubt they both looked cold and ill. Add to that, the car seemed loaded down with as much stuff as they could possibly cram into the interior and still sit in the front seat. It looked as though they'd brought it all with them because the car was positively filled to the brim with household goods.

Which prompted Skye to interrupt with a question of her own. "If you don't mind my asking, where are you and your family living now?"

Hank seemed embarrassed and reluctant to answer. After several long seconds went by, he admitted, "In the minivan."

"The temp last night dropped to twenty-seven degrees. No wonder they're sick," Skye reasoned, appealing to Josh with a knowing look. As she so often did while patrolling the mean streets of Seattle at night, she went with her gut instincts. "I know a place where you can crash until you get back up on your feet. My old studio apartment is not far from here. It's small and a bit cramped for three people but…"

"That doesn't matter," Hank said quickly. "As long as I can get my wife and son out of the cold for a couple nights, I'd be grateful."

Knowing how she felt about that first little place of her own, Josh leaned in and whispered, "Are you absolutely certain about this?"

Skye lifted one shoulder and answered in a low voice, "It's sitting there empty. I haven't been back over there in weeks." It wasn't exactly the truth. She still stopped in now and then to sprinkle water over her rosemary and oregano. But that wasn't the point now. "This family doesn't have a roof over their heads. Why should the space go to waste when they could use a bed? Isn't this exactly the kind of situation we're hoping to improve with this project?"

Josh smiled and shook his head. "I guess it is."

He flipped his gaze back to Hank. "Looks like you've been given a second chance by the missus. But from here on out, I want you to make a concerted effort to get to a pay phone if you're unable to make it to work for any reason."

Hank nodded. "I will. I promise. I can't wait to tell Melina. She'll be grateful, too."

"The studio has a phone so there'll be no excuses not to let us know when or if something should come up in the future and you're unable to make it in to work," Skye added. "Plus, I've known the neighbors in my building for years, lived inside those four walls since I was eighteen. If you bring drug dealers or an unsavory element within five feet of them, I'll string you up myself."

For the first time, Hank responded with a grin, threw up his hands. "Tate told me about you. I'm well aware of your rep for kicking ass. I don't know any drug dealers. Ask Tate if you don't believe me."

"How is it you know Tate?" Skye wanted to know.

"In my single, carefree days, I used to hang out with him and play video games. Now that I'm an old married man, I don't have time for those kinds of things."

"Let's get your wife and son out of the cold and settled into the apartment. Why don't you follow us the four blocks over?"

"That would be great."

"Then let's go."

As soon as they got back into Skye's Subaru, Josh twisted in his seat. "Are you certain about taking a chance on them like this?"

She hoped she was. "It's time, don't you think? I have a nice tiny apartment sitting empty with a lot more space than a car provides for three people. That baby needs to get out of that cold car. If my tiny studio might make a difference to this family, I'd be selfish not to offer it to them."

"But six months ago you wouldn't even consider listing it as a rental."

"That's before I caught the look on Hank's son's little cherub face. That baby isn't sleeping another night in a cold truck if I have anything to do with it."

"I love you," Josh declared, running a long finger down the side of her cheek.

"I know. But you're the reason I can allow strangers to live in my very first apartment, the place I cherished for so long. You think they'll appreciate it? I mean I know what Hank said but…"

"I don't think the Fieldings will trash the place if that's what you mean."

That made her grin. "So you sensed Hank was on the level, too?"

"I did."

"Then I'm feeling better and better about my decision."

Skye pulled her Subaru up to the curb and into the only available parking spot she could find on the street. When Hank drove up alongside and motioned for her to roll the window down, she complied.

"Where should we park?"

"Wherever you can locate a space to slide your minivan. Sometimes it's difficult to find a spot," she pointed out. "You'll probably have to circle the block several more times and keep looking before you find one."

Skye pointed across the street. "That's the building over there. When you park, that's where we'll be waiting on the steps."

"Okay, sure. You guys wait for us in the car while we make another round. That way you won't have to stand out in the damp wind."

Ten minutes passed before Hank and Melina walked up to where they stood in front of a four-story vintage brownstone. Melina toted the baby and what looked like a heavy diaper bag.

Skye didn't know much about babies, but even she could tell Alec still looked feverish. His cheeks were bright red with a rash. He had a runny nose and cough.

Skye unlocked the front door and led the way into a small vestibule out of the cold. They finished going through introductions standing in the lobby.

"It isn't much to look at, I know, but the location is great. It's only two blocks east of the harbor, which means everything is within easy walking distance. Come warm weather, you'll never have to get the car out to go to the store or grab a cup of coffee. When I lived here I rarely had to use my car."

"Oh, it's wonderful," Melina gushed out in a raspy voice that indicated she'd been sick. "Isn't it wonderful, Hank?"

"The mailboxes are around the corner in that little corridor," Skye directed. "I'll give you a key so you'll be able to get mail."

Skye could tell Melina was taken with the idea of staying. Sentiment rushed through her remembering the very first time she'd set eyes on the place at eighteen. "It's an amazing old building. I truly enjoyed my years here. I think it will work for you and Hank, even on a temporary basis, if that's what you decide. "

"I adore it already. It's a fantastic thing you're doing for us. We're so grateful," Melina went on again.

"Hand me Alec," Hank offered, eyeing the set of stairs. "I'll carry him up. You're too sick to be carrying him that far."

Skye waited for Melina to relinquish the baby before starting up the staircase, talking as she went. "I hope you don't think I'm a busybody, but how long have you been without a place to live exactly?"

Melina grabbed the rail and answered in a gravelly voice, "Since the first of November."

Hearing that news Josh's heart went out to the couple just as Skye's had done. "But it's almost Christmas. All this time you've been sleeping in the car?"

"No, no, not at all. When it gets really, really cold sometimes Alec and I sleep at the shelter over on Bayview.

I don't like doing that though because the rules there say that Hank isn't allowed to stay with us. I'm pretty sure it's because that shelter is designated for women and children only. After the second week of that, I decided I'd rather sleep in the car with Hank than without him." Melina let out a croupy cough. "I'm pretty sure my decision is what caused Alec to get sick. I wasn't thinking. I didn't mean to…"

Josh interrupted the young mom. "That's an awful decision to have to make, whether or not you stay together as a family or sleep in a warm bed."

"That's what we thought at the time," Hank said.

Skye shifted gears, changing the subject back to tour guide. "It's a bit of a climb. The apartment is a fourth-floor walkup. That's a lot of stairs to deal with when you have a baby."

"The stairs are fine," Melina assured her. "I'm usually in much better shape when I don't have the flu."

They scaled the other floors in silence because Melina needed to take a break after the third landing. Once they reached the top floor, Skye took out a key to a unit at the end of the hallway. She swung the door back and let the couple go in first.

"It's basically a rectangular box. But there's a little love seat, a bed, a kitchenette with a two-burner stove, a microwave, and a compact-sized refrigerator. As you can see there are dishes, pots and pans, and just about everything else you'll need for putting together a meal."

Melina spun around in a circle and blinked back tears. "Oh my God, it's better than our last place. It's beautiful. I love it. We can really stay here?"

Skye let out a laugh. She'd never had anyone consider her little studio wonderful or beautiful before now. "Absolutely."

"Are you sure we aren't putting you out of your home?" Hank asked, running his hand over the full-sized antique bed that sat in the corner. "This place will suit us just fine."

Melina dashed to the sliding glass door and eyed the rows of plants lining the balcony. "Are those peppermint plants?"

"Skye loves to grow her own herbs," Josh added. "You have fresh mint and sage at your fingertips. And I see they've all been recently weeded," he added with a wink.

"So maybe I've been here a time or two since Thanksgiving to make sure the tarragon doesn't die from neglect," Skye confessed. "Those plants in the corner growing on the mini trellis are cherry tomatoes. They'll bloom in a couple of months."

"We want to pay rent on this place," Hank announced. "We have sixty-seven dollars cash that we've been hoarding for food. I know it isn't much but... It's yours if you'll let us stay here."

Josh noticed Skye's eyes were almost as watery as Melina's. "How about we go back to the job site while Skye helps Melina settle in here with the baby? The two of us will go over the job again, start fresh. We'll discuss the specifics of your getting back to work and what I expect. Meanwhile, I'll come up with a lease for you guys to sign and we'll take it from there."

When the baby started rubbing his eyes and began to cry, Melina said to Hank, "Before you go, could you bring up the port-a-crib from the back of the car? Alec needs to go down for his nap."

"Sure. I'll get the crib and make another trip to grab the box with our clothes."

As soon as the men took off, Skye looked adoringly at the little boy, itching to touch. Instead of that, she pointed out the best place to stick the crib. "There's room to set it up right here by the little kitchen table." She couldn't wait any longer to reach out and run her fingers through the few strands of hair on the infant's head. "How old is he anyway?"

"Eight months. Hank and I were doing fine until he lost his job. We aren't bad parents."

"Of course you aren't. People go through rough times. It happens."

"I'm so glad Hank found this job. I'm glad he didn't get fired." Melina coughed several times before adding, "I'm usually pretty busy with the baby but if you ever need help with stuffing envelopes or answering the phone down at that foundation of yours, you let me know. I'd love to do whatever needs doing to help out."

"Good to know. For now, I'll get you and Alec squared away before I leave you two alone. You both look exhausted, like you could sleep for a week."

"Being here makes me feel normal again." Melina reached into the bag and brought out a bottle of milk. "Look at that. You even have a microwave. I feel like I'm in the luxury suite at the Ritz-Carlton. Would you hold Alec while I heat this up?"

"Uh, sure." Skye reached out her arms and the baby fell into them, curling up against her chest.

That's the picture Josh saw when he walked through the door carrying a box of clothes—his beautiful wife clutching an adorable infant up against her heart. He captured that image and put it to memory, knowing full well Skye wanted a baby. Maybe it was time to bring up the subject of adoption and stick to it. So far, they'd tabled that discussion at least a dozen times, using a variety of excuses.

As quickly as he considered bringing it up, he put the idea on ice. Who in their right mind would bring a child into the mix when mommy went out every night to face the bad guys? How would that even work anyway? Better if he stalled. Bringing up that quagmire topic would lead straight to quicksand for sure—for now anyway.

Chapter Six

Once Josh and Skye got the couple and baby settled into the apartment, they headed to the Artemis Foundation—Skye's three-hundred-square-foot dot of a space in the same high-rise that housed Ander All Games.

If they wanted to catch the man responsible for mutilating three young women, they had a lot of work to do.

From its inception, the foundation had been set up with one purpose in mind—to locate and bring back the missing: those who'd disappeared under questionable circumstances, who'd vanished without a trace. Their age or gender didn't matter.

But somewhere along the way, the dynamics of their mission statement had changed. Families with missing loved ones or victims of violent crimes often became disillusioned with the system that couldn't provide them with answers. When they showed up at Skye's door looking for help, she didn't have the heart to turn them away. Assisting law enforcement to solve certain homicides had now become part of their everyday routine.

Skye understood better than most how family members suffered, many times for years without resolution. Her own parents had been in the same boat—heartbroken from the moment they'd learned their twelve-year-old had been stolen off a playground in broad daylight, with them at a barbeque mere feet away.

But thanks to Kiya and the power of her Nez Perce heritage, that little girl had escaped her captor. She'd managed to outsmart Ronny Whitfield, the sexual predator who had nabbed her.

Since that day, she'd grown stronger. And the night she walked down a certain alleyway only to save Josh Ander from a mugging had been her turning point.

Together the two had built The Artemis Foundation into more than a local clearinghouse, more than just a database, more than a physical place to collect and then sit on a pile of useless data.

To make the most of that data, Josh had put together a team of computer hackers—Leo Martin, Reggie Bechtol, and Winston Reeker. They excelled at banging through firewalls to retrieve and accumulate streams of information that often turned into key pieces of the puzzle used to nab the bad guys.

Always up for doing whatever was necessary to crack a case, Leo, Reggie and Winston had taken to hanging out here. Whenever they weren't upstairs at Ander All Games, they could be found manning the bank of phones or organizing the massive amounts of case files.

This morning, while Josh signed checks, Reggie and Winston tackled the mail together, sorting through mountains of letters containing pictures sent in by families from as far away as Florida.

Skye tacked the photographs up on the map she had on the wall and stacked the letters on the corner of her desk to enter into the database.

Leo strolled through the door, his arms full of books and papers. An imposing figure at six-three, his height made a lot of people gape, but it was likely the dreadlocks down to his shoulders that had them taking a third hard look. Like Reggie and Winston, Leo was young, brilliant, and had shunned the standard path to a nine-to-five job. Working as contractors for Ander All Games, the hours the trio put in earned them plenty of money. Yet each man lived without many of the trappings associated with a six-figure income. They had apartments in the city, and somehow managed to avoid owning a car, although Winston did go everywhere on his ten-speed. All three men shared one valuable trait—a willingness to go the extra mile for the foundation. Each had a good-hearted nature that made for an enjoyable work environment. They often clowned around to cut the tension that built up in the office.

Skye had long decided the place wouldn't be the same without them or their dazzling technical contributions.

Leo let the heap of folders fall into a vacant chair and slapped down a printout of names onto Skye's desk. "That list you emailed me after Gwen DeLargo went missing yesterday keeps growing. Take a look at the statistics I extracted last night while Winston ran the names."

"What am I looking at?" Skye asked, thumbing through the pages. "I gave you the list of Seattle's missing females I'd accumulated over the last few years. I wanted you to make sure I hadn't missed any."

"I improvised and added to your instructions. I went back farther than you had, as far back as fifteen years. Our list shows forty-five young women have gone missing from an area that spans as far north as Bellingham, Washington and as far south as Medford, Oregon. And as you can see, I branched out west to Idaho."

"But these names can't all belong to our killer," Skye stated, not wanting to believe there were so many women who'd gone missing at the hands of their mutilating monster. But something about Leo's face told her he felt different.

"That's what I thought, too. But you know what they say about assumptions. Most of these are teens who went missing from schools, malls, parks, public places, even three from a library. I narrowed down the field, chose not to include those over the age of thirty, or who didn't fit your profile."

"Leo, I appreciate your initiative but there's no way to know for certain these are all connected, no way at all," Skye declared. "Our guy mutilates his victims."

Stubbornly Leo hung in, clinging to his theory. "Just hear me out. All the women on that list share one common, undeniable denominator. No one has seen or heard from them since the day they disappeared, no bodies located, none ID'd, no activity on their social security number or credit cards. Zero. Winston and Reggie were very thorough on that score. They triple-checked the info against the names and dates of birth. So if they haven't been found we don't know they *weren't* mutilated."

"We don't know for sure they're dead, either," Josh added from the doorway. "And a fourteen-year-old rarely has her own credit card to follow a paper trail," Josh continued as he handed Leo a check. "Here you go. Your Christmas bonus."

Leo took the paper, stared down at the amount. "Contractors don't usually qualify for bonuses."

Winston came around the corner. "It's for our work here, isn't it?"

Josh smiled. "You guys often work late into the night. You deserve to get paid for it even if it only comes once a year. " When Winston tried to hand the check back to him, Josh held up both hands. "If you don't want it, donate it to the charity of your choice."

"But all of us came on board knowing this is volunteer work," Winston protested. "Okay, I'm donating it back to the foundation."

"You don't have to do that," Skye added. "Josh and I talked about this. We're able to keep our overhead and expenses to a minimum. We have a printer around the corner who donates paper stock each time we circulate flyers. You guys donate your valuable time every day to the cause. A bonus is long overdue."

"If you're sure. Then thanks, boss," Winston said, finally tucking the check into his shirt pocket.

Skye shifted the conversation back to business. "If that's settled, let's get back to the list. Josh is right, teenagers don't have much of a credit history."

Leo picked up his train of thought. "It's true someone that young wouldn't but most have social security numbers you can plug into the system to see if they've been employed during the years they've been gone."

"And no activity usually indicates... Sinister circumstances," Josh noted as he used the corner of the desk for a place to sit.

"It doesn't bode well, that's for sure. When we compiled the list, we eliminated the ones we came across that you and Skye had already pegged as runaways."

Josh winced. "That was a call we made based on information the families gave us."

Skye folded her arms across her chest. "Just so you know, it was a case-by-case decision. We don't lump kids in that category without strong indicators they bolted on their own. And in some of those disappearances, we're still open-minded enough to keep them in a separate database."

Leo shifted his huge feet. "It's a good move. But after excluding them that left the forty-five names. The most interesting one we ran across is the oldest case and involves the youngest victim. An eleven-year-old girl from Pocatello, Idaho, by the name of Camilla Prentiss who went missing from a neighbor's house where she'd gone to babysit on a Saturday night. Camilla was never seen or heard from again. She just vanished out of the house, out of the neighborhood, out of town. The police files show she had a good home life and no reason to run away."

"But I wanted you to focus on Washington State, specifically the Seattle area," Skye said stubbornly. "So many other unrelated cases complicate matters."

"I know but... There are four more in Idaho that fit, each about a year apart. It's almost like every spring he had to... Make some kind of statement. There's more. There's a string of missing seventeen- and eighteen-year-olds from Oregon to British Columbia, sandwiched in between is Washington. According to info I retrieved online from websites established by some of the families, each girl seemed happy at the time she disappeared and by all accounts was heavily into school life, extracurricular activities and the like. Yet they went missing without a trace from around schools, football and soccer fields, and public parks. It might be a trivial thing, but some had even been seen partying after a basketball or a football game the night they went missing."

"Nothing is ever too trivial because it's an interesting detail we might be able to work into a pattern."

"That isn't all. You should know that even though I found a lot of disappearances, I eliminated those names where the ages didn't fit. Let's say, anyone on the list older than twenty-two, I excluded."

"That could be a mistake in the long run," Josh suggested. "We need to be able to consider all angles. This guy might nab an older girl in a pinch if he couldn't find a teenager."

Leo bobbed his head in agreement. "I've kept that age group in a separate spreadsheet. So, here's the thing. I deleted all those missing from the Gary Ridgway era, since he's been locked up for more than a decade." Leo paused before going on, as if he dreaded mentioning the name. "I also discounted the ones Skye had already pinned on Ronny Whitfield—those Whitfield grabbed and shipped out to foreign countries, which accounted for a good many already on your list. Because of that, Winston and I wrote a specific program that pulled from two key factors—a young age *and* family stability. No one on our list had a reason to run off on her own. Not a single one. Our program has pretty much kicked out cold cases and narrowed it down to those forty-five that could be attributed to your guy."

"Impressive," Skye uttered, letting out an accepting sigh while Josh took the list out of her hands to peruse it.

"Thanks, but keep in mind this list may grow because it doesn't account for any…"

"Who were never reported missing at all," Skye finished. "Never passed onto any cop's radar because they were never put into the system. It's one of the more frustrating aspects of what we do."

Josh went over Leo's paperwork and let out his own pent-up breath. "So this is what was left. If this is the killer's handiwork it shows he's been a busy boy. Let's say he began his killing around the age of twenty. That would make him thirty-five now. I wonder. Does he cover all this area because he lived in all these places or was he moving through these states for work?"

"And now, for whatever reason, he's recently landed in the Seattle area to spread his perverted kind of…"

Leo was in the middle of his sentence when Skye didn't wait for him to finish. "There's just one problem with your leap in logic. While the stats are notable, and probable, the girls on that list are *missing*. We, on the other hand, have three real homicides with bodies that ended up in the morgue, murders that deal with females who disappeared several years back and have now reappeared. That means he didn't just surface in Seattle last month. He's been here for quite some time."

"Then why start leaving them where they're easily discovered?" Josh questioned.

Skye bit her lip. "That's the big empty hole we have to somehow figure out how to fill. Obviously our guy isn't opposed to exploring what other states have to offer. But if Leo's info is even half accurate this is bad news. I thought maybe the guy was just starting out but now there's very little chance of that."

Josh jingled the change in his pockets in an edgy show of deep thought. "Let's keep in mind that Bundy changed his MO multiple times. He'd break into a woman's apartment one week, bludgeon her to death with a metal rod, and then go back to kidnapping them off the street or sweet-talking them into getting into his vehicle the next. He'd pull whatever ruse worked to gain access to a victim. The point is he didn't stay with one method during the years he was active. When his urges got out of control he'd feed them by finding a way to get it done. His victims varied in ages and by the time he landed in Florida, Bundy had become a killing machine like the predator he was."

"Thanks for that recap," Skye muttered, sarcasm laced in her tone. "You know what this means, don't you? We'll have to contact the families of every woman on here and get the specifics of their daughter's disappearance for our own benefit."

She eyed Leo and added, "I know Winston and Reggie did the surface stuff. But I'm suggesting that we delve deeper than the general info you found elsewhere to better understand each victim and come up with a pattern, if there is one."

"A painful undertaking," Leo stated. "I'd like to recommend more training for all the volunteers. Interacting with family members is a tricky landmine. All of us struggle to ask the right questions in a professional way while maintaining a balance and avoid crossing an awkward line."

"We'll work on it. That's why we have a team. When one bumps up against a tough situation, we hand it off," Josh said, a grim reminder of why they did this job. Thinking of his earlier "baby moment," he felt this might be an excellent time for a reminder of another kind. He turned to Skye, draped his arm over her shoulder. "It's time you realize you can't do everything, be everywhere, and take on every single task that comes into this office."

Skye knew Josh meant well but it didn't mean she could let go that easily. Of course, she had to learn to delegate, spread the tasks around to others as the foundation grew and took on more and more volunteers. Practicality had to be a virtue. After mulling it over, she decided it was in the best interest of the missing girls and their families to hand off some of the names.

"I've already been working with Judy Howe on how to deal with digging out the delicate information from a family member. Judy's past with Berkenshaw makes her a great choice to be one of our go-to people able to successfully reach out to relatives. There's a fine line to it. Making contact is difficult. You don't want to give them false hope that their daughter is out there somewhere, that she might've survived somehow. The balance is about gaining as much info as we can and *not* yanking that hope out from under them. For months now, Judy's been practicing her people skills and seeing a therapist twice a week. I think she's ready to tackle this one."

Josh's face broke into a grin. "I agree. Judy's been doing a damned good job of making her way back despite surviving a brutal attack from a sadist. The last time I talked to her, Judy brought up the ordeal herself without any prompting from me. She's making remarkable progress, to think only months ago she lived her life in a reclusive environment."

Skye beamed back. "Recluse no more. I'll call her and get her to come in early today, call Travis, too. All of us will divvy up the list, start working it, obtaining last known addresses for the teens, exact locations of where they went missing, and get current phone numbers for their next of kin, start setting up face to face appointments if we have to."

"I'm going out with you tonight," Josh stated out of the blue. "There's no point in arguing about it either."

She narrowed her eyes. "A serial killer delivers flowers to me personally at home and you think I'd be foolish enough to turn down company or go out by myself? Tsk, tsk, after all this time you still underestimate me."

"Who, me? No way. It's going up against that hard head of yours time and again that has me prepared for battle each time I mention helping you on the streets."

Skye took hold of his shirt with both hands, pulled him closer in front of Leo. She smacked his lips with hers in a fierce kiss. "Besides, we make such a good team and you're my right-hand man," she cracked. "How could I go out at night without you to protect my back?"

"'Bout time you realized it."

Assembling the team was the easy part. Skye had a long list of people willing to help. Longtime friends like Velma Gentry and Lena Bowers had become staples. There were others on standby that could be counted on when the foundation needed to rally ground troops for searches or make phone calls.

Getting down to the nitty-gritty was a piece of cake. But reaching out and touching base with moms and dads who were still hurting from a disappearance was another matter entirely. Some of the couples hadn't even stayed together. Divorce often occurred after the traumatic loss of a child. Statistics proved that. But these particular instances when a daughter went missing without a trace could put a different kind of pressure on a relationship. No closure, nothing to latch onto, meant it was easier to go their separate ways than to deal with the pain together.

On top of separation and strain, it was a sad fact the families of the missing were often pushed aside by members of law enforcement. The same could be said about the media. Once the case grew cold, interest tended to evaporate on both fronts. Unless a family member took matters into his or her own hands and kept the case alive by giving TV interviews, becoming a regular contributor online, or establishing a website or Facebook page, or became a pest in general with detectives, the file, more than likely, sat in a box somewhere gathering dust. After all, it rarely fell into the "homicide" category because without a body, cops often felt they had no reason to pursue the case. Investigators could only follow available leads. If no leads materialized or didn't pan out, there wasn't much more they could do except wait for tips to come in from the general public. Which meant many case files fell into their own abyss, that special circle of hell with no answers.

By early afternoon, reinforcements showed up—Judy, Velma, Lena, and Travis arrived to pitch in. As they mulled over all the names on the list, Velma commented, "Oh, wow. It's for sure that making these phone calls will be a lot tougher than waitressing. These stories just break my heart."

Skye agreed. "I know. The families want so much for someone to talk to them, to find them any kind of resolution. They're usually very cooperative, but tread carefully with the prickly questions." Skye went over the same spiel with these volunteers she'd had with Leo earlier.

Once Lena had gone over all the names there was disbelief. "So many victims. Are these ages correct? Some of these are just kids."

"Kids are the most trusting and vulnerable," Skye said. "But let's face it, any age is susceptible to falling victim to a clever killer. Predators are good at coming up with the perfect ploy to fit the occasion."

"If the phone numbers the team gathered still work and you get to talk to a family member, suggest a meeting, either at their place or coming in to the foundation," Josh directed. He glanced around the room and into the faces of the group. "We don't expect the ones out of state to make the trip here, but any who are close, bring it up in conversation. Let them know our volunteers are here for them if they need to talk."

"You need to mention to the volunteers that many families have already resigned themselves to bad news," Judy added. "So when the phone rings in, let's say

Spokane, and you start talking about their case, prepare for a lot of emotion."

"Good point," Skye noted.

"If nothing else, maybe stirring things up, we'll rattle some cages in law enforcement," Travis said as he looked over his portion of the list.

Skye glanced at her father. "That's one reason I think it's time we bring in Emmett Cannavale."

Travis shifted in his chair, stared back at his daughter. "You know he's part Chinook. He has an interesting heritage and ties to the area."

Josh rounded into the room from the little kitchen area catching the last part. Holding a freshly brewed pot of coffee in his hand he toured the room, refilling cups. "I read something about that in his bio. His Chinook mother married an Italian farmer who'd settled here after the war to start a farm, grow olive trees."

"I can't wait to ask him about that," Skye retorted.

The door opened and Harry popped his head inside but stopped short of walking in. Instead, the detective looked around the front office, saw the crowd there, and motioned for Skye and Josh to come out into the hallway.

Sensing a problem because of the look on Harry's face, Josh made it to the hall first. "What gives? You look as though you've seen a ghost."

"I've got a report of bones washing up on the beach at Alki Point. I'm headed there now, decided you guys might as well ride along. So I swung by, took a chance that you'd want to see what's what for yourself. Get your gear and let's go."

It was on this same strip of Alki Beach that Chief Seattle waited on its shell-strewn shore to greet the first white settlers, arms open in hospitality, heart full of hope for a long, enduring friendship. The year was 1851 when he first shared the food he had on hand, taught the newcomers how to build the huts that would keep them dry and warm during winter and showed them how to make the best use of the vegetation and surrounding prairie land.

Members of Seattle's tribe—a mix of Suquamish and Duwamish—were practiced farmers who tended the land, making sure it yielded a generous bounty of fruits and vegetables each season. The Natives willingly shared whatever they had on hand. Since the coastal land around Puget Sound gave up enough steelhead and game and berries for everyone, Chief Seattle never concerned himself overmuch about the future of his people.

But he should have.

Inevitable progress forced the area tribes to give up their canoes, their villages, sign treaties that would take away their rights, and break up families. Distraught parents learned their children would be packed off thousands of miles away to boarding schools in other parts of the country. Many were never reunited. Missionaries were determined to indoctrinate what was left of them into a new world they neither understood nor wanted.

A short twenty years later in the 1870s, expansion of the land became the primary goal. Railroads, electricity, and settlements popped up, even an amusement park. A steady stream of people from back east took advantage of a circus-like atmosphere in a new frontier and the new technology to get them there. Advertisements enticed the adventurous to leave home and seek out new horizons. Given the idea of owning the land that had once belonged to the Natives, easterners invaded the area in droves. Ultimately development caused the generous beach to shrink in size to what it looked like today, a smidgen of pebbly shore.

The area resembled any other small, bustling community that sat near the water. Traffic bogged down stretches of the roadway. During good weather, tourists flocked to the seashore. A string of businesses—cafes, coffee shops, trendy boutiques, art studios—did their best to attract new customers.

Giant cedar and spruce grew next to cottonwood and towered over the grassy slopes where older bungalows lined the winding neighborhood streets alongside larger, newly built, modern houses.

Today when they arrived on the scene the place looked deserted.

Yellow police tape marred the beauty and the view across the bay and its surrounding wetlands. Crime scene techs milled about the roped-off area with cameras while Roger Bayliss knelt on the ground, feet from the lapping water.

As soon as Harry pulled his SUV to a stop, three car doors flew open, each person taking in the scene before them. It seemed death had touched this serene, peaceful setting where families like to picnic in the summer.

Even from twenty feet away, Skye could see the scattering of bones littering the sand. She'd never seen the medical examiner quite as pale as he was today. She didn't blame his bark when he warned everyone to stay back.

"Before you come any closer, I should tell you we have at least seven vertebrae and five pieces of various jawbones. Small ones."

Everyone there knew what that meant.

"Those bones belong to kids," Skye said in grim realization. "Five jawbones is a lot of children to go missing at the same time."

"How long do you think they've been here?" Josh shouted to Bayliss.

"I can't answer that," the coroner snarled. "In case you haven't noticed, I'm a little busy here."

Josh spun back to Skye in solemn understanding. "Bayliss may not be willing to discuss it but... Those bones are from a long time ago."

"How… How are you able to tell that from here?" But even as she asked the question there was acceptance. It had been almost two years since Josh had acquired the uncanny ability to pick up on certain details about a crime scene, not unlike that of a seasoned member of law enforcement routinely used investigating the worst of the worst. Pros referred to it as a gut instinct. Never mind that Josh had been a gamer for most of his life rather than a veteran cop. "How far do they go back?"

"I don't know exactly. But there's no flesh left on them, no tattered clothing anywhere in sight." Josh scanned the businesses up on the hill and the cross-traffic on the street. He studied the ridgeline down to the seawall. "Nor does it appear that they've been unearthed recently. See, there are no holes anywhere on shore, no massive grave to excavate. No indication the bones were dug up, or planted here at some point, or thrown out in containers or cartons, at least not from the highway, too far to toss them out like that—busy section of street, too busy not to attract attention from all the businesses nearby. If a vehicle stopped to unload that kind of cargo, for the time it would take, someone would see that kind of dump. That only leaves one conclusion."

Skye shifted her feet, considered the factors in his theory. "They came in from the sea, washed up on shore, recently, perhaps even overnight."

Josh rubbed his chin in thought and looked out at the water. "You got it on the first try. I've lived in Seattle all my life, made so many trips back and forth across the Sound that I couldn't even begin to count all of them. There's a marker not far from here commemorating the loss of the *Dix*, a ferry that sank in 1906, carrying millworkers and their families. After spending the weekend in Seattle, the lumber company had a habit of transporting their employees back to Bainbridge for the work week. But that Sunday night the *Dix* hit an Alaska freighter heading to Tacoma. The *Dix* went down within minutes, taking forty-five people with it to a watery grave."

"I remember reading the history. If memory serves, the marker's around that curve in the trail near Duwamish Head. Didn't they finally locate the wreckage of the *Dix* several years back?"

"I think so. As far as I know there were no plans to raise it. But the bodies were never recovered."

"You aren't suggesting these bones could belong to the children from that maritime disaster, are you?"

Josh shook his head. "I'm not suggesting anything. I don't know exactly where they came from. But I intend to do my own research until I find out."

Chapter Seven

At the downtown Seattle Marriott, former FBI profiler Emmett Cannavale, took center stage at the law enforcement seminar to talk about what he'd learned over the years about serial killers.

The fifty-five-year-old retired Fed wasn't all that tall, maybe five-eight, but he had a presence that surpassed physical traits. That Chinook heritage Travis had mentioned earlier was evident in his black hair and dark brown eyes. He regaled the crowd with anecdotes, an easy smile, and could be charming at times to make his point.

The conference room had already filled to capacity by the time Josh and Skye found a seat. They sat among cops from across the state who had gathered to go over stacks of cold cases, hoping to get their chance at hearing the famed profiler's take on a variety of serial homicides with one common characteristic, a sexual overtone to each crime. Each case competed with the other for a resolution. They'd brought their own three slim file folders that held the few facts they knew about the murders of Carrie, Taylor, and Lisa.

Cannavale held court like a professor in charge of his classroom. The crowd, eager and attentive, listened as he went over the usual characteristics of a serial offender. The speaker rattled off his points by citing the list of traits serial killers most often exhibit beginning in early childhood. From abusing animals to going through psychological or physical trauma, such as a head injury, to developing an odd or embarrassing fetish, including voyeurism, to compounding their problems by using alcohol or drugs, Cannavale warned that society invariably faced the making of another Ted Bundy if it failed to recognize the problem in youth.

"Maybe this was a mistake," Skye whispered to Josh from the back row. "This isn't really new info."

"Our goal is to get Cannavale one on one. That's why we came. Right now he's hitting the high points."

"He's going over repetitive ground," Skye grumbled, that stubborn bent to her tone clearly evident. "Look around. There are at least two hundred cops here who brought tough cold cases. Every single one of us in attendance knows serial killers don't stay choirboys forever and the 'expert' is wasting time spouting off about how they got started. Who cares?"

Josh recognized impatience and squeezed her hand. "Down girl. He'll get to us as soon as his speech is done. If necessary, we'll pounce on him during the afternoon break."

Their first shot at talking to Cannavale came during the working lunch when everyone drifted to tables set up in the back to pick up their cold sandwich and chips. The no-nonsense meal suited Skye's mood. But for the first time all day, she did feel bad for the guy who was just trying to grab a bite to eat while he could. Her sentiment, however, didn't prevent her from interrupting his ham and cheese on wheat.

She introduced herself and Josh before making her brief presentation. Getting down to the bottom line, she said, "Today we brought three recent cases that are remarkably similar. We think our killer is making a statement for a specific reason. We just don't know what it is yet."

Without a word, Cannavale picked up his paper napkin and wiped his mouth, opened the first file, then the second, then the third.

"Much of what I say, you probably already know. But for what it's worth, your guy is highly organized, likes to use his hands, and keeps trophies. He has no problem dismembering. By that I mean he's comfortable with a knife. He fixates on the breasts, probably because he has a thing for that particular body part."

Skye didn't try to mask her disappointment. Her face showed all the frustration she felt. Why had she thought this former government guy held all the magical answers?

"Take a seat," Cannavale said, looking up at the couple. "I can see you're both disillusioned. But profiling isn't an exact science no matter how many TV shows present it as such. Why don't you tell me what you think?"

Josh pulled out a chair for Skye before sitting down across from Cannavale and picked up Lisa's folder. "We think he's cutting out the implants because he sees them as intrusions to what he considers the perfect body. What we can't figure out is why he made the girls get them in the first place only to cut them out."

"Maybe he didn't. You might be dealing with a guy who hears voices."

"A schizophrenic?"

"Sure. Ed Gein, Berkowitz, Richard Chase, they were all diagnosed as such. There's also the possibility he's fractured into more than one personality."

"That would be a new one," Skye said to Josh.

"Add in the fact that serials are usually proficient at masking their real self, their true feelings to the outside world, especially with family and friends. I'd say you have a disturbed man, probably white, between twenty-five and thirty-five. He gets off on the suffering your three victims felt. That tells me he's proficient at what he does. Translation: He's killed before these three."

"Which means we're looking at the tip of the iceberg," Josh stated.

Skye nodded. "On that we all agree. He wanted us to find these."

"That sounds like a reasonable conclusion. But keep in mind what I said about the trophy thing. Remember, when they keep the bodies close to them, bodies are considered trophies."

"You think he doesn't like letting go of his other victims," Josh stated in understanding.

"That, or he's like Ridgway, and puts them where he has access, where he is able to go back and forth whenever he wants."

Skye scrunched up her nose. "Yuck, you're inferring that he practices necrophilia on a regular basis. You should probably know the coroner has yet to find semen on, or in, any of his victims."

Cannavale arched a brow. "That's interesting. That suggests this isn't a sexual perversion but something else."

Josh let those two things sink in before adding his own distinctions. "I don't think this guy handles conflict very well."

The profiler picked up the photographs Skye had included in the files and studied them, taking his time with each frame. "You're probably right. Little things could cause him to go off the rails at the slightest provocation when he doesn't get his way. Let's say, for instance, he's walking down the street and decides he wants a cup of coffee. He goes into a coffee shop, stands in line with everyone else and when it comes his turn he places his order. He takes his first sip and realizes they had the gall to get the order wrong, maybe too much milk, or too much cinnamon, whatever. This incident would be enough to send him over the edge, piss him off enough to want to exact revenge in some way."

"So he sees any slight as a personal affront?"

"Exactly. He also sees women as inferior, having only one purpose in life. That probably stems from childhood, and a shameful or embarrassing sexual experience. He made that into an excuse to turn violent. Even if it isn't during his sexual acts, something triggered his serial killer instincts." Cannavale smiled. "I can see by the look on your faces that you'd already figured that much out on your own."

The profiler chose that moment to point a finger at Skye. "Which means your killer no doubt sees you as being out of your league against him, so much so, that you have no right to pursue him."

"It wouldn't be the first time," Skye muttered.

Josh's protective nature stirred inside, his sense of outrage ramping up. "So Skye's not a viable threat, but rather someone he looks down on with disdain?"

Cannavale stabbed a finger toward Josh. "Make sure you have her back because he'll likely come after her in some way."

"The flowers. He sent me flowers and left them on my patio. We thought he was simply trying to get my attention."

Cannavale shook his head. "Knowing where you live? Not a good development at all. My guess is he *is* showing off to get attention but not for the reason you think. Since he's convinced himself you're deficient as a human being, he wants you to know you aren't worthy. Until this guy's in cuffs, I'd take extra precautions."

Josh didn't hesitate. "Believe me, I intend to."

"How long are you in town?" Skye asked.

"Till Monday, at which time I intend to head to the Cascades to spend a long vacation in the mountains with my wife until after New Year's."

"Then if you haven't already made plans for Sunday, how would you feel about a home-cooked meal at my father's place?"

"I never say no to home-cooking. Maybe you both should start calling me Emmett."

"Okay, Emmett. You'll need directions."

Later on the ride home, Josh wanted to know, "Do you really think it's wise to invite him to dinner the same night you're meeting Travis's main squeeze?"

"You know me. I guess we'll find out the hard way if it's a mistake. If nothing else it should be an interesting meal."

Chapter Eight

As it turned out, they picked Emmett up from the lobby of his hotel and explained they'd be eating dinner in Everett at The Painted Crow, the forty acres of ranchland Travis owned that hugged the Washington coastline where he bred and sold American Paint Horses.

"Interesting name. Probably something to do with his spirit guide," Emmett deduced, his attention turning to Skye. "Which makes me wonder. What's yours?"

While Skye zipped her Subaru in and out of the Sunday afternoon traffic, she spared a glance in the rearview mirror at the man sitting in the backseat. "White wolf. And you?"

Emmett grinned in the direction of the driver. "Coyote. Lifelong enemy of the wolf. I see conflict in our future."

Skye shot him an amused look. "Goes without explanation. You might want to include Josh in that statement. It probably isn't a good time to tell you that you're surrounded by wolves—at least in this car." She looked over at Josh. "You should definitely tell him what happened to you and how you acquired your *wolf* tendencies."

"I don't think I have to." Josh angled in the passenger seat so he could meet Emmett's eyes. "You picked up on something the other day when we were sitting across from each other I saw it in your eyes."

"I did indeed. You're perceptive like the wolf, keenly smart and cunning. I'm fascinated to hear how you have wolf blood running through your veins."

"Suffice to say, I wouldn't be here if it wasn't for Skye's spirit guide."

"And the fact that I led us into what amounted to a trap, an ambush with Ronny Whitfield, didn't help matters," Skye admitted.

"Ah, yes. I'm familiar with your background. I discovered in the records that Whitfield died of an unfortunate animal attack." Emmett cocked a brow in Josh's direction. "Your wolf's doing?"

By way of an answer, Josh ignored the question. "Right about now, most people would merely consider all three of us insane or delusional."

Emmett nodded. "But we aren't most people. What we are to some are anomalies. Even now, Chinooks are still viewed as extinct by the federal government."

"That's crap," Skye muttered, passing a slower vehicle that seemed to have a hard time finding the gas pedal.

"I'm sure you're referring to the tribe's historical fight with bureaucratic red tape. I read your extensive bio as well as the book you wrote about it," Josh admitted with a grin. "I'm a huge fan of your work."

Emmett grinned back. "The wolf makes for a worthy adversary because he's insightful and takes his time sizing things up before he acts. And yes, my people briefly won the right to establish ourselves as a tribe and be recognized as such back in 2001, only to lose the recognition within a matter of months. We've been fighting in court ever since. Imagine being from the tribe that kept Lewis and Clark's entire expedition alive, and yet we have to fight for our tribal existence, our very heritage. We're just one of a hundred Native tribes petitioning and working our way through the court system, fighting for federal recognition."

"It's the same with the Duwamish," Josh pointed out.

"Good thing we come from a long line of stubborn people, right?"

Skye nodded in agreement. "We do. Look at me, the Nimiipuu. Just because a bunch of French Canadian fur traders supposedly spotted a couple warriors with a bone sticking through their noses, the nimrods called us Nez Perce, meaning pierced nose. We've been stuck with that tag ever since. Forget the fact that nose piercing wasn't even part of the Nimiipuu's culture."

"Exactly. So do you guys live around here?"

"Not anymore. We bought a place over on Bainbridge Island, a spot where Skye has room to plant a garden if she wants. Whenever we head to Seattle these days we take the ferry."

"I see. So in order to leave you flowers on the back porch, your unsub had to go out of his way to take the ferry to get there? Interesting."

This time, Josh retold the whole story.

"Hmm, you don't find it odd that your wolf didn't sound an alarm?"

Skye and Josh exchanged long stares. "We questioned that back and forth until we decided that maybe I slept through Kiya's fuss. That's her name by the way, Kiya. I'd been up all night so I guess I didn't hear the racket. That's the only explanation."

"Unless this unsub put a block of some kind on your spirit guide," Emmett suggested.

"A block? You mean like a spell?"

"Exactly like a spell to prevent your wolf from picking up his presence."

"But he'd have to be Native in order to know about Kiya, or spirit guides in general for that matter," Josh pointed out.

"Not necessarily. Don't be so quick to rule out other ancient peoples who practiced curses and the like."

"I hadn't considered that. By the way, what do you call your coyote?"

"Coyote."

Skye belted out a laugh. "Now that's original."

She steered the car toward the exit ramp, made a left turn at the stop sign, and drove past towering evergreens and rolling pastureland. The ranch sat among a lush forest of Douglas fir and spruce.

As the vehicle flew under the iron gate-topper, horses grazed in the front corral. Looking beyond the two-story house, steep cliffs dropped down to a narrow stretch of inlet rocky shoreline scattered with conifers and beach grass.

The unmistakable aroma of salt and sea mixed with pine met them as they stepped out of the car.

Travis appeared on the wide porch with a stylish woman draped on his arm. The couple sent up a friendly wave to their guests.

Skye decided she'd need to work on getting used to seeing a female with her father. She couldn't deny they made a striking pair. At five-ten, Travis was quite a bit taller than the petite, thirty-something Chenoa Starr. Skye had to admit Chenoa's warm exotic eyes, high cheekbones, silky black hair, and ready smile were all huge pluses.

Despite all that, it was the apparent age difference that didn't sit well with Skye. From the looks of her, Chenoa had to be no older than thirty-five, which made her more than fifteen years younger than her fifty-two-year-old father. The fact that Chenoa had chosen a tight-fitting, neck-plunging cocktail dress that looked like it deserved its own Academy Award didn't help put Skye in a better frame of mind. The out-of-place attire went a long way to prevent Skye from becoming a charter member of the Chenoa fan club.

Maybe Josh had been right. Maybe this wasn't the best time to bring a guest with them to meet the girlfriend.

As if reading Skye's mind and disapproving thoughts, Josh sent her an "I told you so" look that reminded her it had been a bad idea to bring Emmett along. The look earned him an infuriated glare from his wife. But it was too late to change the dynamics of the showdown now.

"Hi, Dad," Skye finally managed. "I'd like you to meet Emmett Cannavale."

"Ah yes, the former olive tree grower. Nice to meet you. Welcome to The Painted Crow."

Emmett let out a laugh. "Thanks, I plan to retire one day to the family farm my father handed down to me. So do your heart a favor and make sure you stock up on plenty of olive oil in the future. It's good for the ticker. My wife will thank you for it."

"I'd think olive trees are tough to grow here?" Skye said. "What with the cold and damp winters?"

"Our farm uses the hardy Arbequina variety. It tolerates coastal climate really well as long as the temps don't drop below twenty degrees. We take precautions against the winter weather beginning with the November harvest season by layering mounds of dirt around the trunks. It protects the young trees. I'll send you a couple for your own yard. You'll be shocked by how much fruit two trees will give you."

"Would those produce green or black?"

"Spanish olives are actually dark brown, very smooth and buttery in flavor."

"Here that, Josh? We'll be able to grow our own olives."

Josh put an arm around Skye. "Does that mean you'll make those great big ones stuffed with cream cheese?"

She poked him in the rib. "Someone's hungry."

The group drifted through the front door and into a masculine living room, a traditional man's room filled with soft black leather furniture, chrome accents, and mahogany wood. The walls were decorated with several large landscapes depicting Native scenes in oil done by Native American artist Ty Moon.

Making herself at home in her father's house, Skye was about to play hostess and take drink orders from everyone when the charming Chenoa beat her to it.

"Now, what would everyone like to drink?"

With that one sentence, Skye gritted her teeth, found herself clenching her jaw. But despite the instant dislike she'd taken to the woman, Skye resolved to get through the evening without being rude.

That proved even more difficult when Chenoa fussed over Travis like a clucking hen with her baby chicks. It made Skye want to barf.

To make matters worse Chenoa brought out appetizers that looked like they came straight from the freezer aisle—tasteless mini quiches, brown clumps of hamburger shaped like meatballs, and a plate of chicken-stuffed taquitos.

Not exactly a menu that corresponded with the rich, snobby equestrian image Chenoa seemed determined to present to the world.

When the woman kept rattling on about all the blue ribbons and trophies she'd won from her various horse shows, Skye all but lost her appetite. She listened as Chenoa droned on about how a rider had to control a thousand-pound mare using every muscle throughout her entire body—as if the guests were supposed to find that information the least bit fascinating. While Skye sat there feigning interest, she conjured up a vision of Chenoa going head first into a muddy trough.

That made her feel better until the woman announced, "And this year Travis is taking me to the Savannah Classic so I can accept the award for Horsewoman of the Year."

Skye and Josh traded fed-up looks then slanted one over at Emmett, who wore a bemused expression on his face. The profiler seemed a snicker away from reacting to the motor mouth who couldn't seem to shut up about herself.

That alone had Skye on the verge of committing a social faux pas. To keep that from happening, while they waited for dinner, Josh tried to turn the conversation to something more appealing, at least to them. He asked Emmett about highly organized serial killers and the ploys they generally used to achieve success.

Skye lifted her glass of red in Emmett's direction. "Our guy is definitely not one who kills simply at random. He's methodical and takes pride in his work."

"Until he isn't," Emmett offered up. "Methodical, that is. I've studied the cases you brought to me in greater detail. I believe Josh is right about why the killer mutilated those young women. The implants were an affront to him in some way. But he dumped them where he did because he wanted them found."

Realizing they'd gone over this same topic at the seminar, Skye picked up on the gist of Josh's intent, which was fine by her. As long as she didn't have to listen to Chenoa prattle on about her hobbies, she could talk about the weather. But serial killers would make for a better dialogue. "I think the guy wanted to get a reaction and sit somewhere so he could keep an eye on the scene."

"It was the middle of the night. He probably brought night vision goggles," Josh suggested. "In order to do that his spot had to be high above the shopping center."

"Like a rooftop," Skye offered.

"You're looking at someone who wants your attention so much that he may go all in to make sure he gets it, Emmett noted. "Even if it means he'll try a new angle, something he's never tried before."

Josh chewed on that. "And you still believe we might be dealing with several different personalities?"

Emmett nodded. "Consider the possibility of at least three. You'd do well to keep it in the back of your head as you move the investigation forward. Keeping an open mind means less chances to miss a vital chunk of the puzzle when dealing with a splintered identity."

About that time, Chenoa appeared in the doorway to the dining room arm in arm with Travis. "Time to eat."

The cozy couple reinforced how the woman had prevented Travis from mingling with his other guests. One more mark against Chenoa, Skye decided, as everyone moved to the table. After getting comfortable they attempted to pick up the discussion where they'd left off.

But Chenoa headed that idea off with a terse reminder. "Excuse me, but I don't think this is the time or place to have a morbid conversation about serial killers over my delicious lasagna casserole."

"We were just touching on the fascinating concept of personality disorders," Skye pointed out, hoping to either push Travis to finally engage in the topic or drive Chenoa over the edge. "That's one of the reasons we invited Dr. Cannavale here tonight. Tomorrow he leaves town for the holidays and who knows when we'll get this chance again to pick his brain or to talk to him in depth, one on one. You obviously don't appreciate just how special this opportunity is."

Chenoa sent Travis a scathing look. "That's all fine and well but no one bothered running this by me. I had no idea you'd want to spend the evening chatting about something as vile as murderers and the like. It never occurred to me that you'd want to. But it should have."

Skye sent her father an equally lethal glare but out of respect for her dad kept quiet while Chenoa continued to build her case.

"It's simply not a proper venue to talk about mutilations and bones over dinner. In my opinion, it's not in very good taste. In fact, I've heard enough of this kind of talk tonight to last me a lifetime. And I want it to stop this minute."

Skye sent Travis another seething scowl. It was then she noticed her father looked positively embarrassed. She wasn't sure but his demeanor might even border on a degree of humiliation. She was sorely tempted to ditch this whole effort then and there and head for the front door. But something about the pleading look on her father's face prevented her from getting her feet to move. Instead of walking out, she picked up her salad fork and rolled her eyes at Chenoa. "Fine. I wouldn't dream of ruining this delicious pasta dish by discussing such mundane and trivial topics like who might be mutilating and killing young females around Seattle when what we could be doing is counting all the blue ribbons you have hanging on your wall back home."

Chenoa pushed her shoulders back, visibly insulted. "I'm proud of my ribbons. I earned each and every one of them. At least I know how to dress when someone invites me over to Sunday dinner."

Skye looked down at her red fluted-sleeve top and the black trousers she'd worn. "If that dig is aimed at me, I accept. Since the invitation didn't specify a dress code to my father's own table, I put on what feels comfortable to me, especially during winter. Dressing like a fashionista isn't for me."

"Maybe it should be."

"Maybe you should take your fashion sense and shove it up your snooty, tight—"

Josh interjected before she could finish. "This Caesar salad looks tasty. Doesn't it, Skye?"

Skye turned that lethal stare on her husband. "Oh, it does. And the garlic bread is such a nice homey touch. If I know my frozen foods, I believe this is the brand that comes straight from the freezer section, right?" Skye made a big production of tearing it into shreds on her plate on top of the bland pasta dish.

When Travis tried to halt the tension between the two women Chenoa glared at him. Travis found himself at a loss for words and caught in the middle. Sitting at the end of the table he looked on helpless to stop the bickering.

The group managed to get through tasteless lasagna without another major blow up. But toward the end of the evening Skye's neck began to ache from the stiff bent to her spine. Her cheeks began to feel numb as if they'd been frozen into a permanent phony smile.

So she turned to Josh shortly after the meal. "I think it's time to get Emmett back to the hotel, don't you? Emmett, are you ready to go? With traffic, it'll take us an hour to make the trip."

Emmett seemed just as eager to get out of there as she was. "You're right. I have to get going. I have an early wake-up call tomorrow. It was nice meeting everyone."

The three of them said awkward goodbyes and headed to the car.

Skye was too upset to drive so she let Josh take the wheel and settled into the passenger seat. Once they got underway, she offered an apology to the profiler. "I'm sorry for all that. I had no idea the evening would be so…horrible and strained. Josh warned me about bringing you along to a dinner where I had never met the hostess before. But I thought since it was dad's house… It never occurred to me Chenoa would be so narrow-minded and intractable."

Then the truth locked in her throat. When had Chenoa entrenched herself into her father's life? The woman was her dad's girlfriend. Just when things were smoothing out between father and daughter he had to go and… Her head began to ache at the thought of him with Chenoa.

From the backseat, Emmett offered up a cheery outlook. "I should thank you guys. It's the most entertaining evening I've had in years."

"We aim to please. Who knew we'd get fireworks with dinner?" Josh cracked as he pulled out onto the highway. From Everett to Seattle, they easily slid back into the serial killer exchange, spending the time going over all the scenarios that might aid in catching the guy.

After dropping the profiler back at his hotel, Josh headed to the ferry. "What is it exactly that you find so objectionable about Chenoa?"

Even in the dark front seat, Josh could tell her brows were knit in a tension-filled frown. He squeezed her hand. "Where were you just now?"

"Back at The Painted Crow. I acted like an ass tonight. I was so jealous of my father having Chenoa there and acting like the proverbial lady of the manor that I couldn't see straight."

"It's nice that you recognize that in yourself and want to apologize."

"I didn't say anything about apologizing."

"It was implied."

"Not by me. Travis has a woman in his life, who obviously doesn't understand the importance of what we do. So why would I want to apologize for the way I feel about her."

"Then why bring it up?"

"You're my spouse. I'm supposed to be able to tell my spouse how I feel, truly feel about things. I'm simply admitting I didn't handle tonight very well. I'm just venting."

"So you want me to sit here and say nothing, without comment."

"Hmm. Yeah. That's what I want."

"How am I supposed to know that?"

"I don't know. What about that mind-meld thing you're always talking about? You should know what I'm thinking."

"You're kidding? In a real-world scenario, ninety percent of the time I have no idea what you're thinking. Just because you're in a pissy mood about Chenoa doesn't mean you have to take it out on me when I'm simply trying to keep up with your mood."

"My mood?" She blew out a pent-up breath. "My mood reflects how my father went out of his way to find a girlfriend who already acts like she owns the place."

Silence descended between them.

After a full minute passed without a comment, she drummed her fingers on the dash. "Well, aren't you going to say anything?"

"Oh sorry, I was waiting for you to give me permission to speak."

"Screw you."

"Okay. I'm up for that. But maybe we should table that type activity for later. Or maybe we could do it *on* the table. I like that visual. Anyway, I thought I was supposed to wait for you to completely finish expressing your internal struggle with this moral dilemma you're having before I injected my 'clumsy, ill-advised man advice' into the conversation."

"Oh, shut up. I'm feeling guilty enough without having to listen to a pathetic attempt at humor."

She drew in a deep breath, scrubbed both hands over her face. "I'm sorry. I don't know what's gotten into me tonight. Chenoa is a perfectly suitable woman for my father. Other than the fact that she's thirty-five and he's fifty-two, there's no reason they can't date their way to New Year's Eve for all I care."

"No way is Chenoa thirty-five. At least I don't think so. Where'd you get that? Did she tell you that?"

"No, but...I...just assumed. She looks...younger. Do you know how old she is...exactly?"

"I didn't ask her if that's what you're getting at. I learned a long time ago you don't do that. All I know is that she mentioned she'd been riding horses for thirty-five years. I assume she wasn't born on one. Although *you* assumed and here we are."

"Oh, God. I feel sick at my stomach. I'm pretty sure it's because I acted horrible tonight and it's making me feel really small. What kind of daughter am I to feel so petty about my father's happiness? It isn't like me. I'm not a petty person. Why couldn't I just keep my big mouth shut and enjoy the evening?"

He let her battle with her inner demons for several more seconds and then offered, "Here's a thought. You have a phone, why not call him and apologize?"

"Now? With Chenoa still there? I think I'd rather have my toenails removed. Okay, so I'll wait until tomorrow and grovel then. There's only so much eating crow in me. But if you don't mind I'd rather do it when he's alone. When I apologize, I don't want an audience."

"Suit yourself. Does that mean table sex is still on the agenda?"

She huffed out a breath. "You're incredible."

"I know. And I'd be willing to prove it to you as soon as we get back home and hit the kitchen."

Chapter Nine

While Skye and Josh rode the ferry across Puget Sound, the man who'd been born Dillard Barstow sat completely naked in his garden among the trophies and bones he'd collected over the years.

His house sat on a hill surrounded by ten acres overlooking Lake Union. It had a solarium with a skylight and enough plants to fill a landscape nursery. He had a boat—a little thirty footer—he kept docked at the Elliot Bay Marina. He often used it to navigate across Puget Sound whenever he got the urge to dump a body or explore.

It wouldn't do for anyone to see him unloading a corpse near his estate. That's one reason he'd hidden this part of the grounds from view. A retaining wall built from stone gave the bright red Bougainvillea a place to climb to soaring heights. At its base, saucer-sized purple dahlias fanned out among yellow daisies. By using layers of ornamental grass dotted under crepe myrtle and feathery smoke bush, he'd built the perfect "living" wall, evidence of his ability to grow just about anything.

By bringing the bodies back here to what he considered his inner sanctum, he could make the best use of the sloping terrain. The topography allowed him to use the location of his property by sectioning off certain aspects of the land—space he needed for his flower gardens. He might've been partial to his dark brunettes and the deep purple section where they ended up, but he refused to neglect his daisies or roses.

Sitting in the middle of it all in a circle he'd built for this very purpose, he'd swept the outer area clean and spread out fresh mantzourana around the campfire. The smoke rising from the fire pit smelled sweet and aromatic—the marjoram wafting on the wet air. As the blaze flickered around him, he heard the voices. His women were singing, chanting to him in honeyed serenade. Soon they began to dance for him, dance in time to the bouzouki, the pear-shaped lute, he strummed in his hand. Playing as his grandmother had taught him, it was the same ritual he'd become accustomed to performing the night before going out on the hunt.

Inhaling the cannabis he drew the smoke into his lungs. He took out the carving he'd made of the white wolf, rubbed it with a layer of leaves from the mantzourana plants. The herb grew thick and tall among his flowers and marked the graves of those he'd used and then discarded. Ancient tradition taught him to scatter the plant throughout his garden, a gesture that meant the souls resting here would have everlasting peace.

In a wooden bowl, he tossed in the leaves from the wolf's bane and mixed them with Viscum album, better known as European mistletoe. The concoction was so poisonous he had to make sure he kept it from making contact with his skin.

Once he blended the mixture together to a consistency that would stick to the figurine, he used a knife to spread the paste over the wood. When he was done, he placed the statue on the slab of concrete he used for an altar.

It took another round of marijuana and several chews of the San Pedro cactus containing mescaline to take him back in time to the cave of his youth.

Soon he breathed in the damp musty smell and knew he was back—back among the murky shadows that greeted him like a long lost friend. He cherished the peacefulness he found here. The coolness under the dome always lessened the fever pitch he felt growing within him.

Since the age of twelve the cave had been where he kept his personal stuff, all the paraphernalia he didn't want his parents to find. He'd learned at an early age how to perfect secrecy. His father had taught him that. Boys didn't act like he had. His parents had made that clear again and again. The beatings he'd taken had taught him to hoard his special items—magazines, sketches of people at school, food he'd taken from the kitchen without permission.

After his mother discovered his stash in the vent of his room, he'd waited until that weekend to set out on a journey—a journey in search of a place that would belong only to him, somewhere no one else knew existed or had yet claimed. As luck would have it, he'd come upon the cave. It wasn't perfect. It could've been closer to his house and maybe roomier, but it suited his purpose just fine as long as he have privacy there.

For years, the cave had acted as his sanctuary until he left home for good at eighteen.

He remembered one of the first defiant acts against his parents had occurred at the cave when he'd shorn off his own hair then shaved his head in a military-style buzz cut.

Of course, he'd paid for his rebellious streak when he returned home. His father had been shocked almost speechless at the sight of him.

But then Dillard had rarely been able to make either of his parents happy, no matter what he did or how much he tried. It was at his mother's direction that his father had punished him with a beating. Then she'd dealt the final blow herself, one he'd never quite been able to get over.

From that moment on, at every opportunity, his parents had gone out of their way to embarrass and humiliate him. Derogatory comments and insults became the norm.

So if he couldn't be himself at home, he preferred the beatings. With each event, something inside him had snapped. Little by little, he lost control. And there'd been no looking back.

Coming out of his trance-like state, the revelations flowed. Clarity returned.

His parents had demanded perfection in him so it seemed only fair to expect the same of those he brought back to his garden. Only the best and the most beautiful he could find would eventually make it this far to his special place.

"Tonight, we get rid of the white wolf, the pack leader," he uttered as he picked up the knife again. For the final act, he sliced open the pig he'd bartered from the butcher. From neck to stomach he managed to catch enough of the blood in a vial before chanting in the language of his grandmother's tongue. He poured the red liquid over the small figurine and set fire to the carving.

Watching the flames spiral upward, he breathed in more of the marijuana and said, "What began as an anomaly, so shall it end."

Chapter Ten

The next morning, Josh caught up with Hank at the motel busting up rotten drywall in what used to be designated as room number eighteen.

"You're making great strides," Josh called out at the younger man from the doorway.

Balancing a to-go carrier filled with two paper cups—one latte and one cappuccino—and a sack with hot cinnamon rolls he'd stopped to get from a Pike Place coffeehouse down the street, Josh stared at his contractor slash handyman.

Hank hesitated in mid-whack, looked up at him through a pair of protective goggles and stared back, obviously surprised to see the boss here so early in the a.m.

Josh grinned at the guy's nonplussed expression, watched as Hank slung the sledgehammer to his shoulder, rested it there, pushed up his glasses, and moved the bandana from around his mouth.

"Please tell me you brought coffee and doughnuts. Man, you read my mind."

Josh held out the hot drinks, listed the two choices of coffee and jiggled the bag. "Sweet rolls from McCarron's Bakery."

"As long as it's pastry and caffeine I'm not picky," Hank said, grabbing the one with a big C marked on the top. Hank leaned the hammer up against the wall and snatched the bag out of Josh's hand like a hungry child.

"I'm starving. Plus, I was in such a hurry this morning that I ran out the door without my Thermos."

Josh sipped the latte, rubbed his fingers into his temple.

Over the rim of his cup, Hank eyed Josh. "What's the matter? You got a headache?"

"Woke up with it. It's as if your sledgehammer met up with my skull and the hammer won."

"Bummer. I have aspirin in the truck."

"Thanks, but I already washed down four. You look better than you did the other day."

Hank laughed. "That's because I'm getting a decent night's sleep now that we're not living in the car. Crawling into an actual bed at night is huge."

Josh winced at the notion of sleeping in such cramped space—with Hank's height it had to be a tight fit, not to mention the difficulty in staying warm, especially with the cold night air whipping in off the Sound.

"You guys settling in okay? How are your wife and baby doing?"

"They're great. That studio is amazing. Thanks again for cutting us a deal on the rent. We appreciate it. Melina loves the apartment. I don't know how to thank you enough for letting us move in there, have a roof over our heads. And the fact that it's furnished is a godsend. Alec slept through the night last night for the first time."

Josh grinned at hearing another round of gratitude. It was only the fifth or sixth time Hank had echoed that same sentiment. "I hear that's a milestone. You just keep taking care of your family and you guys will be fine."

"The medicine's kicked in for both Melina and Alec. It makes a big difference in the nighttime coughing."

Noticing that Hank didn't exactly have a gift for gab, Josh added, "I'm working on getting you some help."

"What made you decide to take on such a huge undertaking when you're obviously such a busy guy?"

Josh rubbed the back of his neck. "Lately, I've been asking myself that same question."

"It's a good plan. I know when you hired me you mentioned that families could eventually move in here to get off the street. That's what appealed to me right off. I'm pretty sure that's why Tate sent me your way."

"Didn't you say you were a gamer at one time?"

"Used to be. Had to hock my console about six months back though. These days my wife and son's well-being is far more important to me than playing video games."

"That's as it should be. Are you interested in a job at Ander All Games? I start everyone out in testing and they move up from there. It would get you out of the cold."

"Man, if you'd asked me that two years ago I would've probably jumped at the chance. But honestly, I like being outside. Out here, I get to hammer away on things and go at my own pace. I'm no good up against release deadlines."

"Are you sure?"

"It's not so bad working here. I like the idea of taking something and making it better, sprucing it up."

"Okay then, since we're being honest with each other, I'm glad to hear you say that because the idea of spending time looking for another contractor isn't something I want to do right now. Skye and I had our hearts set on being finished with this project by spring, which means you certainly won't be able to do it single-handed."

"I have this friend who could use some extra cash for Christmas. His name's Coy Kingston. But Coy already has a regular job during the week. He's a damn fine carpenter, works over at the Archway seven to four. Could you use him on the weekends? He's a hard worker."

The Archway was a shiny new super mall scheduled to open next summer. "Sure. If he's willing to put in those kinds of hours."

"Hey, when you have kids and want to get them something special from Santa, you do whatever it takes. Now when you get ready to install the new plumbing I know someone who wants to bid on the business."

"But if you know a plumber then why…"

"Why don't I work for him? Good question. I'll tell you the truth. He's my stepfather and a bit of a prick. But hey, I thought I'd do the family thing and put in a good word for him."

"By the way, Skye and I are having a Christmas party on the twenty-fourth. I know that's Christmas Eve but we're getting all my employees and her volunteers and their families together for eats and drinks. If you're interested, you and Melina are welcome to come."

"I doubt we could get a babysitter."

"No problem. Feel free to bring the little one. I'm sure there'll be other parents in the same boat."

While Josh hung out with Hank, Skye swung by her old apartment to do the same with Melina—her sole purpose, to make sure the two had enough to eat.

As she made her way up to the fourth floor studio, it seemed odd reaching the front door and knocking instead of using her key. From inside she heard the wail of a baby's cry.

When it took Melina a while to answer, she realized she should have called first. And then realized the young mother might have her hands full.

Just when she'd decided it was a bad time for company to drop by and she should leave, she'd taken two steps back down the hallway when Melina opened the door.

"Oh, hi. Come on in. Alec is a little fussy. That new tooth coming in is giving him fits."

"And that's the main reason I stopped by—to see if you needed anything."

Melina slid Alec into a well-worn infant rocker. "What I could use is another pair of hands. Want some coffee? I made use of your coffeemaker. It's wonderful having a kitchen again. I love putzing around and fixing meals again." Her voice began to falter as she busied herself at the sink. "There's no way I can begin to thank you for letting us live here."

Uneasy at the emotion, Skye took off her jacket and sat down at the little table she'd refinished herself. "I'd love coffee. Look, Melina, there's no need to keep thanking me every time we see each other." Sitting there, taking in the room, she saw how it had changed in just a few days. It was now jam-packed with baby things—a portable crib, clothes, toys, stuffed animals. The place even smelled like baby lotion. "The apartment was vacant. Josh had been after me for months to rent it out. But for some reason, I always resisted. Now I know why. I was saving it for a family like you and Hank. It's yours for as long as you need it."

Melina got down two familiar cups from the cabinet and brought one over filled with steaming coffee. Before Skye could pick up the mug, Melina grabbed her in a hug. "We'll take good care of it, I promise. I love it here. It's a fantastic place. I know it holds sentimental value for you."

It seemed silly not to admit it. "Am I that obvious?"

"Kind of. But it's sweet. Your first apartment in the city is always special. I should know, I remember mine."

To change the subject and get out of the emotional box she found herself in, Skye asked, "Have you and Hank been married long?"

"Two years. We were doing fine until he lost his job, then we lost the apartment, and things began to slide downhill. Now, for the first time in a long time, things are looking up. If I have to, I'll get a job to stay here."

"Will it come to that? What would you do with Alec?"

"There's Hank's mom. Since I'm no longer breastfeeding, I could drop him off at the day care center she works at in Renton."

Skye laid her hand over Melina's. "Hank has a good job. Josh says he's a good worker. The motel project will likely be around through June. So why don't you relax until after the holidays and reassess your financial needs then. By the way, we're having a Christmas party on the twenty-fourth. Josh and I want you guys to come."

"A night out? That sounds wonderful. I'll need to get Hank's mom to sit with Alec."

"No need. Bring the baby with you. I'm sure other kids will be there."

That night, after spending nine hours cooped up inside an office, Skye dragged Josh out into Seattle's streets. Four hours into the venture they hadn't stumbled across anything that looked the least bit sinister so they packed it in early. The ferry got them back to the island in time for bed a little before midnight, a rare occurrence.

But then, Josh hadn't been feeling well all day. Several times he'd mentioned he might be coming down with the flu.

After turning in, he'd conked out next to her. But Skye hadn't been able to settle down. For something to do, she decided to get up, fix a cup of chamomile tea to help her sleep, maybe play a round or two of *Princess Kilda* to rid herself of the pent-up frustration she felt.

Now was a great time to get her first look at the new game Josh had downloaded to her iPad. She'd played the beta version several times on her phone before, but now that it had been released to millions of gamers, her curiosity had taken over. She wanted to see *Princess Kilda*, the final product, in action.

The minute her feet hit the floor, Atka was right there next to the bedside table, tail wagging, tongue drooping, wanting her head scratched. Skye obliged but held one finger to her lips for quiet before the dog woke up Josh. The puppy had finally grown into her feet but still had a tendency to knock things aside with her tail.

With the dog trailing her, she tiptoed downstairs to the kitchen where she grabbed her iPad and a bottle of water. Flopping onto the living room sofa, she waited for the game to load while Atka stretched out, covering her feet like cozy slippers.

"You go back to sleep," Skye murmured to the pooch as she keyed in her password for log in.

Once she got her first look at the main menu, there was no mistaking the similarity to Kilda's eyes, the deep violet, or the other traits she shared with the heroine—head bobs, style of movement when fighting, instincts and interaction with the bad guys—they were all things Skye recognized in herself. Josh and his team hadn't missed a trick.

Skye grinned at his creativity and began to try her hand at the first level. After a series of aimless hunts through trails and forests, she suffered a few defeats before finally getting the hang of all the upgrades Josh's team had put in before releasing it to the masses.

Changing weapons to a long broad sword, she faced a string of formidable opponents. Then out of nowhere, three different challengers appeared at once, all trying to blindside her. Surrounded, she managed to dodge and engage the trio of warriors and ninjas in blade to blade combat. Numerous times Skye took Kilda to the edge in each battle before ending the skirmish by annihilating all of Kilda's enemies as well as their well-defended bases.

Pleased with her progress, Skye fell into the real-life 3D graphics, an enchanted land that brought out the best of both survival and escape. After an hour or so of taking on higher level enemies, she got more adept at brandishing the magic lasers, and did a better job searching, then uncovering the hidden gems stashed away in the little golden boxes available for more power.

While the clock ticked toward two a.m. and she became more deeply engrossed in the game, she didn't notice when Kiya appeared. But Atka did. As soon as the dog detected the wolf's presence, the malamute stood to attention. It wasn't until the pup moved next to Kiya at the living room window that Skye glanced up. By this time Kiya was all but getting ready to leap through the plate glass.

Skye heard the floorboards squeak overhead right before Josh bounded down the stairs two at a time.

"Someone's outside," Josh announced from the entryway, still looking half asleep. "Why didn't the security system go off?"

Setting her iPad aside, she met him at the front door as he peered through the peephole. While the canines took up guard next to them, she took her turn after Josh, looking through the little hole onto the porch and to the darkness beyond. "Maybe whoever it is didn't reach the perimeter yet. Should we flick on the lights and let him know we know that he's out there snooping around?"

Josh looked back at the animals. "The crowd's all here on alert. Don't let them bark or howl while I go out there and…"

The piercing look she sent him said it all. "I'm not letting you go alone."

He slanted his head in response, sent her a measured stare of equal mulishness. He ticked off the points with one hand. "It's better if you stay here and keep Atka quiet while Kiya and I track his scent. Atka still wants to chase off into the wild without staying on course. It's a fact. Two, I have better night vision than you do."

At the first hint of annoyance he saw in her eyes he knew he'd hit a raw nerve. "Once again, that's a fact. It's not my doing either, it's just there. And besides, this guy might be trying to draw both of us outside for a reason. We won't let him do that. One of us needs to…"

"Okay, okay, when you're right, you don't have to drone on about it. Take your phone. Text me with any updates."

"Good idea."

Before she could get another word out, Josh kissed her on the mouth, opened the front door, and let Kiya dash into the night ahead of the pack. Josh took off in pursuit, speeding into the darkness, running headlong as fast as the wolf. Light as air, with a sliver of moon for a guide, he flew over damp ground, bounded through the verdant hillside. Night sounds hit his ears—the hoot of an owl, a chorus of crickets, a squirrel scrambling up a tree. He got a whiff of ocean, but then skunk fumes mingled with the sweet smell of wild mint. Before he ever left the yard, he spotted a lizard scaling up the bark of a tree.

He smelled man before he actually heard the rustle of footsteps running through fallen leaves.

Their visitor was sprinting toward the road. Following the scent, he chased it into the thicket of woods, past down timber and fetid undergrowth.

Josh heard the sound of a car door open then slam, heard the engine start up. He picked up speed, hustling through a field of scrub. By the time he reached the road all he saw in the misty fog of night were the taillights from a vehicle taking off toward town.

"Damn. We don't dare lose him, Kiya." He should've known the wolf had no intentions of giving up at this spot. His link to Kiya kicked in. Man and wolf shared the same mindset, their interwoven, indomitable spirit urging them on. The wolf howled at the slice of moon and tore off in rapid strides into the night.

It had been a long time since Josh had chased after a car, if ever. But his pack instincts had him doing so now, his feet barely touching the pavement, Kiya in the lead.

Left alone in the house, it didn't take long for Skye to become impatient. She skirted each room on the bottom floor as well as upstairs, checking windows and locks with Atka shadowing her every step.

On high alert, she and the dog stood watch near the door until she decided that wouldn't do. She went to the study, unlocked the gun safe and took out the loaded Glock pistol Josh had insisted they keep at home. Circling back to the living room, she dug out her nightstick.

Armed now, she felt better about taking up a position inside the entryway. It didn't last long though before she got antsy. She wandered into the kitchen to make a pot of coffee but then decided against it.

She waited, walked each room again listening for any sound outside or inside the old house. But nothing she did got her mind off Josh.

He'd been gone for more than an hour when she heard footsteps on the front porch.

Peeping outside, relief welled up when she saw that it was Josh. She opened the door to an out-of-breath runner.

"Are you okay?"

He nodded, bent at the waist with his hands resting on his knees to better catch his breath. As soon as he could talk he whooshed out one long string in explanation. "With Kiya's help I did a perimeter search. We couldn't peg who was out there, but someone was definitely in the woods lurking around. We followed the scent all the way through town, thought for sure he'd end up at the ferry terminal, easy enough to corner there. Even though I hoped that would be his first mistake—not knowing the ferry doesn't run this late at night. But no such luck. The trail ended south of town. Whoever it was had a boat stashed somewhere along the banks. That's my guess, anyway. I'm certain it was our unsub though."

The vision he'd had in New York suddenly popped into his brain. The one that had brought him home early. The uneasiness of it had him snaking his arms around Skye. He nuzzled her throat. "I'm sorry I lost him."

"Don't be ridiculous. I can't believe you ran all that way to the ferry. That's gotta be two miles at least."

"More like two and a half."

"You're sure he's off island though, right?"

"I'm sure."

"Then let's head to bed. You must be exhausted. You still look flushed."

"I feel like I ran a marathon."

They started up the stairs wrapped up in each other.

"When I came downstairs tonight I saw you were in the middle of playing the game. So, how does it compare to the beta version you tried several weeks back?"

"Five stars, easy. I understand now why the buzz on the Internet has been so positive. I was so wrapped up in Kilda's character and capturing all the treasure I lost track of two hours."

"Music to a gamer's ears."

Chapter Eleven

The white wolf had almost caught up with him. He'd barely made it to his car and then on to the thirty footer he'd moored near a private dock in the southern part of the island.

Dillard Barstow didn't like close calls.

Why was it taking so long for the curse to kick in? Was there a reason the spell hadn't worked?

Ander had pursued him at a fierce pace and didn't appear to be weakening. He'd have to repeat the ceremonial ritual.

It wasn't easy to carve out the time.

Five days a week Dillard toiled away at his day job. But the job paid pocket change when compared to what he generally made from his sex trade operation. Since he'd given up his side business—for the most part anyway—he could focus on his weekends. Weekends belonged to the hunt. He could always find time for the hunt.

Like tonight.

He'd started his Saturday evening donning his usual disguise. He'd taken his clever use of camouflage and cruised along the dark streets that served the UDub campus, sticking to the neighborhoods he knew best, the ones that had served him so well in the past.

This time of night—between the hours of nine and midnight—things were just beginning to pop.

He parked his van a couple streets over using his permit at the same lot where he made regular deliveries to the school. Without fear of a ticket, he hit the pavement and headed to the area known as sorority row.

If you were persistent enough you could easily snag a coed, drunk and disoriented, coming in from a night of partying and doing her best to find her way back to a dorm room—alone.

His first choice was always a dahlia with black hair. He didn't mind the occasional rose if he were in the mood for a redhead. But sometimes he couldn't afford to be picky. When looking for a perfect flower, he knew he might have to settle for a daisy. As long as the girl had an All-American type body—no sleazy tattoos, no unusual piercings, or fake boobs or damage to skin—he could overlook most other imperfections.

A gaggle of females passed him, tipsy and boisterous. As usual, he went unnoticed by the women. The snub caused him to toss his shoulders back and persevere. His grandmother had always preached that it took patience to be successful at the hunt. So like any good predator, he bided his time and waited for the best opportunity to strike.

Surely among these targets he could find his next blossom ready to bloom. After years of perfecting his pursuit, he knew to avoid the girls who traveled in packs. Instead, he focused on lone females.

But after three hours of tracking several prospects he turned up empty-handed. Unfulfilled, he headed back to the truck. Circling the U District again was the only option. It was on his sixth trip through the streets that he spotted a woman at a nearby supermarket, walking out the double doors to her car. Since the place wasn't well lit, he shot a quick U-turn for a second look. Taking another pass through the deserted lot to get a better look at the redhead made him realize he might've hit the jackpot. A rose, with perfect stems, this young female carried her sacks of groceries out to a well-worn Taurus like a star athlete.

Her hands laden with bags, she struggled to get the door open. Zeroing in on her every move, he began to think the night held a lot more promise than before.

The security cameras covering the lot were a problem so he avoided them by staying close to the outer perimeter.

He chortled with glee when the young woman had trouble starting the engine. Instead of offering to help and risking the capture of his image on surveillance, he drove out the side exit, pulled to the curb, and waited.

By the time she finally got the old thing to turn over and threw the car into gear, his edginess began to creep in. He closed out the voices by fighting off the panic in his throat. He took several deep breaths to calm himself.

While dealing with his anxiety, he realized he'd lost sight of the Ford. To catch up, he stepped on the gas. A few minutes later, he caught sight of the car's exhaust. Heading north, he decided to keep his distance by remaining several car lengths behind.

Excitement coursed through his veins as he followed the pretty thing to Mercer, a busy residential street smack-dab in the middle of a trendy neighborhood known as Capitol Hill.

Dillard watched her make a turn onto a side street. When she pulled into a driveway in front of a colonial-style brick, he decided she was worth the investment. Ten or fifteen more minutes of his time wouldn't matter in the larger picture.

So he pulled to the curb and turned up the heat in the van. While the hot redhead dashed inside he drummed his fingers on the steering wheel. A hundred thoughts flashed through his brain. Reason and logic warred with his urges. She'd be a perfect addition to his garden. He'd put her with his other roses. His pulse quickened thinking about it.

Just as the anxiety started to ebb, something occurred to him. She hadn't driven the vehicle into the garage as he'd expected. Which meant if she intended to stay here for any length of time why had she kept the old sedan running?

Then it came to him. This house wasn't her final destination. This was a quick stop to pick up something and head somewhere else. Since she'd had trouble starting the car at the grocery store, she likely didn't want a repeat of that happening here.

No point in picking up another trail this late in the game when he already had the very fine rose in his sights. But he might have to alter his methods.

The holding pattern had him continuing to tap the steering wheel keeping his fingers busy. While his mind raced with possibilities, a series of irrational messages flashed in his head. The voices grew louder. Despite the confusion, his predatory instincts ramped up. His determination spiked.

Minutes went by before the front door opened again and the woman came out. This time she clutched a bundle to her chest wrapped in a blanket.

A baby.

He'd sensed something different about tonight but he'd never dreamed it would include a toddler—a child who could belong to him.

Lost in that lofty goal, he lost track of time while the mother had strapped the child into a car seat. He completely missed the Taurus backing out of the drive and roaring off. Blinking out of his fugue state, he needed to catch up. He pushed down on the accelerator causing the van to screech down the street. Ahead, he spotted taillights at the stop sign on the corner.

"Patience," he muttered, slowing down to a crawl. "Let her get where she's going. Don't fuck this up."

When the Taurus took off, he stayed put, backing off to give her the necessary space. It wouldn't do to have her think someone followed her or spot the tail. He kept the van at a slow twenty-five falling behind even farther as they wound their way through the neighborhood.

To his surprise, mother and baby didn't go very far. The redhead finally stopped in front of an eclectic building that offered small, renovated apartments built over first-floor shops with a parking garage next door.

Shadowing her all the way to the lot meant another wait for her to get out of the car. He watched as she unstrapped the kid from its special seat before making his move. Checking his image in the rearview mirror, he made sure his disguise was still in place.

As she entered the building carrying the groceries and her sleeping child, he caught the door before it closed shut and followed her inside to the tiny lobby, past the mailboxes, and up the stairs.

"Are you new?" the redhead asked over her shoulder. "I don't think I've seen you here before."

Adjusting his voice to a whisper, he played out the part. "I just moved in yesterday. You look like you have your hands full. Want me to take your bag, help you to your front door?"

"That's nice of you but I can manage. After all this time, I'm used to it."

Pretending came easy as he continued the climb. "When you have a baby it must take ten extra hands to make it from the car to the door."

By the redhead's silence Dillard could tell she'd started to grow suspicious. Before reaching her apartment on the third floor, she picked up her pace. He saw that she cuddled the baby tighter.

The timing had to be perfect.

From his pocket he withdrew the hypodermic needle and readied his method of attack just as the redhead stuck the key in the lock. As the door squeaked open, he put the syringe up to her neck, plunged the tip into her skin.

He shoved her inside before she collapsed on the floor of the entryway. Nimbly, he caught the baby up in his arms and grabbed the grocery sack. The darkness of the apartment forced his eyes to adjust. Once around the place he made certain they were alone and used his leg to move the unconscious redhead farther into the room before pushing the door closed. While he bounced the baby he decided how best to get them back out to his truck.

That's when inspiration struck.

He crammed the baby down into the stroller, picked the redhead up off the floor, slinging her dead weight over his shoulder.

When she let out a low moan, he patted her ass and said, "Be a good girl now and don't scream. Otherwise I'll have to cut you and leave you behind. So be the good mommy I know you probably are—because I'm taking the baby anyway."

Chapter Twelve

Unaware of the latest abduction, Josh sat inside his office with another type of mystery on his mind—the bones found on the beach at Alki Point. How had so many ended up at that particular spot?

If the bones were from some kind of serial killer, where had they been all this time? Not only that, but if a serial killer had murdered so many children why had there been no public accounts of so many disappearances noted in public records. He'd stayed up late into the night researching old newspaper articles on the subject. The lack of information had caused him to move on past the serial killer angle to his initial gut reaction that day on the beach.

He'd spent the first hour of his morning surfing the Internet, going through the list of all the maritime disasters in the area. The only other explanation, other than the *Dix* going down, pointed to the *Pridewin Star*, a steamship that sank in the general area in 1897 carrying mail, freight, and passengers on their way from Seattle to the Klondike gold fields of Alaska.

On a foggy night in August, the *Pridewin Star* had veered too close to shore striking an underwater rock formation. It went down within ten minutes taking all eighty-eight souls onboard to the bottom of the ship channel. The manifest had included the usual supplies to help miners get through the cold winter. But for years rumors persisted that among those lost had been children slated for use as cheap labor in the mining camps. Back then, it had been common practice for poor families to farm out their kids, especially boys aged six to twelve, to work farms or whatever jobs they could get. Once there, the kids would send their wages back home to help with expenses.

On the phone with a grouchy medical examiner Josh had spent ten minutes trying to nudge Bayliss toward some sort of dialogue. At the risk of pissing the surly coroner off more, he tiptoed around what he wanted. "Look, I've been searching the Internet to see what I could find. You've had a couple days now to assess those bones. I'd like to know your conclusion." Before Bayliss could interrupt, he went into his theory about the *Pridewin Star*.

After summing up, he expected an argument, but was shocked to hear Bayliss accept what he'd managed to cobble together.

"I considered the *Pridewin Star* as the source of the bones. But I admit spending too much time on the idea these kids came from the *Dix*. There's really only one way to be sure though. I've decided to call in a batch of archaeologists to solve this one."

"Okay, that's good. How long before we know something definitive?"

"Months. It's the simplest way to some kind of resolution. I could do testing on them but let's face it, I know by the looks of them they're at least several decades old. Who knows why they surfaced when they did."

"Probably the heavy rain we've had this month. I appreciate you taking my call."

"No problem. I'm always available for a reasonable discussion. As long as you know it could take as long as a year before we know anything."

"I understand. Will you let me know when you get the results?"

"Sure."

Josh heard a click in his ear, abruptly ending the call. As he hung up the phone, he glanced up and saw Travis standing in the doorway. "What brings you to Seattle?"

"Country Kitchen was shorthanded. I often become fry cook in a pinch. Plus, I wanted to talk to Skye. Her attitude Sunday afternoon toward Chenoa was disappointing and appalling to say the least."

"So you noticed?" Josh said with humor.

"Noticed? It's been two days and I still feel the frost. Chenoa's convinced Skye hates her."

"Look, I don't want to get in the middle of this. The best thing for both of you is to sit down and work this thing out."

"I will, but first I want your advice on what to say. Chenoa's a big part of my life now. I'd like the two of them to get along. No more get-togethers like Sunday night."

"For what it's worth after talking to Skye, I think she knows she was out of line."

"Really? She said that?"

"If you just talk to her and explain how important Chenoa is in your life. I'm sure you'll be able to broker a peace between the two of you. How serious is it with Chenoa?"

"I was leaning that way before I got the two women in the same room together. I wasn't sure any of us would survive those four awkward hours. I'm sure that profiler thinks we're off the charts."

"He's seen worse."

"Is that what he said? Never mind. I don't really want to know. I think about a repeat of Chenoa and Skye together and get pains in my stomach. What if they don't ever get along? What's the point in moving forward with Chenoa? I don't want an encore performance of Sunday night. That's for sure. Seeing firsthand how the two most important women in my life don't seem to be able to stand looking at each other is frustrating."

"Then what do you want from me?"

"Your wisdom, your insight into Skye's mindset would be a start. Why was she so upset?"

Josh cocked a curious brow at his father-in-law. Something about the man's desperation reminded him of the time he first met Travis. "So I shouldn't point out that the two of us didn't exactly have the most auspicious start?"

"We get along well enough now, don't we? If you have any idea why Skye had such a negative reaction to Chenoa you should tell me."

With some reluctance, Josh hit the same high points Skye had gone over with him Sunday.

Travis shifted his feet. "What does age have to do with anything? Before you ask outright, Chenoa's forty, will be forty-one in two months. And yeah, I've known she's a little too focused on herself, her achievements with her horses, her own horse ranch. But she was raised around horses. I don't mind it so much if she'd stop obsessing over her own self-importance. At times, the animals are the only things we have to talk about. The clothes thing is a separate preoccupation altogether and annoys me more than I've let on."

Josh sent him a puzzled look as the floodgates seemed to open and Travis let loose with a long list of issues he had with his new girlfriend. Obviously, Travis had been holding back. But for how long? As Josh sat there listening he got the impression the relationship had been going on a lot longer than a few weeks. He let Travis complete the tally before he sat back in his chair and steepled his fingers together.

"Sounds like to me the two of you don't have all that much in common after all, except for maybe the four-legged animals you sell and she likes to ride. Are you sure this is the woman you want to go to the mat for with Skye?"

Travis let out a long, exasperated sigh. "See, that's the thing. I'm torn. Sunday night I couldn't even do a decent job of refereeing."

"You shouldn't have to referee, Travis."

"That's what I thought you'd say."

"Did you know Skye rented her apartment?"

Travis dropped his jaw. "You're kidding?"

"Nope." Josh went into the story about Hank and Melina Fielding.

"That's sound like the only situation where Skye would've let go of that studio. So this Fielding guy is also your contractor on the motel job?"

"I intended to ask you about contractors Sunday evening but things took a different direction and got a little weird. I need your advice about the whole project. Hank's made some progress but hasn't hired a work crew yet. If you could take some time to point him to one or two decent carpenters, I'd really appreciate it."

"I'll stop over there while I'm in town. You trust this Hank Fielding?"

"Let's just say that I hope he works out for the sake of his wife and baby. I don't think Skye would have the heart to evict them if things go south. But as long as Hank shows up and makes an effort, continues to make progress on the renovation, he'll have a job. If not, we'll have a sticky situation on our hands. So let's hope Hank is a workhorse."

Skye brought Atka to the office with her every day and right now the dog needed a potty break. She'd just snapped his leash in place and stepped into the hallway to head downstairs when she spotted Travis getting off the elevator.

"I need to talk to you," he said.

"Okay. We're headed outside. You're welcome to join us. How's the girlfriend today?"

"What do you care? You were rude and insufferable Sunday night. You've never once embarrassed me the way you did until I saw your ugly side during dinner. And in front of a man I respected and admired, not to mention the woman in my life."

She pushed the arrow button for down and said quickly, "I know. I'm sorry."

"Don't tell me, tell her," Travis snapped.

"I will. Happy now?"

"No."

She frowned at the elevator when it dinged. The doors opened, she stepped into the car with an attitude. But then she realized her father didn't look so much angry as distressed. Losing patience, she snapped, "Do you plan to tell me what's wrong any time soon or do I have to play twenty questions?"

"Chenoa's pressuring me to get married."

Since that's the last thing she'd expected him to say, her mouth fell open. "What? After dating for two weeks? What kind of woman does that? It's ridiculous. And you expect me to apologize to her for being rude? I think this woman is the one who should back off twisting your arm about marriage at such an early stage in your relationship."

"Uh, I've known Chenoa for a lot longer than two weeks."

Even though they'd reached the lobby, that statement had Skye stopping dead in her tracks. "Oh really? How much longer?"

"Add a hundred more weeks to that and you'll have the whole picture."

She felt her jaw tighten as she grinded her teeth. Distracted with the disclosure, she almost stumbled out of the opening, but caught her balance in time before her foot got lodged in the gap between the elevator doors. Atka lurched forward, pulling her into the building's atrium and beyond to the revolving doors.

While Christmas music drifted from the overhead speakers, Skye tossed her father a frosty glare. "Let me get this straight. Are you telling me you've been dating that woman for two full years and I never heard of her before last week?"

"You might try calling her something else besides *that woman*."

"Why? I'll call her whatever I want."

"Skye, in case you haven't noticed, Chenoa's part of my life now."

Suddenly it all became clear. The way Chenoa had taken over the dinner party, not like a newcomer but rather a woman who was used to being at her lover's house. Skye felt incredibly foolish. Why hadn't she wondered before now about her father's personal life? Because before now, it had never occurred to her that he had one.

"Oh, I saw how much a part of your life she is for myself Sunday night. She's incredibly self-absorbed. What exactly do you two have in common?" Skye held up her free hand and added, "Never mind. I don't care. I think you two are all wrong for one another."

"Why do you say that?"

"It's obvious she walks all over you. You barely contributed anything to the conversation Sunday night. Not only that, she talks about herself constantly." Again Skye held up a hand. "It's your life. Do what you want. But I've never known you to let anyone pressure you into doing anything you didn't want to do. So you obviously want to… Marry *that woman*, no matter how self-centered she is."

With that defiant attitude hanging between them, they made their way through the revolving doors outside onto a grassy area designated for pets. It wasn't the chilly December air that had her feeling so raw but the idea her father would even consider marriage to such an arrogant, narcissistic woman.

"You obviously don't approve of Chenoa," Travis accused.

"What difference does it make? I'm not the one hooking up with a woman whose name sounds like she works at a strip joint."

"Chenoa is *not* a stripper," Travis insisted. "She's classy in her own way."

"I'll take your word for it and alert the media. If you're lucky the announcement might make *Seattle Today*."

"Now there's the smartass girl I love. I'd like your word that you'll try harder to get along with her. That's why I'm here."

She lifted a shoulder. "What do I care? Your type of woman is obviously a snotty female who looks down her nose at the rest of us. If she's the kind of person you want as your significant other, who am I to stand in your way to happiness? Be sure to let me know when you decide on the big day. I'll make sure I've gone shopping and picked out a suitable outfit for the occasion."

With that, Skye stalked off into the chilly December wind leading Atka to do her business somewhere else.

Eight hours into the kidnapping, Skye and Josh were still oblivious to the crime. It hadn't made the news yet and since no one had contacted them through the foundation, the two went about their business as usual looking for any homicides Leo might've overlooked that fit their serial killer's method.

They sat huddled together in a small conference room at the Seattle PD going through boxes of cold case files looking for any other victims who'd suffered mutilation before death.

While Atka napped under the table at their feet, Josh grumbled, "Our tax dollars need to be better spent on keeping these kinds of details current. Imagine being able to log on to a software program and pull this kind of information about decades-old cases and be able to use the details for comparison. I mean, I'm aware there's Encase® Forensics, a database that allows sharing of evidence. But our tax dollars need to be better spent computerizing the city's cold case files."

"Maybe you should get Leo, Reggie or Winston to expand what they do for us. You guys could sell the application to Seattle PD and make a fortune. Speaking of Winston, does he seem distracted to you lately?"

"I haven't noticed anything out of the ordinary, other than, I'm pretty sure he has a major crush on one of the testers."

"Which one?"

"Rhonda Braddock."

"The little blonde? Aww, that's sweet."

"It would be if she returned the interest. I don't think she does."

"Why do you say that? Is Rhonda with someone?"

"I have no idea. I do my best to stay out of the personal lives of my employees." He cut her a hard glance. "You'd be wise to follow suit."

"But since Winston is so sweet and also a volunteer at the foundation…"

"Skye, let it go. I know you'd just love to play matchmaker. Pairing him up with Rhonda is a mistake," Josh concluded. "Start interfering in the personal lives of people and you…"

"Suffer the consequences when it doesn't work out? Yeah, I get that. Okay, so maybe I'll let Winston get his own women." Suddenly she snatched a file off the top of the stack and thumbed through it, scanning the police report. "So back to the reason we're here. What does your gut tell you about whether this unsub will go dormant anytime soon?"

Josh shook his head. "That's just it. My gut says no. I don't think he will. The three found dead, I'm betting they weren't his only victims. Correction. I'm sure of it. In fact, I think he's settling in for the long haul and heading for spring if we don't catch him."

"What makes you say that?" Before he could answer, Skye waved the folder in the air. "I knew it. Found one. Remember that girl left near the dumpster behind Pine two years ago? Apparently she was never ID'd. They buried her as a Jane Doe in a potter's field with a number on her grave marker instead of a name."

"And?"

"The Jane Doe had breast implants. They were cut out."

Josh gritted his teeth. "Helluva painful way to go. How old was she? Does she fit the pattern? Do you think she might be on Leo's list and we haven't connected the dots yet?"

"Approximate age nineteen, five-foot-two, a little bitty thing with breast implants that were most likely size D cup."

Josh raised a brow. "That's insane."

"I'd hate to carry that excess top-heavy weight around, especially when I seriously doubt it was her idea to begin with."

"Why weren't they able to ID her by the implants?"

"That's the major question. I think you should be the one who contacts Bayliss and bug him about Jane Doe to jog his memory since you have such a good relationship with him. He doesn't like me."

"Bayliss doesn't like anyone."

She chewed at her bottom lip before getting up to look out the window. Staring at the view across the bay, she wondered aloud, "Something tells me this Jane Doe fell through the cracks somewhere, which means there's a flaw in Leo's list. We have to consider the fact that it only covers the *victims* who were reported missing by their families. What if this particular victim's name doesn't appear in the system anywhere? It does happen."

Josh skimmed the details of the autopsy report. "Did you read this? Bayliss noted her overall physical condition appeared as though she'd been indigent for some period of time. This Jane Doe was basically butchered. Poor kid, poor luck, a runaway who happened to get kidnapped and then reappeared after a period of time, dumped like trash, just like Carrie, Taylor, and Lisa. I think you've found one we add to the list. We just need to find out who she was, then backtrack to learn when she went missing."

"A runaway who simply had no family to speak of, or she dropped out of the system, went off the radar for some reason, and when she disappeared, no one noticed she was gone. None of that explains how an impoverished kid ends up with breast implants."

"Then we'll find the answers."

Inspired now with success, they were elbow deep in paper and files when Harry walked into the conference room.

"I have bad news and worse news. We have another missing woman. A nineteen-year-old single mother by the name of Ashley Kendrow didn't show up to work this morning at her job at a fast food restaurant. Her family got worried when they didn't hear from her and couldn't reach her and called the police. That's the bad."

"Do I even want to know the worse part?" Skye asked with dismay.

"Probably not. Ashley's gone missing and so has her eighteen-month-old daughter, Kiki. Approximately thirteen hours ago, the teen picked her baby up on schedule from her mother's house. The mother babysits Kiki while Ashley works the late shift."

"What makes you think this case belongs to our unsub? Maybe it's just a custody dispute. Maybe the father persuaded them to run off with him or he kidnapped the kid and did something to the mother."

Harry sent Josh a look that spoke volumes. "That's the first thing we checked. We tracked down the baby's father, another nineteen-year-old, and found out he's never been a part of the kid's life, doesn't even visit, and doesn't pay a significant amount in child support."

"Okay, maybe the single mom left on her own," Josh started.

"Not without taking her purse or the baby's diaper bag or taking her clothes with her," Harry insisted. "We found Ashley's personal items, all those things I mentioned, right there in the living room. It looks like she made it home, put the baby to sleep in the crib and then she and the baby just vanished."

"So he's morphed into new lows, new dynamics, by targeting a mother with a baby?" Josh pointed out. "Didn't Emmett predict he'd try a new angle?"

"What did we expect from this lowlife? You said it yourself. Bundy did whatever it took to obtain his goal. Got a pic of the teen?" Skye asked Harry.

The detective slid a copy of Ashley's driver's license photo from the folder and handed it off.

After studying the woman's features—pretty auburn hair, beautiful blue eyes, and a milky complexion—Skye shoved it toward Josh.

"So we'll hit the streets if you want like I did with Gwen. See what we can find," Skye offered, spearing looks at her partner for affirmation. Instead of that, she saw confusion in Josh's gray eyes.

Josh expected to pick up on something from the picture but was disappointed when it didn't happen. "What about the baby?"

Harry pulled out another snapshot of a toddler with an adorable face much like that of her mother's. "The family calls her Kiki. But her real name is Kiyanna Diana Kendrow."

There was a vibe in the compact room that spoke volumes. Harry noticed it right away and scratched his head. "What gives? You two have never needed my permission before to wander around Seattle at night. What's up?"

"Not a thing."

Harry shrugged. "Okay by me. I get it. You guys keep your secrets. Continue with whatever means you need to locate these offenders, I don't care. Get me results and leave me out of the how."

Skye smiled at her longtime friend. It wasn't the first time Harry had made that kind of declaration. She reached over and tugged at his arm. "We'll get the word out, ready the volunteers to distribute flyers, the usual drill. In the meantime, do you mind if Josh and I talk to Ashley's family?"

At the frown he saw form on Harry's face, Josh held up a hand. "Before you jump to conclusions, don't take the question as an insult to your investigative skills. Know that talking to the girl's family is our best shot at taking this case from the ground up and getting somewhere with it."

"I'm sure it is. But it doesn't make me feel any better about you two going over there. Makes me think I'm getting too old for this job. Couldn't you just read my notes?"

"Yes, but Josh is right," Skye reiterated. "We need face to face contact. Maybe they saw or heard something they forgot to mention. It doesn't hurt to get a new pair of eyes to look at the situation from another angle. What about Ashley's vehicle?"

"Already towed to where the lab's processing the interior," Harry grumbled, pushing his notebook toward Skye to read. "I'm not happy about this, though. You'll find the mother's address in Capitol Hill while the actual abduction took place at Ashley's third-floor walkup less than five minutes from where she picked up the baby."

Skye quickly perused Harry's scrawled handwritten notes before taking out her cell phone. Using her camera phone, she snapped a series of photos so she could have them with her for referral.

"What are you doing?" Harry asked.

"I'm saving them for posterity's sake. If the kidnapping occurred at Ashley's apartment building then we'll need access, the sooner the better. If that's where she and the baby were snatched, we need to get a quick lay of the land."

Chapter Thirteen

Once outside the police station, Josh and Skye stood on the sidewalk in a slice of late afternoon sun that streamed down on them from a break in the clouds.

She glanced over at a troubled Josh while doing her best to rein in Atka, tugging at the leash, anxious to get going. Skye took the time to breathe in the fresh air and said, "It'll be Christmas soon and I haven't even finished my shopping."

When Josh said nothing in return, she studied his face. Over the last few minutes she'd tried to make sense of his behavior. She decided on the direct approach. "What was that back there? You looked positively blank."

"That's because the images aren't coming clearly to me like they were before. We know this guy's highly organized so it stands to reason he plans his abductions down to the letter except for maybe the victim he targets, but not this one. I don't think he planned on the baby."

"So you think Kiki was a surprise? He spots Ashley somewhere along her route headed home, follows her to her parents' house instead, and that's when he learns there's a baby."

"Things have changed inside him. When he spots Kiki, he realizes the baby's the bonus. He uses some kind of ruse to get close to them, but I have no idea what it is," Josh muttered, his tone mixed with irritation.

"Why do you think the images aren't coming? You just told us more than we knew before. Granted, it isn't much but every tidbit helps. You know that."

"You don't get it. That info is about as vanilla as it comes, a non-picture. We're dealing with a violent sadist. I should be getting more. Instead, I'm getting nothing of real value." He tapped the side of his head. "Up here."

"So it comes and goes. That's no reason to panic."

"Look, since mixing blood with Kiya, I take this gift seriously. The blankness started when I woke up with a headache this morning. It's as though something's blocking me."

"Aw, come on. The old Superman-doesn't-see-through-lead principle?"

"Hey, for the first time in two years my senses aren't sharp. Everything seems fuzzy, out of focus. I can't bring anything into a clear picture. I think that's why I lost the guy the other night at the house. Not only that, but the smells around me, are blending together. Usually I'm able to differentiate one from the other. There's something off. I always dream about the hunt. The last couple nights my dreams are unclear, more like smoke and mirrors. I'm just not able to tell what's real. Maybe I'm losing the power I had. Maybe I'm losing my connection to Kiya."

"Let's hope not. The timing would suck. Besides, why would it happen now, during this particular case?" She grabbed his arm. "Wait a minute. Emmett mentioned that maybe our unsub blocked Kiya that day at the house when he delivered the flowers."

Understanding spread across Josh's face. "The son of a bitch is blocking me in some way. He's using some Native remedy to weaken my ability to keep us from catching him."

Skye's face hid her uncertainty. "Whoa, I'd rather not think like that. I prefer to consider he's some type of warlock rather than having Native blood running through his veins."

Should she admit the whole idea sounded far-fetched? "Look, maybe you're having an off day or something. The condition could be temporary or stress-related due to the headache. Maybe you're still jet-lagged from the trip. You haven't been sleeping very well. You admit the last two nights you've gone *Sleepless in Seattle*. It doesn't take much for sleep deprivation to kick in. You know that. There are any number of reasons you could be experiencing these lapses."

Before she could go on, Josh cut her off. "There's a hot dog vendor right over there at the corner not twenty feet from us and I'm not able to smell the onions from here. Get it now?"

Skye flashed a grin and cracked, "Not even the chili? This *is* serious."

But Josh didn't find it funny.

That's when acceptance began to sink in, slow and steady. She paced a few steps away before coming round again. "So when you were going through those boxes in there, you couldn't pick up on anything from any of the cases we found?"

"For the most part all I got was a blue-grayish screen in my head and a lot of frustration."

"But that wasn't the way it was at first. Just a couple days ago you picked up on several key factors early on. Okay, okay, I'm beginning to understand. Then we'll have to go back to the way things were before and rely on Kiya and Atka to hunt this guy down. We'll revert back to my old-fashioned method and put our faith on Kiya's nose and your muscle. You do still have the ability to leap tall buildings in a single bound, right?"

He finally returned her grin. "My muscle is just fine. And there's nothing wrong with my legs. But there's one more thing you should know. I feel that something's off, wrong, like Kiya's trying to warn me about a dangerous situation but I'm having difficulty tuning it in."

"Hmm, isn't that the same thing you said to me several days back? Listen to Kiya. I suggest you do the same and sit this one out. Let me go visit the Kendrows solo."

"Not a chance."

She shrugged. "Then I guess we swing by Ashley's apartment afterward. Maybe we'll get lucky and you'll pick up on some vibe from the place where it happened."

⋐⋐ ⋐⋐ ⋐⋐

Inside the colonial brick belonging to George and Marion Kendrow, they sat in a tidy kitchen doing their best to console Ashley's worried parents.

Wringing her hands, Marion, a youthful-looking redhead in her mid-forties, couldn't stop gushing about her daughter. "We tried to get her and Kiki to stay here. But Ashley's always been extremely independent. That's one reason when she found out she was pregnant, just before turning eighteen, she decided to raise the baby by herself. After Kiki was born there were times Ashley held down two jobs. I didn't take money to babysit and with the hundred or so we were able to pitch in each month for groceries and gas, she was able to get her own place and pay her bills. She'd recently been accepted to Cornish College for summer classes. She loved to create her own designs. She was so creative."

"Your daughter sounds like an amazing, determined woman despite her young age."

"Oh, she is."

George, a plumber by trade with graying hair thought so, too. He sat with his head in his hands, cringing each time the phone rang in the background. "We've had to rely on my sister to field all the calls from reporters, crackpots, and the curious who won't stop calling. Don't they understand we need the lines to remain free so that if Ashley needs to reach us she'll be able to? They don't seem to understand how special Ashley and Kiki are. Why do these people come out of the woodwork at a time like this when all they do is throw stupid questions our way, and then disappear? Instead of asking ridiculous questions they should be doing more to find them. You wouldn't believe how rude they are."

Skye gripped George's hand. "I know. But right now the media plays a major role in getting the word out."

"We didn't come here to add to your burden, Mr. Kendrow," Josh assured him. "What we need is for both you and Mrs. Kendrow to think back to that night. When Ashley came into the house did she act particularly nervous or scared, like someone had bothered her before she reached your house? Did she act as though someone was waiting for her in the car?"

George finally raised his head to bob at his wife. "Marion is the one who saw her that night. I had an early job to get to the next morning so I went to bed around ten o'clock." His voice broke. "The last time I saw Ashley was when she dropped off Kiki to go to work that afternoon."

"Did she say anything lately had been out of the ordinary then?"

"Nothing," Marion said, dabbing at a tear. "And when she picked up Kiki she was in a hurry to get home, get the baby tucked into bed. That was her mindset. Because she had to get up and go to work the next day, she was in and out of here within a few minutes. There was nothing to indicate she was in trouble at all."

"Did you see anything, hear anything at all outside?"

Marion started to shake her head but then thought of something. "She left her Ford running in the driveway. She mentioned that it hadn't wanted to start up when she stopped at the grocery store for diapers and baby wipes. Do you think the man could've been waiting in the backseat for her when she got into the car with her hands full of the baby?"

Skye squeezed Marion's trembling fingers in reassurance. "I don't think so. The detective on the case knows what he's doing. Harry Drummond's convinced there's every indication Ashley and Kiki made it back to her apartment. You said that she went shopping before coming here to pick up Kiki?"

"Yes, for diapers."

"Is that important?" George asked. "Did someone follow her from the store?"

"Honestly, we don't know yet," Josh said. "But it's a possibility."

Marion twisted the Kleenex she'd taken from the box, blew her nose. "Ashley's our youngest. She's extremely bright and maybe at times she's been a little reckless. But she's a mother now, a very good one. And little Kiki, Kiki's our adorable bundle of joy. Please, please, do whatever it takes to help us find them."

Skye and Josh traded hopeful looks. It was Skye who told them, "We'll do everything possible."

Because of that dubious promise, they were determined to get a resolution no matter what they had to do to get it.

Twenty minutes later, they left Atka in the car while they met one of Seattle's finest who let them into Ashley's little one-bedroom apartment on the third floor. The uniform cop handed them each a pair of latex gloves and paper footies to go over their shoes.

Once they got inside, it seemed evident that despite the busy mom's schedule the teen somehow managed to keep the place tidy and orderly.

Looking around though, it was clear that a child lived here. A stroller sat empty in the entryway. A tot-sized table and chairs were set up next to the kitchen. "I guess when you have a curious toddler, self-preservation means keeping a clean house," Skye reasoned, doing her best to look for anything out of place.

Josh took in the cramped quarters, especially the bedroom. Wall-to-wall furniture included a full-sized bed for Ashley, Kiki's crib, a dresser stuffed to the gills, and the assortment of baby paraphernalia it took to raise a child. Baby books lined the shelf next to family photos. There was a crate that acted as Kiki's toy box. A slew of bright hair ribbons hung from the mirror. An assortment of stuffed animals—a rabbit, a bear, a Washington husky— were piled up in one corner of the room.

Josh gritted his teeth and turned back toward the living room and entryway. "There's no sign of a struggle here."

Skye scanned the apartment, doing another recon of the premises. "Are teenagers normally this much of a neat freak? This place is almost spotless."

"Not the ones I've known. I sure wasn't."

"Could he have cleaned up while he was here?"

"Why would he?" Josh asked.

"I don't know unless he drew blood." For confirmation, Skye took out her cell phone, swiped her way through to the photos she'd taken of Harry's notes. She began to skim his words, his first impression of what he'd considered a crime scene.

Skye ran a gloved finger across the counter. "This kitchen is cleaner than ours. If Ashley made it back to the house, where's the paper sack with the diapers and wipes Ashley's mother said she stopped to buy? Harry's notes confirm she was at the market. Surveillance cameras at the all-night grocery store verify Ashley was at the checkout paying for her items at 12:20 a.m. and walked out to her car—alone."

"Doesn't mean someone wasn't lurking nearby and followed her out of the lot once she got the car started," Josh pointed out.

Skye nodded in agreement as she continued to read Harry's scribbled description of the crime scene. "Wait a minute. Harry noted there was no baby seat found in Ashley's car. The guy must've thought he needed it for Kiki. So let's say he took the diapers and wipes as a necessity. If you're gonna keep the baby you have to be willing to change diapers." She turned to Josh. "You said it earlier. The unsub didn't plan on kidnapping the baby, but after he saw her, he wanted her."

"That indicates he wants to keep the baby long term, which is either a good thing because Kiki's alive or a sickening fact for down the road." Josh automatically reached his hand out to touch the stroller. As soon as he made contact, white flashes speared his vision, going off like multiple rockets.

With her back to Josh, Skye was still deep in analytical mode. She busied herself going through Ashley's stuff and rambled on, "Tell me again why we think this fits our guy's profile. Our monster mutilator kidnaps a baby? Because I'm not seeing it, Josh. Not at all. Yes, we need to find mother and baby. Yes, we're dealing with abduction here, no argument. But is this really connected to the same guy who murdered and mutilated our three victims?"

For an answer, Josh unexpectedly doubled over at the waist as if he'd been hit with a baseball bat. His breath hitched. He forced out each word in agony. "The guy used the stroller to get Ashley and the baby to the car and then brought it back so no one would see it in the parking lot."

Skye turned to look at him, saw his body bent in pain. She closed the distance, grabbed the nearest chair and helped him into it. "What's the matter with you?"

"Massive headache from hell, excruciating stomach pain," Josh answered, rubbing a hand through his hair, which throbbed at the slightest touch of his fingers. "This is our guy. That's the one thing I'm sure of," he tumbled out, right before blood began to gush from his nose.

Skye dashed down the hallway and into Ashley's bathroom to get a towel. By the time she came back, she found Josh had slipped out of the chair, clinging to it, still in terrible pain.

While she pressed the damp cloth to his head, she rubbed his back. But then an instinct kicked in, a sense that they were near something evil. "It's being here in Ashley's apartment, this close to the person who abducted her and the baby that's overwhelming to you. I'm calling Travis. This guy is obviously dabbling in some sort of black magic that's making you sick. But I don't think it's Native. There's a chance he thinks it is, though, which is just as powerful."

"Son of a bitch. I'll be all right, just give me a minute."

Skye used speed dial to reach Travis at the ranch. Once she got an answer she stumbled through the details about Josh's sudden, declining health. "Do you have any idea what our killer could be using to eliminate Josh's power to this extent so quickly?"

"Has he pissed off any ancient magicians lately?"

"Come on, cut the jokes. Josh is in pain here. This is really serious."

"So am I. This sounds exactly like a deadly version of one of the fifty-five ancient katares, or curses that originated in the Mediterranean thousands of years ago. Reciting the words to one is supposed to bring on extreme pain, various types of medical issues, coma, and in certain cases even death to its intended target."

"Well, there's good news. So this guy is using some type of ancient spell to get us to back off? What do we do about it? And why did he go after Josh and not me?"

"I thought Emmett Cannavale explained that the other day at the house. This guy believes a woman is an inferior being. You don't make a worthy enough opponent to mess with."

"I guess I forgot that part. Okay, well, whatever this thing is, round up the elders. Josh needs a cleansing and fast. You'll set it up, right? I gotta go catch this asshole and find a young mother and her little girl before he decides to cut them up for kicks. Did you make all the calls I requested?"

"I have everyone lined up like always. In fact, I'm headed to the foundation now to meet with Lena and Zoe, and Velma and Judy to formulate a plan."

"Fine. You rally the infantry. I'll take care of the recon."

"Skye?"

"What?"

"You and Josh be careful out there."

"I'm always careful."

After disconnecting the call, she turned to Josh, laid her hand on his forehead. "You're temp is beginning to spike. I don't think it's a good idea for you to go out tonight."

"Stop trying to ditch me. We have to go. Look around you. Somewhere out there this bastard is holding a mother and a baby. We don't know for how long. We're running out of time."

"Then we should get moving."

As Skye helped Josh down to ground level, they began to go over scenarios. "So what do you think happened here? Did Ashley allow someone in that she knew and that's why there's no sign of forced entry or a struggle?"

"Or maybe she didn't perceive the person she let in as much of a threat," Josh surmised. "Why would that be, though? Was it someone Ashley recognized, who looked familiar from the neighborhood? Was he or she wearing a uniform she trusted? Was he posing as a security guard or maybe worse, a cop?"

"A frightening thought. Keep in mind a mother will likely comply with anyone and do anything to keep her child safe from harm."

"He no doubt used the baby to get her to go with him."

When they reached the car, an excited, tail-wagging Atka greeted them with a series of boisterous yips. Freedom from confinement had the dog sniffing the air.

Before setting off on foot, they relied on Kiya to pick up Ashley's and the baby's scent from the adjacent parking lot. Standing at the corner, the pack—Skye, Josh, and the two canines—began to roam through the neighborhood, winding their way past Volunteer Park, following the white wolf due west.

The Sunday afternoon was coming to an end by the time Kiya trotted past Thai food places, taco shops, and shoe barns, her entourage dutifully in tow. Buses rumbled down Tenth Avenue in an effort to keep to the regular weekend routes and places like University Village, UDub, and touristy destination points that were always popular on Saturdays and Sundays.

As the sun dipped in the west, Skye noted the direction they'd taken. "Why are we headed toward Lake Union and the waterfront? Kiya, where are you taking us?" she muttered as she followed along. Skye turned back, noticed Josh sweating profusely and more out of breath than before. She stopped and waited for him to catch up. "This can't be right. Why would a kidnapper keep his victims in the middle of the city? This is way too out in the open, too many people, too many neighbors, too many distractions around to be where a serial killer might set up shop."

Feeling worse with each step, Josh shook his head. "No, leave it to Kiya to find him. She knows where she's going. You've always trusted her instincts before, do it now. The area might be high density and busy with boat traffic, but keep in mind this guy probably doesn't stand out in a crowd so no one notices him much."

"Okay, I'll take your word for it along with Kiya's nose. You can't both be wrong."

The pack hiked over terrain that sloped down to the harbor. Once under the I-5 greenbelt, the wind kicked up. Skye noted a storm moving in over Puget Sound.

The four kept moving, eventually dumping out onto Fairview. But Kiya abruptly headed southward as the clouds opened up in a deluge. Pouring rain obstructed their view to a line of yachts and houseboats floating on the water.

Kiya left the pathway and crossed the street into a busy parking lot. The sloops beyond bobbed in the distance, beckoning the wolf to veer farther into the marina. Atka suddenly tugged on her leash and took off toward Kiya until the canines were side by side. They left the pavement and circled into a private dock to an unassuming two-story houseboat painted a bright blue.

"The property looks vacant."

"Looks are deceiving."

Together Josh and Skye stepped onto the wooden mooring following Kiya's lead. Skye heard what sounded like a baby's wail. The canines broke away and ran to the front door. Both began to paw and scratch at the wood.

Fearing he wasn't up for a fight physically, she turned to Josh. Whispering in a low voice, she asked, "Are you okay with kicking it in then going around back when he bolts?"

Josh nodded. "We both know he'll take off."

Without further discussion, he promptly picked up his foot and smashed it into the door. Splintered pieces of wood went flying as they burst through the doorway, prepared for anything. But all they saw in the small room was a screaming toddler on the sofa, sitting next to a very still female form.

That's when they heard an engine start up and roar off, the noise coming from the parking lot they'd walked through earlier.

At the sound, Kiya and Atka skidded through the back door, Josh running behind them in pursuit leaving Skye to deal with the baby and her unconscious mom.

But Skye needed to make sure the house was clear before dealing with the victims. Taking out her nightstick, she tiptoed through the rest of the first floor. Once each room checked out, she made her way to the steps going up to the next level.

The galley was the first room at the top of the stairs. When the smell of gas hit her nose she took the stairs back down two at a time. Scooping up the sobbing little girl, she yelled for Josh.

"We have to get out of here. Now!" The terrified child kept reaching back for her mother, all the while screaming at the top of her lungs.

"Shhh, its okay, baby. Let's get you and your mommy out of here."

Josh came back in through the back door with Atka. Winded, he rested his hands on his knees trying to get his breath back. "He's gone. I couldn't catch up. I called 911. Cops are on their way."

"We have to get out of here. There's a gas smell coming from upstairs. This place could blow any minute."

"Go. Take the baby. I've got Ashley," Josh offered.

"Are you sure? You barely look like you can stand."

"I don't have a choice," he wheezed out as he hauled the mother up and into his arms. Together they followed Atka out of the floating house and into the rain. They took off—Skye holding Kiki, Josh toting Ashley—down the dock ramp and back to the safety of the parking lot.

Behind them, the explosion shook the ground as they dropped on one knee to the wet pavement. The fiery blast caused flames to shoot up so high they lit up the night sky for blocks.

Skye stood back watching, clutching the toddler—rocking her back and forth, trying to comfort her enough to settle down. But the chaos around them did little to help. Sirens went off. People were screaming. A crowd began to gather around the marina.

And the four of them were getting drenched as the skies opened up and the rain came down harder. The drops hit Ashley's face. As the water began causing the teen mom to stir, Josh lost his grip on Ashley. As she slipped out of his grasp, he sat her upright, held her in place while he tried to rally his own strength.

"Are you able to walk?" Skye shouted over the storm. "If so, we need to move to the corner of the lot and as far away as we can get from the smoke."

"Good idea," Josh choked out, helping Ashley move through the rain. They'd just reached the grassy strip near the street when a van came out of nowhere. It jumped the curb and barreled straight for them.

Josh glanced up, saw the van without headlights swerving into their path. Despite stumbling over his own feet, he managed to shove Skye and the girl out of the way with his body, in time to take the brunt of the force full on.

Still clutching Kiki to her chest, Skye looked up and saw Josh sprawled out ten feet away on the concrete—blood oozing from his nose and mouth.

Chapter Fourteen

Travis rushed into the waiting room at Harborview and spotted Skye, head bowed, her fingers rubbing her own temples. "Is Josh gonna be okay?"

Looking up and staring into her dad's eyes, she bit her lip, trembled a little. "I don't know. The ER doctors sent him up here to X-ray for his shoulder and to Imaging for the brain scan. They want to make sure he didn't suffer a head trauma. He's still in there. They're keeping him tonight regardless so they can do another brain scan tomorrow and check for internal bleeding."

"What happened?"

"We'd gotten out of the houseboat, Josh carrying Ashley and me holding the baby. We were a safe distance back when Josh had to sit down. Ashley started coming to and Josh helped her get to her feet. So I suggested since she could walk, we head to the far corner of the parking lot, next to the street and put some distance between us and the blast. Out of the blue this delivery van jumps the curb. Not one of those paneled jobs either but the bigger kind that carries major cargo around town."

"Like the postal trucks?"

"Almost but not quite. Anyway, Josh shoved Ashley out of the way just in time to keep them both from taking the blow full on. The driver headed right for Josh. If Josh hadn't jumped in the air when he did, the van would've hit him straight on, full body impact. Instead, he came down on the driver's side and bounced off the side mirror. I'm pretty sure the van grazed his left shoulder. That wasn't what did the damage though. It was making contact with the pavement that caused him to hit his head. He lost consciousness and hasn't come around yet. He could be... He might be dead right now." Her voice broke off as the waterworks flowed.

Between sobs, she continued, "The bastard took off at a high rate of speed heading east toward the I-5. By now he could be pulling into Canada." She scrubbed her hands over her face before adding, "It was all such a blur I didn't even have time to get a plate number."

"Not even a partial? That's not like you."

Skye glowered at her father. "It all happened too fast. I was focused on Ashley, who could barely walk because she'd obviously spent hours drugged out of her mind, and an eighteen-month-old toddler who wouldn't stop crying. I let Josh take the lead. I should've been in front. I knew he was struggling and I let him take point."

"Cut it out," Travis urged, sliding his hand in hers. "Like Josh would've wanted you in jeopardy. You know better than that." Travis sat down next to her, wrapped her up in his arms. "He'll be fine. You'll see. He's tough. Didn't he come through the transformation without losing his mind? A lesser man would've had major issues with all the changes to his body. Not Josh."

Travis leaned in to kiss her forehead and lowered his voice. "The elders are on their way. They'll gather here later tonight, perform the cleansing ceremony we talked about. We'll get Josh back on track. You'll see. But first we have to find a way to sneak them all past the night nurses."

For the first time in hours, she smiled at her dad. "I'll see what I can do. Thanks for coming."

"That's what family's for." When a doctor showed up, Travis nudged her in the ribs.

"Mrs. Ander, I'm Dr. Lynch, the neurosurgeon called in to assess your husband's condition. If you'll come with me I'll go over the results of his MRI."

"Did he wake up yet?"

"That's what I want to talk to you about. He took a hit to his head and has a mild concussion. But he hasn't regained consciousness yet. We aren't sure exactly why."

Skye slanted a glance back at Travis as if to say, "the elders need to get to work and fast." But she said nothing about ancient curses or Native remedies as she followed Dr. Lynch into a small room off the nurses' station, where the doctor already had Josh's x-rays lit up on the display for viewing.

"So, are you saying his brain's okay and there's no obvious bleeding to worry about? Because the guy in the ER said that might be a problem. And if he's not awake yet…"

Dr. Lynch pointed to the MRI. "As you can see there's no indication of bleeding so far from the tests we ran. Your husband shows contusions and bruising though, here along the temporal lobe. So far, swelling hasn't occurred. If it should, there are ways to handle the pressure without being too invasive. But let's not worry about something that hasn't happened yet."

When they were joined by another physician, Skye narrowed her eyes. "If there's more, I need to call Josh's mom and dad. They'll want to be here with him."

Dr. Lynch nodded. "That's a good idea. Right now, I'm going to hand you off to the orthopedist, Dr. Vollmer, who'll talk to you about your husband's shoulder, which is dislocated. He also has two cracked ribs."

As he turned to go, Dr. Lynch patted Skye's hand. "Don't worry. Your husband is in good hands here. I'm sure they already mentioned downstairs that we'll keep him until everything checks out from head to toe."

"About that, do you have any idea why he's still out?"

"After viewing his test results, I don't have a reasonable explanation for it. He shouldn't be out for this long based on what I saw on the MRI. But if there's more injury, it'll surface soon enough. We'll know by morning if it's more serious than what we first thought."

After Dr. Vollmer went through the injuries to Josh's shoulder and ribcage, Skye asked to see him.

"Sure. Give us ten minutes and we'll have him in a room by then up on the eighth floor."

Skye took advantage of the time to make the call she'd been dreading to Josh's parents.

She spent the next ten minutes reassuring Phyllis and Douglas Ander as best she could that Josh was receiving the best care possible. She'd see to it. Knowing the couple wouldn't understand Native customs or ritual cleansing ceremonies, she encouraged them to get to the hospital now to see their son, hoping they might be gone by midnight. It wouldn't do for them to cross paths with a group of Nez Perce shamans, let alone go into an account of what Josh had kept hidden from them for two years. In Skye's mind it was hardly the time to disclose what had happened to their son that day in the woods—a metal pipe to the head tended to do irreparable damage.

She doubted the Anders would put much faith in legends, spirit guides, or Kiya's role in the whole transformation process. Instead of full disclosure, Skye bypassed all that. "You don't have to spend the night with him because I'm staying put until he wakes up. They're taking him up to a room on the eighth floor now so we'll meet me up there."

When Doug questioned her over the phone about the hit and run she confirmed what had happened. "But don't worry. I intend to find the son of a bitch who did this to him."

After ending the call and heading back to the waiting room, Skye bumped into Harry in the hallway. "I hope

Ashley gave you enough of a detailed description to get a decent composite."

"Ashley didn't see much, Skye. How's Josh doing?"

"Unconscious. They're moving him upstairs. How are Ashley and the little girl?"

"Will he be okay?"

"I hope so. I'm not leaving him alone until I know he's okay."

"I know you have your hands full right now and I don't want to monopolize your time but... I need to talk to you about Ashley's ordeal."

"Let's hear it," she said wearily.

Harry took her through the teen's version of what happened. "When she reached her apartment and got out of the car, Ashley was followed up the stairs by a female with long dark hair."

"What? This guy has an accomplice?" Skye shook her head. "I'm beginning to think this isn't the same guy who mutilated the others."

"Maybe not but I learned just now that the doctor took a rape kit. The results were negative. She was drugged for most of the time he had her, I doubt she'd remember it anyway if she had been."

Skye aimed a disbelieving look in Harry's direction. "This might be a first. Why kidnap her if not for sex? To sell her for later? That's the only thing that makes sense. I don't get it, Harry." She marched off a few steps and then turned back. "What about Kiki? Did they complete a rape kit on the baby?"

Harry nodded. "Results turned out the same, negative."

"So if this wasn't about rape, then what? Our guy keeps both mom and baby at this houseboat for almost twenty hours, but doesn't beat her, mutilate her in anyway, or take advantage of her. He leaves them alive all that time. Come to think of it, the lab didn't find any semen on the other victims either. Why is that?"

"Maybe this guy's impotent."

"Maybe. But then why go to the trouble to abduct young women if he doesn't plan to use them sexually? Sex trafficking would be a good reason to do that. Maybe twenty hours wasn't enough time to complete the transaction."

"That's what I'm thinking."

"How about Kiki, how is she doing through all this?"

"Kiki checks out fine... Medically. Emotionally she seems terrified and traumatized."

"Bastard," Skye muttered. "Hopefully, Kiki will get back home to the Kendrows and her mommy soon and life will smooth out some. At some point, both of them will eventually forget what happened altogether. Okay, so maybe that's optimistic."

"We have survivors. I'd say that's more than reason for optimism."

Skye rocked back on her heels, beginning to feel better. "So let's move on to the owner of that houseboat."

"Some guy named John Stockman. He says someone must've picked the lock and broken in, and must've brought the girl and baby in there to hide out. Stockman says he doesn't use the houseboat all that often, mostly for entertaining. It's a second home for him. The last time he was there was about two weeks ago."

"Hmm, and you believe him?"

"So far his alibi checks. He's a local businessman with ties to the city council and mayor."

"Yeah? Well, so far I've got a husband who's losing ground by the hour, no answers as to who ran him down, a houseboat that blew up with us within feet of it, and I'm not real happy about any of it. So, I'm sure you won't mind if I choose to remain skeptical at this point about a guy with 'political ties' when two kidnapped victims are found in a house he owns."

"I'm right there with you. How about we keep tabs on Stockman? He might have a connection to our unknown subject."

"Or subjects. Fine. You keep an eye on him because as you can see, for the next couple days, I've got my hands full. Josh is staying put until he wakes up. And I'm not budging until he does."

"He's in a coma?"

Skye stabbed a finger in the detective's chest. "Do not use that word."

Just then, Lena and Zoe hurried up to them. The stylishly dressed woman wrapped Skye up in a bear hug, swaying back and forth. "I'm here now, honey. It'll be all right. You'll see."

Skye stared at the woman, she'd known for years. Lena wore a pair of black pants with a teal blouse under a festive red jacket. Skye noted she'd lopped off her dark brown hair into a spikey cut that made her look far younger than her fiftyish years. "What are you doing here?"

"Travis alerted us to what's going on. Zoe and I got here as soon as we could. How's Josh?"

"We were just getting to that," Harry said.

They all four turned to stare when Travis appeared with a band of Skye's fellow tribesmen trailing behind him. Travis pointed a thumb over his shoulder. "They'll wait for as long as it takes until the coast is clear to get access to Josh's room. Whenever you say the word, we're ready to go."

Lena looked confused. "Why do all these people need to get into Josh's room?"

Skye explained the situation, and hopefully, the solution.

After listening to the reasoning, instead of doubting Skye's judgment or the ritual itself, Lena simply replied, "Zoe and I want to be in there for support."

Skye smiled at the lady she considered a substitute mom. "We could be planning an exorcism for all you know and you want in?"

Lena grinned back. "If there's a chance it might make Josh better, absolutely. I mean what could it hurt to send healing vibes out into his space?"

"My sentiments exactly. Besides, I don't like it that the asshole we're chasing is using Josh like this. So let's do this thing."

Chapter Fifteen

But before the elders could get underway with the ceremony they had to wait for Phyllis and Doug Ander to leave Josh's room.

For three hours Skye stalled for time. Standing beside Josh's bed, nervously hoping his parents would eventually feel comfortable enough to leave their son in her care, she wanted to get the show on the road. But noting the worried look on their faces, she didn't blame the Anders for sticking around well past the witching hour. After all, their son had been comatose for more than six hours now.

"I don't understand why he doesn't wake up," Phyllis wondered.

Doug touched his son's cheek, felt his forehead and then searched Skye's face for answers. "It's as if something else is at play here. Is there a reason there's a roomful of Nez Perce elders lined up outside the nurse's station hoping the way will soon be clear when we leave?"

Skye looked over at Phyllis then back at Doug and decided to level with them. "Okay, you deserve the truth. Here's the deal. At the risk of sounding completely off the charts and you thinking I'm nuttier than peanut butter, Travis and I think the killer we're after is utilizing some kind of ancient curse to keep Josh sick and out of it. There, I said it."

Doug looked stressed and baffled until the light bulb went off. "So that explains why there are a bunch of elders—I haven't seen since the wedding—sitting out in the waiting room. If this ancient curse is a factor then why have you wasted all this time? Let's get the tribe in here and try making him better. For God's sake, help Josh come back to us."

"Right," Skye said. "I don't know what I was thinking." She angled her head toward Travis. "You round up the medicine men while I distract the nurses."

Doug waved her off. "Don't worry about the nurses. You get this thing started and Phyllis and I will take care of them. Just see to it that my boy gets better."

"You heard the man," Skye said to Travis. "I'll set the stage with everything we need. You think it'll work without being physically inside the lodge?"

"That's the next thing we'll try if this fails, but it is mid-winter, the perfect season to bring about the healing power of the wéyekin."

To the Nez Perce the wéyekin ceremony was the backbone of their spiritual culture where powerful medicine could be found in a quest for their guardian spirit, the spirit that resided in the peopleless land. Since children from seven to thirteen went in search of their Power, wéyekin offered protection throughout their lifetime. During illness or hardship they called on their wéyekin for help. Even though Josh had come late to the party, this was one of those times. He might not be Nez Perce by blood but his adopted people believed he was a full member of the tribe. So, the elders had come to call, to appeal to his spirit guide, the wolf, for healing.

Standing beside his bed, Skye had a hard time dealing with how gray Josh looked. Since the hit and run, he seemed to be going downhill faster. Taking his hand in hers, she placed a kiss on his brow before stepping back so the tribe could work their magic.

The elders entered the room in order of tribal hierarchy. They began to utter in their Native tongue, chanting for the spirit of their ancestors to heal and protect. Two lit candles while two more began playing their flutes. The beat of drums sounded as the scent of cedar and sage wafted on the air, replacing the sickly hospital disinfectant odor.

The shaman directed the tribe to stand in a circle surrounding Josh's bed. They took up the same refrain. "Ee ah hay, ee ah hay, ee ah, ee ah hay. Tonight we call this room our lodge. We call to the peopleless land to use its forces of nature, its powerful energy, to enter here tonight where we meet and heal our young friend, Josh Ander. We ask the land to help in driving out the source of the evil spirits causing the sickness to befall our friend. We ask that Josh Ander regain dominion over his own human spirit. We call to the warrior wolf spirit inside him to fight strong once again and be with us again the way he was before. We call to his wolf spirit to chase away whatever evil keeps him sleeping. Heal like the strong wolf you are, Josh Ander. Ee ah hay, ee ah hay, ee ah, ee ah hay. Let the light shine in your eyes once again. Let your strength return tenfold. Ee ah hay, ee ah hay, ee ah, ee ah hay."

The singing continued until the first rays of sunlight peeked through the vertical blinds.

If the roomful of people thought anything physical would change in Josh right away, they were greatly disappointed. Skye knew it might take a while for the healing powers of the Great Spirit. But Phyllis and Doug and Lena and Zoe were disheartened at the lack of response in Josh.

Skye looked around at the faces of their friends. "I'm glad all of you came. I'm not sure what I would've done tonight if you guys hadn't been here with me to see me through the night."

"What happens now?" Phyllis asked.

"We wait. Until then you guys get out of here and get some sleep. Lena, I need you at the foundation for the next couple days heading up things. In fact, any of you who are able to spare the time, it'd be great if you could check in with Lena for specific assignments. Travis, if you could take Atka home with you, I'd really appreciate it. Last trip out to the car for the dog was at three a.m. I'm sure she needs to go out again."

"Don't worry about Atka. You just take care of yourself. Try to catch a nap if you can."

A nurse came into the room, looked around at the standing-room-only crowd and rolled her eyes. "I've been patient up to now. But there's a shift change due in thirty minutes. Be out of here before the day shift goes on the clock. That means anyone who isn't immediate family gets the boot."

"They're all family," Skye returned with a smile. "And I love all of you for coming."

Once they'd all drifted out to the elevators, Skye sat down by Josh's bedside and held his hand. Tears streamed down her face. She'd walked down alleyways and faced child molesters and every kind of murderer, but she was never as scared as she was right at that moment.

Harry found her like that.

"You look like you could drop. Is there anything I can do?"

"No, not really. But thanks for asking. Thanks for coming. What are you doing here so early?"

"I thought you'd like to know that the lab picked up useable DNA from Ashley's and Kiki's clothing."

"Touch DNA? So we'll know pretty quick if it came from two donors, if it's male or female, or if it matches anyone in the system."

"You know the drill. It's more than we had two days ago."

"Okay. Then as soon as Josh is able to walk out of this place, we'll want to talk to Ashley, delve a little deeper into her ordeal, find out what she remembers."

"He'll be okay, Skye."

She stared down at Josh. "You bet he will."

Several hours after the cleansing ceremony had ended and Harry had left her alone, Josh's eyes fluttered open.

His first clear picture was of Skye, head resting near his chest, asleep. He feared if he moved, he'd wake her so he remained perfectly still just watching her. Instincts though were back in full throttle. He laid his hand on her hair in a gentle, light touch.

As if sensing he was awake, Skye lifted her head, meeting his gaze.

"You have beautiful eyes," he murmured. "Have I told you that lately?"

"No, I don't believe you have." She ran a hand over the bruises on his forehead. "Would you like some ice chips? You still feel feverish to me."

She scooped up the plastic hospital pitcher, clinked ice into a cup, and then spooned the pieces up to his mouth. "How do you feel?"

"Like a truck hit me."

She pursed her lips in a grin. "You have a concussion from where you met up with a block of concrete called a curb. Your head is so hard the concrete lost. And the city plans to bill you for forcing them to send out a repair crew on a weekend."

Josh tried to laugh and was immediately reminded of the pain in his left side.

"That's from a set of cracked ribs," Skye explained. "Looks like you'll be sidelined for a few weeks."

"Nonsense. I'm already healing. I feel my body regenerating already. Don't look at me like that. It's Kiya's influence. You of all people know it is."

"I'm not denying it. I'm delighted you're on the mend."

Her brave front didn't fool Josh. "I'm sorry I worried you."

"Comes with the territory." But when she pressed her lips to his, there was urgency there. Truth. A connection of spirit. "Fact is I was terrified when I saw you lying on the pavement crumpled and hurt like that. There have been times over the years when what we do weighs heavily on me and I wonder if it's the right path. Today was one of those times."

"We don't let evil stop us, though. You know that."

"Yes, but it took a lot out of me seeing you injured."

"It should motivate us more to catch this bastard."

She kissed his forehead, worked her way slowly down to his lips. "Oh, it does. Count on it."

Chapter Sixteen

In Everett, an exhausted Travis unlocked the front door to his ranch house a little after seven in the morning with Atka leading the way into the foyer. Travis unhooked the malamute's leash, watched the dog head straight for the couch to curl up for a nap.

"Great idea," he muttered to the canine. "But I've got too many things to do. Might as well start a pot of coffee to stay awake." When he reached the kitchen, no one was more surprised than he was when he rounded the corner and found Chenoa already up and pouring creamer into her coffee mug.

"Where have you been?" Chenoa demanded.

Right at the moment, Travis wasn't in the mood for one of her infamous inquisitions. "Why ask? You know where I was. The question should be where were you? I called and told you the elders were performing the cleansing ceremony to help Josh wake up. It took a little longer than we'd planned."

"How long does it take to say a few words over a guy who can't even hear you?"

Travis's forehead knitted into a scowl. After being up all night those words nicked him a little too deep. "Since you're Native I'd think you'd respect the traditions of our forefathers a little more than you do."

Chenoa waved a hand in the air. "I told you upfront that I'm not really into all that. I still don't understand why it took all night. You should've been home hours ago. I really don't get it."

"I know you don't. But it was a little more detailed than we originally thought. Besides, things got complicated at the hospital. And I had to come up with excuses for your absence. At the very least you could've made an effort to stop by for a visit."

"Why would I do that? I just met those people the other day. It isn't like I actually know any of them, or that they know me. It would've been an uncomfortable situation for me."

Travis took out a cup from the cabinet, poured coffee, then dumped in four teaspoons of sugar. "'Those people' are my family. How, exactly, do you intend to get to know them if you don't make an effort?"

"And I told you showing up at the hospital isn't the best time to do that."

Travis got down a bottle of aspirin, knocked back three. He felt a headache coming on. "We'll discuss this when I get back."

"You just got home. I waited all night for you. Where are you going now?"

"While Josh is in the hospital I doubt Skye will devote much time to the foundation. So I've decided to step in to help. You could come with me," he suggested, clearly hopeful she'd take the opportunity to develop an interest in Skye's work. It wasn't the first time he'd given her the option. But that hope evaporated when Chenoa opened her mouth.

"When do you plan on spending time with me? I have a lot on my plate right now. The horse show is in two weeks. We were planning a trip to Savannah. What about that? Right now, I don't have time for anything but that."

He'd heard the same lame excuse for two years. "This isn't about you or me. Skye and Josh are on the trail of a man who doesn't mind kidnapping babies or mutilating young women. The killer's getting so desperate he tried to run down Josh. For me, this is a lot more important than your horse show."

"Since when? You love watching me compete."

He used to. "No one loves horses more than I do. But I'll say it again. This is my family we're talking about. Skye and Josh do important work that's vital for the very survival of some of these kids. They need my help and I'm not walking away from them to see a horse show. I take care of my own. If you don't know that by now you obviously don't know me well at all."

He started for the bedroom to change clothes but stopped. "So does this mean you won't come to the foundation today with me at all? Because I want to be clear here."

"No. I have no intentions of sitting around stuffing envelopes all day inside some boring office when I could be spending time with my horses. If you think I'd be happy going through the names of missing or murdered women, you don't know *me* very well."

Travis sighed. "I see. You know what? I should've realized before this minute how selfish you come across. You aren't willing to come to the hospital to visit my son-in-law. You refuse to volunteer your time at the foundation. Have I got that right?"

"So?"

"So I think we've reached an impasse."

"Oh, come on. Things were fine between us until you had to go and introduce me to your precious Skye. The minute you had that dinner party and found out your daughter didn't like me, things changed between us."

"You're right. I'm embarrassed to admit it but I thought it was Skye's problem. I even went to see her and called her on it. We had words, an argument if you will. But yesterday when I got the call that Josh had been hurt, seriously injured—the kind of situation that draws families together in times of crisis—you refused to come with me to the hospital. I should've known it then. While I sat there waiting for the elders to show up, I began to think back over the last two years. I didn't like what I remembered about us. I didn't like our relationship very much. Not just that but I didn't like myself very much for putting up with you for so long."

"Why, you ungrateful jerk! Why don't you admit it, Travis? You just don't want to get married."

"I can't argue with that. Not to you anyway. It's over between us, Chenoa. Whatever you have in my house, you have until this time tomorrow morning to remove everything you've brought here."

"And what happens if I don't pick up my stuff?"

"Then you'll find a stack of boxes sitting by the gate. Now if you'll excuse me I need to feed my horses, take a shower, get dressed, and head back to Seattle. I'd appreciate it if you'd lock up before you go."

Travis was still fuming from the confrontation when he walked into the Artemis Foundation.

Chenoa's refusal to rush to Harborview with him and check on Josh had been the tipping point. There had been other times during their relationship when she'd used stall tactics to avoid meeting Skye. That's why it had taken him two years to get them together. The fact that he'd always made excuses was clear to him now.

Chenoa had never seemed to understand his devotion to family. But refusing to help out when Josh was laid up was pure selfishness on Chenoa's part.

"What kind of woman does that?" Travis said to Atka as he started for the kitchen, only to see Lena Bowers and Zoe already there. They'd stopped to get fast food and had spread their breakfast out on the table to share with each other.

"Does what?" Lena wanted to know as she withdrew Styrofoam containers from a plastic sack. "Want half of the omelets? We have plenty." As an added inducement, she added, "It's from Country Kitchen. Velma bagged it herself."

"It does look good and I am starving."

"Then pull up a chair," Zoe said, stuffing her mouth with a bite of cheesy egg.

"How come you aren't in school?" Travis asked Zoe.

"Uh, because I was up all night," she reminded him. "I told Lena I wanted to stay at the hospital and make sure Josh was okay. I couldn't have concentrated anyway knowing he was hurt. And it's almost Christmas break. We aren't doing much."

"How did you guys beat me here?"

"When we left you were still inside with Skye. And besides, we live closer to the foundation than you do," Zoe pointed out. "Then there's the fact that Lena has a tendency to lead-foot it wherever we go."

"I do not. I was well within the forty-five-mile-per-hour limit coming from Harborview to the parking garage."

Zoe guffawed with teenage laughter. "You were racing down Ninth Avenue doing fifty-five and you know it. Even a new driver like me knows that's begging for a ticket."

Lena rolled her eyes and tossed Travis a grin. "Ever since she got her learner's permit she's convinced she's an expert." Lena pointed a finger at Zoe. "Keep giving me a hard time and I shouldn't plan on letting you behind the wheel to practice any time soon."

"Okay, okay. You weren't speeding." Zoe snickered and added, "Even though she was."

Travis sat back, sipped his coffee, amused at the bickering.

"Any leads yet on this serial killer Josh and Skye are after?" Lena asked.

"They think the houseboat owner, John Stockman, might be involved."

Lena's face showed surprise. "Wait a minute. He's the man who owned the houseboat? Could that be the same guy who owns Dandelion Eatery, the fancy restaurant four blocks from here?"

"That's the one. You know him, too. I know him because he's one of the members of the restaurant association I belong to. I don't know him well, but I do know John."

"Everyone knows John. I can't believe he'd be involved with kidnapping a mother and a baby. That's not the man I know."

"The thing is he claims he hasn't used the house in weeks and that someone must've broken in after the kidnapping. Skye's not buying his story. Then there's the female accomplice Ashley Kendrow saw. How the mysterious woman plays into this mix is still part of the puzzle. It might mean a couple pulled off the abduction. At this point, no one really knows anything for certain."

Zoe's radar zeroed in on the gossip and speculation. She decided to toss out a few helpful hints. "Maybe the kidnapper doesn't have an accomplice and acted alone. Maybe it isn't a man at all but a woman who wanted a baby."

Travis cocked his head, stared at the teen. He knew one day Zoe wanted to be just like Skye. He took out his phone. "Hmm, I wonder if Skye's considered that. I'll text her and offer that up."

Lena picked up her mug, held it up to her lips. "Knowing Skye like I do, I'm sure she's already thought of that. And she's rarely wrong. But I've known John Stockman since he was the line chef at Baker's Grill. It's difficult for me to think he could be a party to anything like that. Do they plan to pick him up anytime soon?"

"I don't think he has anything to worry about there. They've questioned him but there's just one problem. The houseboat is in pieces. The cops have picked the rubble apart looking for anything that ties John to the abduction.

So far they've found no probable cause to arrest him for anything."

"Then I guess Skye will have to bide her time before she gets the opportunity to talk to him and clear this whole matter up."

"I wouldn't worry too much about this case. If anyone is able to find out what this guy's up to, it's Skye and Josh," Zoe emphasized, obvious hero-worship in each word. "I hope this case is over soon and Josh is okay by the holidays. They promised they'd take me skiing with them to Mt. Baker the day after Christmas. Josh said he'd teach me how to do a double cork."

Travis needed a translation. "A what?"

Lena laughed at the confused look on his face. "Josh promised they'd go snowboarding and he'd show her how to do a double flip."

"Ah. That makes sense but—"

Lena sent her daughter a wry smile. "I think Travis would have to agree with me that you probably need to give Josh a few more days to recover before expecting him to attempt snowboarding or skiing."

Travis winked at Zoe. "Lena's right. Remember, the last time we saw Josh, he was in no shape to 'double cork.' But I'm sure he'll make it up to you after the first of the year as soon as he's feeling a hundred percent."

Tears formed in Zoe's eyes. "Josh will recover, right? I mean, he'll wake up, won't he? His coma's just temporary, right?"

Travis reached over, put his hand on top of Zoe's. "Why don't you text Skye and ask? I bet you'll be surprised to learn his condition is already greatly improved."

Zoe jumped up, took out her cell phone, keyed in the question all in one energetic motion. As soon as Skye replied, the girl promptly wrapped her arms around Travis's neck in a hug. "I knew those guys who showed up could do it. You guys are awesome!"

Travis grinned and hugged Zoe back. "Sometimes when it works, we are indeed awesome."

Chapter Seventeen

Wednesday morning after the latest MRI, Skye checked Josh out of the hospital. Even though he limped wherever he went, Josh refused to head home to Bainbridge to take it easy.

"It's a mistake not to go home and rest."

"Do you want to get this guy off the streets as soon as possible or not?"

"Of course I do but that's beside the point. I need you at a hundred percent."

"Don't worry about me, I'm fine. Today let's focus on talking to Ashley and getting everything we can out of Stockman."

"Then explore the possibility that we're dealing with a woman as our killer."

"There you go. A full agenda. I feel better already."

Skye swerved to the curb in front of the Kendrows' colonial brick with something else on her mind. "Remember when Emmett mentioned this unsub might have several different personalities? I'm wondering if we need to slant the questions to Ashley with that in mind."

"What you're really saying is that you think this guy has at least one personality inside him that's female."

Skye raised a brow. "Not that I'm actually buying into the whole split personality thing but let's float that on the water long enough to see what Ashley remembers. At the very least we might be dealing with a cross-dresser."

"It's weird how we're so often on the same page."

"Yeah, I know." Skye stared at her husband trying to determine the amount of pain he was in. "Do you need help getting out of the car?"

He shook his head, eased himself out of the passenger seat leaning on the car door for support. His ribs might be hurting and bruised but he could do this. He tried to breathe air in deeply, but got considerable pain for his effort. "I'm already feeling much better."

Skye sent him an amused look. "Good to see the bump on the head didn't crack the stubbornness out of you."

Minutes later, they were ushered into the living room by a grateful George and Marion.

"How can we ever thank the two of you for bringing us our girls back?" George gushed. He aimed a gaze at Josh, tapped him on the back with care. "And you got yourself run over in the process. I'm sorry for that."

"But I'm bouncing back," Josh said with a grin.

"We got lucky," Skye deemed, eyeing what looked like a check in Marion's hand. "I can't accept that unless it's made out to the foundation."

Marion placed her hand on Skye's arm. "George said you'd say that so that's exactly what we did. It's drawn on George's plumbing company account. You ever need help again, all you have to do is let us know. You hear about this kind of thing happening to other people, but we never thought it would ever hit this close to home."

"Now we know it happens to ordinary people," George finished. "Ashley's still a bit dazed by it all."

"How about something to drink?" Marion asked.

"We're fine, thanks," Skye said, looking past Marion over at Ashley sitting on the sofa while Kiki played nearby with a set of blocks.

Skye stepped closer to the couch, lowered her voice. "I'm sorry we have to be here right now. I know you're still reeling from what happened to you. We know you've talked to the police in depth but Josh and I need to jog your memory for anything else you might remember, anything at all."

Skye looked back at Ashley's parents. "Is it okay if we talk to your daughter alone without a lot of distractions? Is there any way you could take the baby in the other room for a few minutes?"

"Sure thing," George said scooping up his granddaughter. "Marion and I will fix Kiki some mac and cheese for lunch. How's that?"

"That would be great. Thanks. We'll let you know as soon as we're done." Skye went over and sat down next to Ashley on the sofa and clasped the girl's hand in hers. Ashley still hadn't said a word or looked up at them. Gentling her voice even more than before, she suggested, "Let's step back for a minute and try to go back to that Saturday night. Do you think you could do that for me?"

Ashley covered her face with her hands. "I don't know how helpful I'll be because I was drugged. I don't remember all that much."

Skye nodded knowing she'd have to prod Ashley along. "You'd be surprised what the subconscious picks up. Just relax, close your eyes if you have to. It's critical to go over everything you heard, anything you saw, to the point of recalling smells and then how you felt at the time you caught the aroma."

Ashley bit her lip while tears filled her eyes. "If you guys hadn't gone looking for me when you did and busted in when you did, I wouldn't be sitting here right now."

Skye wrapped her arms around the girl. "Josh and I know exactly how you feel. But we aren't here for thanks. One thing that's been bothering us… You're absolutely certain it was a female who followed you up the stairs that night? You're positive it was a female who followed you from where you parked your car in the lot to your building? Was it a female who came through the door behind you? You actually heard heels on the pavement as this person followed you inside?"

Ashley considered that. "Heels?"

"Heels, like a woman would have on if she were coming in from a Saturday night out."

"Ah, let me think." The teen mom closed her eyes, but then shook her head. "Honestly? No. I'm not sure of anything. The entire thing is so fuzzy. I'm sorry."

"Rohypnol tends to do that to a person. It's known on the street as 'the forget me pill' for that reason," Josh said as he slid into the chair across from Ashley.

"Is that what was in the shot she gave me?"

Skye sat up straighter. "Now see, right there you used 'she' instead of using the word 'he' to describe the person. That tells me your first impression, your gut reaction, was that it was indeed a woman."

Ashley thought about that. "That makes sense. Now that I think about it, she did have long brunette hair with a red band running across the top. You know, like the kind that tries to hide the fact that you're wearing a wig or extensions but you know it anyway."

"That's excellent detail," Skye told her. "You're doing great. What about her hands? Were her nails painted, manicured? Did she have on rings, jewelry of any kind?"

Again, Ashley thought back. "Ah, I remember her long, sparkly red earrings because they dangled down from her ears at about neck level."

Josh waited a beat. "Do you think you could relay that description to a sketch artist?"

"Detective Drummond asked me that at the hospital. My mind was too cluttered to be of much help. But now that I've had a couple days to recoup and get back home, I'm thinking, yes."

"Great," Josh said in optimistic fashion before prompting Ashley for more. "Anything else? What about the woman's skin tone? Was it light or dark or something in between?"

"Well, she'd done a decent job on her makeup. She had good skin. But I guess if I had to say, her skin leaned to something in between light and olive. So what was it, Rohypnol in the shot?"

Now that the teen mom was beginning to open up and felt more comfortable doing so, Josh filled in this part. "We think the Rohypnol came first. It was in the needle that night, although the hospital did find a cocktail of drugs in your system. One of them was Rohypnol, traces of etorphine were also discovered. But for the long haul, it looks like what she used to keep you out of it most of the time was sevoflurane, a type of ether." He held his hand in front of his nose. "Do you remember having a cloth mask on your face at any time?"

"I don't know. I'm not sure. I did have trouble breathing at some point. At times, it felt like I was drowning."

"Interesting. Okay, do you remember if this couple— assuming there was a male waiting somewhere around the apartment building for the female to grab you and bring you out to the car—did they appear to have medical training? Like a nurse, a doctor, or a paramedic might have? After all, she plunged a syringe into your neck with the effectiveness of a pro."

Ashley's brow crinkled in concentration. "Couple? Come to think of it, I only saw the woman that one time. Then the few times I woke up, a man was right there hovering over me. He seemed agitated a lot and a little socially awkward."

That detail nagged at Skye. "I see. So you're saying during your ordeal at the houseboat the only person you saw was the man? What did *he* look like? Different colored skin from the woman? How tall was he?"

"Now that I think of the blurry images I have in my head, he was very similar looking to the woman. I remember lifting my head to see if I could get a look at Kiki, and he had the same skin tone as the woman had, and he was about as tall, the same mannerisms."

Josh and Skye traded glances.

"What do you suppose happened to the woman?" Ashley wanted to know. "That has to be important."

"If there was a woman," Skye muttered.

Josh decided not to go down that road in front of Ashley so he picked up the slack. "Okay, is there anything else you remember at all?"

"Well, the only thing I know for certain is that Kiki wouldn't stop crying. She seemed to aggravate the man constantly. Even when the guy did his best to do something for Kiki, like trying to get her to eat, his effort came off mostly clumsy. Kiki wouldn't have anything to do with him at all. He got angry with her. That's what I remember the most—Kiki crying and crying, and me, wanting desperately to get to my baby."

Josh put forth an idea to Skye. "Maybe he grew frustrated with his inability to take care of Kiki. That's why he kept Ashley around for twenty plus hours. Even drugged, she might come in handy if he needed her at some point to help him with Kiki."

The teen mom swallowed hard, visibly shaken. "Are you saying that eventually he planned to kill me?"

Skye sucked in a deep breath, let it out to gain a measure of control. In situations like this she'd found honesty was the best path. "Sorry. We didn't mean to let that slip. But you deserve the ugly truth. We feel pretty sure that was the goal."

"It's okay. Somewhere in the back of my mind I already knew. I'm not going back to the apartment. I've decided that Kiki and I are moving in with my parents. At least, until you catch this guy."

"I'm sorry," Skye reiterated. "Monsters have a way of causing us to alter our lives in a way we never intended."

"It isn't your fault. You guys saved us. If you hadn't showed up when you did…" Ashley's voice broke.

"Group hug," Josh suggested with a laugh. "Just not too tight my ribs still hurt."

The three came together, arms wrapped around each other until Ashley felt like letting go.

Ashley turned to Josh. "When I asked the nurses at the medical center, they told me you were really sick, in a coma. How did you recover so fast? I mean, you look like you're in pain but you're out walking around."

"Head injuries are a mystery of science," Josh said with a grin.

"But after you saved me, when the raindrops woke me up, you looked sick like you had the flu or something. That was before the van hit you."

"I must've had a mild case and then my flu shot finally kicked in," he joked.

For the first time in days, Ashley burst out in a laugh. "You guys are so cool."

After that, they left Ashley recovering in Capitol Hill and rode back to downtown tossing ideas back and forth.

"Let's go over what we know," Skye managed. "Ashley never saw the man and woman together. So it's possible they are one and the same like Emmett suggested."

Josh nodded, went on to another question. "Why hold Ashley and Kiki at the houseboat in a place where the neighbors are within a walk to the next dock? Are we supposed to believe our kidnapper just happens to pick Stockman's houseboat to hole up? Coincidence? Planned? Did he know who lived there beforehand? Had he been there before and knew the place on sight?"

"That's bothered me since I walked inside the boat. Let's say for a minute we believe Stockman's story and he knows nothing about the kidnapping, that he's simply an innocent man caught up in something he had no part in. That could mean our guy must've encountered some obstacle or problem the night he grabbed Ashley and Kiki, something unexpected, something that convinced him he had to hide out at that spot, at that particular time. After all, the location is less than a mile from Ashley's apartment."

"There's just one major problem with connecting Stockman to our serial. Harry said he checked out."

"Then maybe we get the team to dig deeper. While they're at it, do a sweep of the neighborhood around Lake Union."

"Sounds like a plan. If we have to, we'll get everyone together and go door to door canvassing the area."

"Something else to consider. If this guy is in the habit of holding multiple victims at the same time, like Cannavale alluded to, then he'd need space for that. A houseboat wouldn't cut it. It's far too small for that sort of confinement especially with neighbors next door who'd no doubt hear every loud noise or scream."

"That means we're talking about a larger primary location, the main place where he keeps his victims, those trophies he likes to revisit. And that takes money."

"It bothers me that we can't figure out what connection Stockman has to our killer. Because there has to be one."

"Not necessarily."

"What else do you know?"

"You trust Harry, right? He called last night. We had a long talk about Stockman. Harry didn't just check the man out nine ways to Sunday. Harry's convinced the guy is on the up and up. The background revealed Stockman owns a restaurant that specializes in serving organic dishes. The business checked out, too. No links to organized crime or kiddy porn or sex trafficking. That's the bottom line. Half of Seattle knows Stockman as a legitimate restaurateur, including Travis. In fact, Lena also knows him, vouches for his business acumen, his friendship."

"What's your point? People have alternate egos? If Stockman has different personalities Lena and Travis might not pick up on them. Besides, Harry made a point to let us know Stockman came across a little too laidback about his boat blowing up. According to Harry, Stockman was on the phone to his insurance agent that night, which touched off the initial red flag."

"My point is it's a perfectly normal routine action for a business owner to call the insurance company when he or she has a valid claim. And second, we need to move past Stockman as soon as possible. We waste less time if we eliminate him upfront," Josh insisted. "Are you forgetting there isn't a speck of evidence found so far that points to Stockman abducting Ashley and Kiki?"

"I hate it when you're so reasonable, especially when all I want to do is grill this restaurant owner guy over a circle of hot coals. Why do you have to be so reasonable all the time anyway?"

"Because if we go after him aggressively, Stockman will simply lawyer up," Josh pointed out. "It's unproductive."

"Then tell me this. You know as well as I do, the pathology of a killer stays the same. It almost never changes. Why did this one change his method? Why go after Ashley and Kiki? Why hold them on this houseboat right in the middle of Lake Union at the end of a busy weekend instead of taking them back to his place? It's not like The Jungle where the first two victims were found and it sure as hell isn't a shopping center after it's closed up for the night. Why change his pattern?"

"All reasonable questions. I think in order to resolve any of them at this point we go back to square one. We meet Stockman face to face, determine for ourselves if he's legit."

She squeezed his hand. "Now see, that's the guy I know and love."

John Stockman turned out to be nothing like Skye expected. The man was in his forties with a receding hairline and a little goatee and looked as though he might have hosted his own cooking show on cable TV.

"I told the cops everything I know," Stockman stated. His body language said it all. The man was tired of answering questions. "My attorney says I should just stop cooperating with you guys."

"We aren't cops," Josh replied.

"I know who you are. I've seen you both on the news before. As a business owner, I've even contributed to your foundation."

"We thank you for that," Skye said doing her best to assess the man. He looked harmless enough. But that didn't mean he hadn't been involved in some way. "If you're familiar with the work we do, then you shouldn't be too surprised by our questions."

"Yeah, you do good work. But you're on the wrong track this time with me. I'm a responsible guy who pays my taxes on time. I'm good to my employees. I visit my mother twice a week and now everyone may stay away from my restaurant because I had the misfortune to have someone illegally enter my second home and blow it up. I've got nothing to hide."

Josh stared down the owner. "Convince us. You do understand that it looks suspicious that a serial killer picked your houseboat out of all the others to pick from and held two of his victims inside for almost twenty-four hours. You've read the papers. You know one was a toddler. We want to know from the source if you might've knowingly loaned your place out to a friend or family member and just don't want to own up to your part in all this."

"Which means you're choosing to cover for someone," Skye added. "Friends and family tend to do that for one another in a situation like this."

"I'm not covering for anyone. Maybe it was someone I had over for dinner. I give lots of parties there. I even rent the place out for weddings, especially in the spring and summer and early fall when the weather's good."

"Could you throw together a list of the people you've invited there and get it to us?"

"You're kidding? That would take…an enormous amount of time. I don't know every single person that's been on my houseboat. Besides, how far would you want me to go back? A year? Two? Five?"

"I see your point," Skye finally said. "But I'm curious about one thing. Why wouldn't you want to do everything you could to help us catch this guy? If you're so innocent in all this, cooperating would go a long way in my mind that you're telling the truth."

Although the interview lasted several more minutes, the guy continued to stick to the same song and dance—his houseboat had been broken into and taken over by a stranger. Period. End of Stockman's story.

With nothing more to go on, they left Stockman a business card with contact info on it, and urged him to put together that guest list from the parties he'd given.

1. As they walked back to the car, they kicked around Stockman's steadfast position trying to find a hole in it...somewhere.

"It's so unbelievable though," Skye asserted when she couldn't come up with anything else.

"Which part? The part where our serial deviates from his methodology or the part where Stockman maintains the kidnapper was a stranger. Either way, the facts are this. Our guy obviously rigged the house to explode and then took off."

"And then tried to run you over with his truck."

"I have the bruises to show for it, too. So have we eliminated Stockman as a suspect yet?" Josh asked when they reached the car.

"You're pulling me kicking and screaming into that slot, aren't you? I don't like it. Fine," she grumbled, grudgingly giving in. "But I'm withholding total elimination in case we get anything new, which I'm adding to my Christmas wish list."

Chapter Eighteen

For three days, Dillard Barstow had hidden away in his special place. Most of the time, curled up in a ball. He still had a hard time getting the sound of that crying brat out of his head. He cringed whenever he remembered any part of the ordeal. Most of the time he'd spent with the lovely redhead he'd had to keep his hands over his ears. Nothing he'd done to quiet the little girl had helped to shut her up. Not bringing enough of the tranquilizer with him had been sloppy. He wasn't sure how it had gone so wrong so quickly. But from the moment the child had come awake in the car and started screaming, the whole thing had come undone.

The squalling infant had caused him to lose control of the situation. It had deteriorated from there.

Sometime Monday morning he'd realized he should be grateful, grateful he'd looked out the window in time to see the Cree woman and the white wolf sneaking up on him. He attributed that luck to the spell he'd woven to ward off his enemies. He should've used his grandmother's unique talent for curses years earlier to block his adversaries. The fact he'd been able to pick up on vibes had saved him from getting caught.

Somehow, in spite of the spell, they'd managed to find him, though. He'd never had to bolt out the back door before, never had to go on the run. He'd never escaped with such fanfare or driven a truck into another person before. Now that he'd had time to gather himself, it all had been rather exhilarating.

Okay, so kidnapping a mother and baby had been the stupidest thing he'd ever done. It'd gotten him out of his rhythm, off his game. Wasn't that the euphemism the sports jocks used? Whatever they called it, picking a woman with a baby had been a huge misstep. He was ready to admit that now and move on past his failure. Over the years he'd had a few. Each time, he'd found it best not to dwell on those for long.

Now that he'd pulled himself together he had to get to work. It wouldn't do to go off the map for much longer without raising suspicions. Besides, he had a delivery to make first.

And it was a long way over to Bainbridge Island.

Dillard drove his other vehicle, an inconspicuous white Chevrolet, off the ferry and sailed through downtown Bainbridge past its quaint shops and boutiques.

The Ander-Cree property spread out along the coastal tidelands, nestled among a thicket of evergreens. He parked the car a mile away in a clearing and followed the same path he'd taken before. When he'd been on the island last time, his panther, Oreias, had led the charge over the land. But for some reason his panther seemed to be fading, getting weaker in his mind. Just as the other voices grew stronger, Oreias appeared thin and frail, even sickly, as if the animal could no longer help him. After all their adventures together had Oreias found a reason to abandon him?

Without his guide, Dillard trekked over wet ground alone. He maneuvered through tangled brush and scrub, which meant he avoided the busier, better-known hiking trail. Making his way over rough terrain took an extra half hour to reach the woods at the back of the house. But to deliver the package was worth all the effort.

It took Dillard even longer to set up and stage the scene for the most impact, especially since he had to stay away from the terrace and away from the prying eyes of the recently-installed surveillance cameras. Instead of leaving the package on the patio table, this time he opted for a more subtle approach, choosing the towering birch at the perimeter near the pond to make his statement.

It was a gift, after all, and one he hated to part with. But sometimes one had to relinquish his treasures for much greater gain.

By two that afternoon Skye had been able to talk Josh into heading home. They'd arranged to meet the team later at the house to go over strategy.

Winding through town, Skye chattered away about the progress transforming the motel.

"While you were in the hospital, Hank checked in with you Monday morning and I took the call. He wanted to reassure us that he had a better handle on things now that Travis found him two reliable carpenters. Their hard work seems to have taken some of the pressure off Hank. Plus, he said that since they were living in the apartment now and out of the car, Alec and Melina are on the mend."

"I admit I was worried about keeping Hank around."

She steered the Subaru down the driveway of the farmhouse, hit the remote to the garage door and waited for it to open.

"I know you were. You had every right to feel that way. But let's face it, second chances make you feel warm and fuzzy when they work. And giving out second chances this close to Christmas, you get the bonus round."

"Is there sex involved with the bonus round?"

"You bet, when your ribs have completely healed, we move to the double bonus round."

"Damn. I knew there'd be a catch. You should probably describe in detail the double bonus round to give me incentive."

Skye filled the interior with laughter. "Since you know I'm worth the wait I can do that."

She went around to the trunk, grabbed Josh's bag and helped him out of the front seat. Together they made their way inside the house through the mudroom where she stopped to help him shed his jacket.

Once in the kitchen, Skye pointed out, "We need to pick out a Christmas tree, one from that lot at the corner of town. They have the most gorgeous noble firs."

"Those are your favorite. I invited Hank and Melina to the party we're having on Christmas Eve."

"So did I. Hmm, I wonder if I have to invite Chenoa."

Josh grabbed an apple from the bowl on the counter, started munching away. "Probably. You should make a peace offer to Travis tonight when he shows up with the whole gang. Inviting Chenoa to our house means you're the bigger person."

She set the bag down, scooted it out of the way. "I'm already the bigger person. What is she five-two? Anyway, when he drops off Atka later, I'll make amends. How's that? But do you ever wonder why it took him two years to tell me about Chenoa? If you ask me, his secrecy is inexcusable. Ever wonder why he keeps things to himself like he does?"

"I get the sense he's always been a private person."

"That doesn't explain why he didn't bring Chenoa to our wedding? That was the perfect venue to let me know he had someone in his life."

Josh sat down at the kitchen table. "I wondered when you'd pick up on that little trickle of information and it would turn into a torrential flood."

"You don't think that speaks volumes about their relationship? That my father felt the need to hide her away for so long?"

"I do, but I think you and Travis need to have a heart to heart before I wade into those muddy waters."

She went to the kitchen sink to wash her hands before starting a pot of soup. Her eyes drifted out the kitchen window to the backyard and beyond. "What is that hanging in the tree? Do you see that?"

"What?"

"There's something hanging in the tree at the edge of the backyard."

Josh spun in his chair to get to his feet. That's when he zeroed in on the staged scene in the tree. Although the birch stood forty yards from the house, he was able to make out the ghoulish sight and its symbolism.

Skye followed Josh out the back door and onto the patio, unable to take her eyes off the white wolf pelt with the head still attached hanging from the lowest branch, a bright red scarf wrapped around its neck, the wind whipping both around like flags.

They stood frozen in place studying the remains of the large animal until Josh finally said, "It looks like this sick bastard took advantage of our absence."

"He couldn't help himself. He just had to make a bold statement. I'd better call Harry."

But neither one moved. They continued to gaze out at the tree and the appalling imagery.

"There's actually an upside to this," Skye said, walking closer to the edge of the yard. She took out her cell phone to capture a photo.

"What would that be?"

"Maybe he left DNA."

Chapter Nineteen

The cold December breeze whipped across the water as the gang stood on the patio and watched the crime scene techs take down the macabre display.

While one investigator backtracked through the woods, the other bagged and tagged the animal remains. As it turned out, it wasn't a wolf at all, but an Alaskan husky. The killer had gutted a beautiful white dog and tied a scarf around its neck, then left the carcass dangling from a tree.

Once Josh and Skye got a closer look, they were able to examine both in greater detail through the clear plastic evidence bag.

It was hard to miss the tattered and windblown burgundy-colored scarf wrapped around the dog's neck. It had initials stitched into the fabric in black thread. The raised letters 'JS' posed a problem.

"He's bragging to us there's a victim out there with those initials," Josh said as he sent Leo a sideways glance. "I don't remember a victim on your list with the letters JS? But then my brain's been fuzzy for a few so my memory might've lapsed."

Leo went inside to retrieve his messenger bag and came back out waving the paper.

"I think you're right. I don't think the name of this victim's on there," Skye finally asserted. "He's definitely showing off again by trying to tell us we missed this one. I'm sure he hated the idea of parting with it."

Leo scanned the info he'd printed out days earlier. Shaken by the scene in the yard, the grown man stuttered out, "There's no name on here with the initials JS. The only Js reported have to do with a Jennifer Layton and a Susan Jamison."

Skye rocked back on her heels. "How far have we gotten through the list?"

"About midway," Travis announced from the doorway. Joining them outside, he stopped to watch the flurry of activity at the tree. "Lena let me in and caught me up to speed on what happened here. She had to put Atka in the bedroom with Zoe because the dog's been acting spooked ever since we got off the ferry. I didn't trust Atka not to dash out the door. I didn't think the crime scene techs would appreciate that."

"Good call. I'll say hello to Atka in a minute because she's bound to smell the pork roast in the crock pot Lena brought," Skye said with a wry smile. "These days Lena keeps the group fed whenever we're looking at an all-nighter, like tonight."

Travis grunted at that and eyed Josh. "I thought you installed surveillance cameras around this place."

"I did, taking in a three-sixty panoramic view, but there are limits even to that. Our killer made sure he kept away from the house and stayed at the edge of the property. Hence the display he fashioned away from the house. You can bet next time I'll include the woods."

Instead of grumbling more, Travis moved next to Skye. "There's a reason we're making such slow progress on the list. Each call takes time to explain to whoever answers the phone why we're calling. After all that, we have to go into detail about what we need from them."

"I understand there's no way to make it go any faster," Skye noted. "It's the nature of what we do. I'll contact the relatives of Layton and Jamison myself and see if either woman ever owned a red scarf like the one our killer left. But I doubt it belongs to them."

"We could get lucky," Josh said.

She slanted him a knowing look. "Let's hope you're back to your old self because this is a helluva 'welcome home' party."

The old farmhouse filled quickly with volunteers—a long list of people who wanted to contribute in some way. Tate had brought his new girlfriend, Gabriella Thorenson, or Gabby as Tate fondly called her. Tate and Gabby had met at a victims' rights group where Tate had needed help getting past the murder of his co-worker and his then girlfriend Maggie Bennett. Gabby had been attending the meeting because she'd lost a cousin to violent crime. The two had formed a natural bond. Using advocacy as their common ground what had started out as a friendship had developed into something more serious.

Leo, Reggie and Winston had bummed a ride off Judy from the office and were fascinated by her Berkenshaw survival story. Josh had been right. Once Judy had finally made the decision to leave her apartment and get involved at the foundation, the woman had come into her own around the other members. These days, Judy never held back with her thoughts and wasn't shy about sharing her own theories.

In fact, the entire group seemed to click, a rare thing with so many different personalities in play.

Harry and the crime techs finished up the work in the backyard and left a somber atmosphere behind. They all agreed it was past time to catch this bastard. To do that, they had to keep digging and stay focused. That meant they needed food to fuel their minds and bodies.

So they made sandwiches out of Lena's pork roast and ordered two pepperoni pizzas to feed the masses. They ate while sitting in front of their laptops in the living room. Bodies spread out over furniture and floor, the sturdy coffee table used as a bench. Limbs dangled from chairs in a laidback style as everyone scrunched together wherever they could to make room.

While stuffing their faces, they discussed the scene with the Alaskan husky, each contributing an opinion or coming up with ideas as to why someone would go to such lengths to make that kind of statement.

"He had to take most of the afternoon off to make the trip over here from the mainland," Winston pointed out. Winston, the most introverted of the bunch, adjusted his glasses. Like Judy, lately he seemed to be opening up more and more each time he got together with his colleagues. Tonight, the programmer had been downright chatty. "When you consider our unknown subject has mutilated and killed in the past, it isn't surprising he'd create a bold scene like that. There's something that bothers me though. I think it's significant he used a white dog. The symbolism represents something important to him. If we could find out what that might be, we'd be ahead of the game."

Josh exchanged a quick look with Skye. No one knew about his link to Kiya. Josh meant to keep it that way. He decided to run a bluff. "Maybe the statement is simple. The killer found a neighbor's white dog, one that looked similar to Atka, our malamute. The husky and malamute breeds are often mistaken because they share the same basic characteristics. Maybe this asshole intended it as a threat to our dog. Instead of writing a note this time with flowers, he came on our property to shove it in our face."

Fortunately for Josh, Tate jumped on that. "That's gotta be it, makes perfect sense. Why else would he kill a dog and hang it in your backyard?"

But Josh noted Winston didn't seem inclined to buy that theory.

"We're still running down the owners of all the white cargo vans in the state," Reggie promised. "The problem is that type of vehicle is very popular with business owners.

There are fleets of them registered to corporations and any commercial enterprise that makes deliveries. But we'll keep on it."

To Josh's relief, Winston seemed willing to move on to another topic. The hacker adjusted his glasses and stated his premise. "Before we left the office I ran some numbers and discovered something we might be able to use. While looking over the database I came across an interesting fact. I've studied the case files of the names on our list and going over the dates they went missing, it appears that eighty-five percent of the time, the abductions occurred on a weekend, either on a Friday or a Saturday night. We've used this model in other cases…"

Skye dropped her fork. "Winston, that's major. It means our killer has a regular job that takes up most of his time during the week. I bet his schedule frees up his weekends to spend hunting victims. But that's assuming the names on the list are connected."

"When you put it like that, this guy sounds so ordinary," Lena pointed out. "His coworkers probably have no idea that this monster sits in the cubicle next to them." Lena dished out salad from a huge bowl. She passed around plates piled with crisp lettuce and topped with ripe cherry tomatoes. She shoved one at Skye, then Travis, who gave her an odd look. "What? You don't like salad?"

"No, no, I like veggies just fine," Travis stammered. Not for the first time he stared at the cheerful Lena who always seemed willing to pitch in no matter the mission. Lena had been involved in the foundation from inception—answering phones, organizing the office, putting up flyers, and sending out emails to law enforcement agencies when warranted. She was even willing to work weekends. That was so unlike Chenoa's selfish bent that it made him fumble with his food.

"There are several different dressings to pick from on the table," Lena said. Then she eyed the man with closer scrutiny. "Are you okay? You look almost like a deer caught in the headlights."

"Uh…"

Before Travis could complete his thought, Skye spoke up. "In case you haven't heard by now, Josh and I've decided to throw a Christmas party on the twenty-fourth. You're all invited." She speared her father a sharp glance and added, "And yes, that includes Chenoa. Please bring Chenoa. I promise you I'll be good."

"We broke up," Travis declared while pouring honey mustard dressing over his greens. Without looking at Skye, he picked up a slice of pizza and added it to his plate.

Josh leaned over, slung an arm over Travis' shoulder. "Woman troubles?"

Travis faked like he intended to elbow his son-in-law's sore ribs but stopped short of actually making contact. "Let it go. Chenoa was always impossible to deal with. I've accepted the fact it was never going to work out in the long term."

"It's better to find out now than later," Josh sang, scooping up pork roast onto a plate. Even though he noticed Skye hadn't said a thing, he could tell she was trying to think of something to say, maybe like a profound sentiment, without breaking into a wide grin or doing a happy dance in the middle of the living room.

"You two really called it quits?" Skye asked, as she sat gaping at her dad, unable to believe what she'd heard. "Was it because of me?"

Travis glanced around the room. "Look at all these people who showed up here tonight. They're working sixty-hour weeks on a case they have no real vested interest in other than to catch a bad man. They're willing to do what it takes. Chenoa was never going to be part of this or any part of my life that holds any real meaning or value, the part that means the most to me. It's simple really. I don't know why I didn't see it before now or why it took me this long to come to terms with it."

"Then she's missing the best part of you," Skye noted, right before she got up to place a kiss on her father's cheek. "I'm sorry."

With one free arm, Travis wrapped it around his daughter's waist. "It's not the end of the world."

Skye followed her father's eyes to where he watched Lena. "Now that one there is special," she whispered. "Lena has a good heart. She's also incredibly down to earth, gorgeous, and hot."

"No argument there. Hey, I'm simply considering my options."

Skye recognized interest along with her father's tendency to drag his foot toward Lena. That's why she pulled him out of his chair and into the kitchen so they could finish the discussion in private. "Are they lining up around the corner and I missed seeing the rush? Where are all these *options* of which you speak?"

"Okay, so maybe I'm exaggerating a tad. I thought it might be nice to stay within my tribe this time around, you know, find someone I relate to on a tribal level."

"I see. So Chenoa filled the Native requirement. But it didn't mean she was the right person for you. I spent one evening with her and didn't see a single thing you two shared in common except a love of horses and the same living quarters."

"It's not like you to rub my failures in my face."

"That's just it, Dad. Chenoa isn't your failure. People sometimes never mesh no matter how hard they try. A relationship isn't supposed to be such hard work. I wish you'd told me about her sooner. Why didn't you?"

Travis let out a heavy sigh. "Because I guess some part of me knew it wasn't working out and if you two actually met I'd have to face it. The truth is I've never quite gotten over your mother, not completely anyway."

"Mom was a wonderful person. But she's been gone for fourteen years now. You deserve to find a woman who gets your strange sense of humor, who shares your passions, your love for life and all things ranch-related."

"I have a strange sense of humor?"

She grinned. "You have a knack for using that deadpan delivery of yours to scare people off."

"Good to know. It doesn't seem to scare off Lena."

"No, Lena's made of sterner stuff. Besides, she's had your number for years."

"Is that a euphemism? What number is that?"

"Surely you aren't that clueless. Why do you think Lena used to hang out at the diner so much, so often?"

Travis looked awestruck at that newfound bombshell. "Not because of me. The two of you connected. You worked there."

"It certainly wasn't all because of me. Of course it was you. Think about it. She'd lost her husband and her son. For a long time she was in a bad place and lonely. Eating so many meals at Country Kitchen didn't send out any kind of clue for you? You never wondered why a great cook like Lena kept coming back to eat your greasy fish and chips or to order that tuna melt she always gets?"

"Why didn't she ever say anything to me all this time?"

"Maybe she didn't think you were interested. Look, she and Zoe will be here for the Christmas party. Wear something besides your jeans and boots that wows and dazzles."

Adamant, Travis stated, "I'm not wearing a tie."

"Did I say anything about wrapping anything around your neck? No. Just put on a nice shirt, a nice pair of pants and a jacket. I know you own them so dress up a little for the party. That's all I'm saying."

Later, everyone decided to stay the night. They camped out in different parts of the house. Lena and Zoe shared one of the bedrooms, as did Tate and Gabby. The programmers spread out in the living room freeing up the last remaining guest room for Judy. Travis bunked down in the den.

Before they all headed to their various parts of the house, Josh turned to the group and said, "Get plenty of shuteye now because we'll be working overtime on this case until we catch this bastard. Be ready for the weekend. This guy is no doubt gearing up for an active Christmas and New Year. So plan to stop him in his tracks by all means necessary."

"Thanks to Winston, we already know the unsub loves to use the weekends so... We need to be ready for anything and everything," Skye reiterated.

"Could we get the cops involved this time, for maybe a stakeout around UDub?" Winston suggested. "That might help."

"Great idea. I'll set it up with Harry. Also, you should know I sent an email to Emmett Cannavale with a list of why he should help us on this case."

"What about his planned vacation to the Cascades with his wife? You really think you could talk him into changing his plans?" Travis asked.

She grinned. "I already did. You forget sometimes that I'm very persuasive when I'm motivated."

Josh draped his arm around her shoulder as they made their way upstairs. "You amaze me. Who else could convince Emmett Cannavale to come back to Seattle to give up his upscale lodge reservation to work this case this close to Christmas?"

"Hey, never underestimate dangling a unique serial killer in front of a profiler."

"But Emmett's agreeing to give up spending downtime with his wife in a luxury hotel with room service at his fingertips, especially this time of the year, is unusual to say the least. I mean, it's great for us, but maybe not so much for his relationship."

"What can I say? He's a cop who loves the idea of going up against a sadistic killer. What cop doesn't bite on that kind of challenge?"

"Come on, how'd you do it? What's the catch? What did you have to promise him?"

"Not much."

He playfully nudged a finger into her ribs to get her to come clean.

"Okay. Okay. He gets dibs on any book deal that comes along *and* he wants full access to interview him first after capture."

"Ah, shouldn't you run that by Harry first?"

"Already did. Harry says it's not a problem. Now the tricky part is that Harry's leaving the force at the end of the month so… After the first of the year, it's not really up to him to grant that kind of exclusive access. But since we have to catch the guy first, I'll deal with that slippery slope when it comes up. I'm willing to take my chances if we get Emmett onboard."

"You're sneaky."

"I know."

"And motivated."

"Guilty."

"Why don't we explore that slippery slope another way?"

"You're so bad. Did I mention it's good to have you home from the hospital?"

Chapter Twenty

The next morning, still cozied up in bed, Skye looked over at Josh who had cracked open one sleepy eye toward her. He scrubbed his hands over his face and tried to sit up. "That was one short night."

"We went to bed late. You do realize we have a houseful of people who'll be starving as soon as they get up."

"I say we make them scrounge for themselves." With that statement, he flopped over on top of her, pinning her body to the mattress. "It occurred to me that I didn't get my official 'welcome home' present last night."

Laughing, she tried to buck him off. "What is it with you and your welcome home euphemisms? What about your ribs and your head?"

"My body's already healing, just like it did after the transformation. Don't worry, I'll take it nice and easy," Josh teased.

"Okay, so what about our houseful of guests?"

"Let them get their own action. So instead of you screaming out my name in wild abandon, you'll need to muzzle your enthusiasm," he said, running his tongue down her neck.

"Wild abandon? Where do you get this stuff?"

He shushed her next word with little nibbles, tugging at her lips.

"Are you sure you're up for this so soon after the hospital?"

In answer, he pressed her further into the mattress, ran her hand down his body. "What does that feel like to you?"

"It feels like you don't give a hang about having a dozen houseguests."

"How'd you guess? I spent three days on my back without you. I intend to enjoy you to the fullest and recapture what I missed."

She linked her arms around his neck. "Then we'd better get busy before the entire house wakes up."

"Now that's what I wanted to hear."

A short half hour later, Skye pushed her hair off her face and scooted out of bed. "So how do I pull off breakfast for ten exactly? Any ideas? Because I'm not sure we have enough of one food item to serve across the board let alone enough cereal or eggs to go around. We haven't been to the market to buy a supply of groceries since this thing started."

"Make it a free-for-all, party atmosphere. Throw together a batch of whatever we have on hand. If there's a box of Bisquick, we make pancakes. Take what's left of a loaf of bread and whip up French toast. Use up the rest of the Life cereal and Cheerios in the pantry. Scramble eggs. Throw bacon in a skillet. Get creative."

"Fine. Then I'll need all hands on deck reporting for galley duty."

Josh tossed back the covers. "Okay, I'll go round up Travis for another pair of hands."

Later, while Josh broke eggs into a bowl to scramble and Travis threw strips of meat into a skillet, Skye manned a griddle bubbling with hotcakes on one end and French toast sizzling on the other.

"Imagine finding milk still in date and bread that isn't growing mold," Skye noted with glee.

"But we have to thank Lena for the bacon," Travis pointed out. "She must've snuck that in with her pot roast last night."

"Lena's good at sneaking things in that way," Zoe piped up. "We stopped at the store last night after we got off the ferry, the little food store in town, and picked up a few things so we wouldn't starve. Any chance of getting a cup of hot chocolate?"

Skye pointed to the pantry. "You'll find the mix in there. I'll put the kettle on."

"Got it handled," Travis said as he reached over, turned the burner on next to the pan he was tending.

By the time the other guests began to drift down from upstairs, the kitchen smelled like a blend of cinnamon and bacon.

Reggie sniffed the air and said, "I wish I lived here all the time, fresh island air out the back door and bacon frying in the pan. This could be home sweet home."

"What's on the agenda today?" Leo asked, grabbing one of the plates set out on the counter. "I mean, are we storming the walls around Lake Union, hitting the streets, what?"

"That's exactly what we're going to do," Josh said filling up a platter with fluffy eggs and shoving it toward the programmer. "We knock on doors around the area where the Stockman houseboat used to be. Don't go near the crime scene, though. Make sure you don't interfere with the investigation in any way. When asking questions, identify yourselves as working for the Artemis Foundation."

"We could sure use ID badges for this kind of event," Winston proposed. "I could design one for us that we wear around the neck."

Skye picked up on the hacker's eagerness. "Good idea. I don't know why we didn't think of that before now. Be sure to include the foundation's logo on anything you design. When you come up with a draft, run it by me or

Josh." She turned from the stove to face everyone else. "The purpose of fanning out around Lake Union is to circulate the flyers Travis had printed up. It has all the info about what we think the delivery van looked like that tried to run down Josh. Ask if anyone's seen it in the area before Sunday night. Show them pictures of Ashley and Kiki. Find out if anyone might've seen the guy dragging them into the houseboat."

"But wouldn't the police have already covered that?" Lena wanted to know, stepping around the crowd as she made her way to the coffee pot.

"Harry needs all the help he can get. Think of us as his support system. Josh already cleared this with him and I think it's an excellent way of sweeping the neighborhood a second time. Some of the neighbors weren't home the day the cops did the initial canvassing. If it works, we might adopt this plan moving forward into what we do and how we react after other disappearances."

"Is this the reason you guys have been training us on how to talk to and connect with families that have been through the worst possible scenario?" Winston wanted to know.

"That's part of it," Josh answered. "Working at the foundation, we interact with the community in a variety of ways. One of those is the hope that when we talk to people we have the potential to get them to open up. Part of opening up is to jog their memories, get them talking about traumatic events from the past, sometimes days, sometimes years in the past. You all know Judy's story." Josh looked over at the woman in question and smiled. "Judy knows how difficult it is to go back in time, and relive events best forgotten. But she also knows how valuable cracking a memory is in helping solve a case. What we're looking for around Lake Union is to locate witnesses. Today we pass around the sketch Ashley came up with, ask if anyone was in the neighborhood lately that stood out, ask about any unusual activity that attracted attention."

Winston nodded. "Then we'll plaster the neighborhood with everything we've got."

Within hours, ten reliable foot soldiers from the Artemis Foundation converged on the neighborhood around Lake Union. Going door to door they canvassed one houseboat after the other. When that turned up nothing, they fanned out to the expensive homes that dotted the steep hillside above the lake.

They chatted up anyone out on the docks, out washing a car, out for a jog, or anyone who looked as if they were willing to talk. But asking people to recall anything strange within the last week only resulted in the same rehash of the Sunday night explosion. And that from the ones who'd been outside. Most had been parked in front of the television watching Sunday football during the dreary afternoon and heard nothing out of the ordinary. Some hadn't even been home because they'd been out finishing up their Christmas shopping. Whatever the reason, the results of the sweep were disappointing.

By five o'clock as darkness descended, the stalwart volunteers reluctantly gave up and headed back to their rides, wondering if their efforts had been in vain.

Winston summed it up best. "I can't help but wonder. Is he out there somewhere watching us now, hoping to find an opportunity to strike? I'm still not over him gutting the dog."

"We're all bothered by the fact our killer is a butcher." Downhearted, but still determined, Leo added, "Let's hope we nab this son of a bitch before he finds another victim."

Chapter Twenty-One

Their last mission of the day was to hit the streets. The sun had already gone down. Traffic had thinned out. As Josh and Skye patrolled their beat they enjoyed the stunning view of the downtown Seattle skyline. It was a perfect evening except for one thing.

Kiya had been a no-show.

Roaming back alleyways and over concrete viaducts that night, the wolf's absence was worrisome to both, but it was hardly the first time. Kiya would appear when they needed her. They had to believe that.

While they weaved through landscaped greenbelts, the subject matter turned to Josh's probe into the *Pridewin Star*.

"You're talking about the bones of children," Skye said in horror. "You're saying this steamship went down, this *Pridewin Star*, more than a century ago and carried children slated for cheap labor in the mining camps?"

"It was a different time back then. Poor families often relied on their kids to bring in extra income by sending them away to work wherever they could get a job, boys especially. Many were children of immigrants and not missed. Bayliss believes these bones belong to males between the ages of six and thirteen. He's confirmed a few sets already."

"The age certainly fits your theory. But it's sad to think that even if the boat hadn't gone down those kids were headed for a life of unimaginable hardship. We should find a way to honor them in some way."

"Like the commemorative plaque that marks the spot where the *Dix* went down? Good idea. But Bayliss still has some convincing to do with skeptics in the area. Some people don't want to be reminded about using kids as cheap labor. That's one reason he called in a forensic archaeologist from California State at Chico to verify the age of the bones."

"I'm in the Bayliss camp. That man's like a terrier with a pork chop. He won't let go of a theory until he's down for the count. By the way, have you heard from Hank or Melina? We've been so busy I haven't had time to check on them."

"Want to swing by and say hi?"

"I'm sure this time of night the baby's fast asleep."

"So that's the only reason you'd want to stop by? To see the baby?"

"You know me too well. That little boy is so cute. I could easily think up a reason to drop in every other day, but I don't want to be viewed as a pesky landlord."

Josh found that funny before turning serious. "We could adopt one of our own. Although sometimes I wonder just who in their right mind would bring a baby into the mix we call our lives."

Skye stopped walking. "You mean because mommy and daddy would go out every night to face down bad men? Need I point out to you that there are lots of mommies and daddies who are in the same boat? They're called members of law enforcement, otherwise known as cops. They often go out and encounter the criminal element every day."

Hope rocketed up inside him. "So you're saying we need to think of this as routine, a normal occurrence that couples face who have dangerous jobs? That we could work out the logistics of such a daily event if we went the adoption route?"

"That's a wordy way of saying it, but yeah. We could find a way if we really wanted to do it."

Josh steered her around a homeless man asleep at the entrance to the alleyway. At least he hoped the man was still breathing. It was hard to tell. "You can't even say it," Josh pointed out.

"Say what?"

"Become parents. We could find a way to become parents."

She huffed out a deep breath, making a mini fog form in the chilly night air. "I guess the prospect of becoming parents is daunting. I could easily panic about the idea if I thought about it long enough."

To lighten up the mood, she added, "But that's silly when what I need to be concerned about right this minute is having eighty people over to our house on Christmas Eve. You do realize I need a party planner in the worst way. Where will I get one at the last minute? Someone with a flair for red and green."

"That's it." He grabbed her close. "We'll hire one. We'll do a theme. Everything in red and green colors including what the guests wear."

"Like a costume party for Christmas?"

"Yep. We'll see how creative our family and friends get when they have to dress in costumes. We'll make it mandatory at the door. Anyone wanting to get in has to have on some outrageous getup with the required color combo. Anyone not wearing red or green pays a tribute at the door to the charity of their choice."

"Like an entry fee. I like it. There's just one small problem. I don't see Travis coming as an elf." She tossed out a quiet laugh at the idea of her father in green pants and a red shirt, more in relief that they'd moved on beyond the adoption topic. "Hmm, we'll need to recruit a Santa Claus. You know who'd make a good one? Reggie Bechtol."

"Reggie? Because he's a tad on the pudgy side?"

"No, of course not. It's his personality. Did you know he offered to play Santa for Alec Fielding? Reggie found out the family was having a rough time of it and took up a collection among the programmers to buy them a Christmas tree. The guy has such a good heart."

"Okay, I'll ask him. Speaking of a tree, we need to get one."

"It'll have to go on the list. We're running out of time."

Josh knew they were no longer speaking about the Christmas season. "Then we need to up our game."

Chapter Twenty-Two

Inside the little kitchenette at the Artemis Foundation, Josh noticed Skye standing near the window deep in concentration. He knew that look, that formidable determined set to her jawline and knew it wasn't good news. "What's wrong?"

"I just got off the phone with a woman named Polly Claypool in Corvallis, Oregon. Polly's name appears on our list as next of kin for Lindsey Claypool. Lindsey went missing four years ago this coming March fourteenth. She hasn't been seen since." Skye shifted to meet Josh's eyes. "After a lengthy discussion with the mother I think the Pine Street Jane Doe might be Lindsey."

Josh rubbed the back of his neck. "Why do you say that?"

"Because Polly gave me a detailed description of her sixteen-year-old daughter. It fits the police report here in Seattle right down to the shoe size and hair coloring. Polly said Lindsey was a high school sophomore who went missing after a basketball game. According to her mother, the junior varsity cheerleader was a member of the National Honor Society and active in drama club."

"You should contact Harry with your suspicions. If Lindsey went missing four years ago that means it took two years for her body to surface here in town. Where was she all that time?"

"These murders have all the signs of sex trafficking, the victims discarded after fulfilling their purpose. Look, I think we need to go out again tonight."

"Then we will."

"No squabble about the timing? We were planning on picking out the tree."

"Nope, no argument from me. No doubt our guy's on the prowl because I'm picking up on some of his negative energy. It's like a black hole that keeps getting bigger. It won't go away unless we stop him."

"We're on the same page then. It's building up and I'm not sure how we stop it, him." She glanced back at Josh before staring out the third-story window again at the towering skyline. "The thing that gets me is how this guy keeps these girls for so long? Where does he contain them? He has to be a sex trafficker who moves them through his system and then takes them back." She contemplated that before answering her own question. "The only explanation I can come up with is that in doing business, this guy exchanges them or trades them up for another or a better product."

"That's disgusting. Maybe that's why I've sensed his urges growing stronger lately, ever since he left the scarf and the stuffed animal hanging from the tree. There's no question in my mind that what happened Wednesday was a ramp up."

From the doorway Emmett sauntered over to the coffeemaker, made himself at home by taking a mug and pouring himself a cup of coffee. "That's because his main personality is likely losing out to the one who wants to take over."

"Split personality disorder is a difficult concept to wrap my mind around. It's so bizarre," Skye muttered under her breath.

"You have a nice setup here," Emmett went on.

"Thanks," Skye said. "This place is all Josh's doing."

Emmett smiled a little and continued, "Together you guys make an impressive team. You've even managed to pull together a roomful of volunteers who take the work very seriously. That's not an easy task to pull off."

"And now we have you onboard as well," Skye tossed out with a wicked grin. "What exactly can you tell us about this sadistic asshole and these 'so-called' personalities of his?"

"What he's likely experiencing, the experts refer to as 'commando' hallucinations. It's where the person hears voices telling him when and how to act and giving him a window. I'd say Josh is right. At this point the unknown subject's veneer is beginning to crack. There's always one personality stronger than all the rest anyway. And it's usually not the one he grew up with. The pressure of knowing he failed with the Kendrow kidnapping is weighing on him. He feels badly in need of a victory."

Skye held up her coffee cup. "See, this is the reason we're hitting the streets tonight. We have to be out there when he strikes again."

"I wish every cop in America could get results like you two do," Emmett admitted. "I mean we've discussed the whole spirit guide thing, but to be honest, I wouldn't mind a ride-along."

"Or in this case, a walkabout," Josh quipped.

"You should come with us," Skye suggested. Scowling into her mug, she thought of a different approach. "Answer me this. How does someone like our messed-up killer splinter into two personalities in the first place?"

Emmett picked up his iPad, scrolled to the screen he wanted. "I'd say the guy we're after likely suffered long-term abuse from a family member in the same vein as Carroll Edward Cole—Cole's tally when finally captured was sixteen victims that they know about."

"I've never even heard of Cole," Josh admitted.

"Most people haven't. The public loves to focus on the Bundys and the Dahmers, or drifters like Ottis Toole and

Henry Lee Lucas. Those killers loved the spotlight and milked the press. What they tend to ignore is all the others. The ones who were just as active but never received the same amount of dynamic media coverage. The ones who slip under the radar are the cross-dressers like Hadden Clark and Carroll Cole."

Over the profiler's shoulder Skye read the details on Cole. "Among her other offenses, Cole's mother forced him to dress up like a girl. Dual personalities seemed to be a side effect of horrific child abuse. Hmm, then we wonder how they develop into such sick perverted offenders."

Emmett dipped a shoulder, lowered his head. "What makes you think our guy suffers from just two personalities? It could be three, four, or more."

Skye started to respond to that and then just let her mouth drop open.

It was Josh who thoughtfully stated, "So this guy is so broken that he's losing a grip on the only persona he's ever known—the one he was born with."

Emmett nodded. "Count on it. He's likely been heading down that road for years."

"So what do we do?" Skye tendered.

Before Emmett could answer, Josh did it for him. "What else? We go back to the beginning. Where's that list Leo compiled for us? The one we've had everyone focusing on for days."

Skye left the room and was gone several minutes before returning. She tossed a folder on the table in frustration. "You want to start back at the beginning? Good. Because the first name on that list is Camilla Prentiss. City and state, Pocatello, Idaho. Status, missing fifteen years. Camilla disappeared at the age of eleven after being left alone on what should've been a routine babysitting job for a family named Grainger. The Graingers lived a couple streets over from the Prentiss family. According to what little police notes I could get my hands on, Mrs. Prentiss allowed her young daughter to babysit only if Camilla agreed to call every half hour to check in. Somewhere between seven and seven-thirty the night before Easter, someone entered the Graingers house through the baby's window—the lock had been busted—and abducted Camilla. The Graingers had gone out to eat at their favorite restaurant, leaving a girl they'd left in charge before with their child, only to return less than two hours later to find the baby alone in the house and no sign of Camilla anywhere on the grounds."

Josh picked up the folder, went over again what Skye had recapped. "When did you find time to get the police files on Camilla?"

Skye lifted a shoulder, crossed her arms over her chest. "That folder isn't the complete file. But when you were in the hospital I had to do something to keep my sanity. Reggie showed me the ropes, a couple of tricks to drill down to obtain what I could. The thing is, we don't even know for certain if any of the girls on that list are tied to our killer. If the two of us go storming off to Idaho we could easily miss an opportunity right here at home."

Josh glanced over at the profiler. "She means going out tonight might yield a better lead while the trip to Pocatello is a long shot at best."

"Then how about this? Why not let me take the trip to Idaho and do the legwork. Let me do my part in catching this guy," Emmett offered.

"That'll work," Skye said in agreement.

"Good. At the very least I'll shake things up in Pocatello in an official capacity. The local PD always appreciates interference from the Feds," Emmett wisecracked with a cutting grin. "Not."

Josh slapped Emmett on the back. "As long as they're willing to give us an update on the Prentiss case, I don't care about stepping on toes. It would be nice if Pocatello cops could share what evidence they have."

"Then you guys should stay in town and try to pick up a trail while I push my way in with the Pocatello PD."

Skye turned to Josh. "Okay with you?"

With a nod to Emmett, Josh agreed. "The road trip's all yours." But to Skye he tossed out a suggestion. "I think we should go back to Lake Union."

"Why? The volunteers exhausted that area yesterday. It seems Stockman's houseboat was nothing more than a fluke, some convenient place our guy spotted and dashed inside with Ashley and Kiki in tow."

"I don't think so. I think he'd been there before."

Skye arched a brow. "Since when? You and Harry claim Stockman is clean as a whistle."

"I'm not talking about Stockman. At some point, I believe our killer had been there, on Stockman's houseboat, as a guest."

"Well, that's certainly a giant leap."

Her skeptic nature didn't bother Josh. In fact, her doubt gave him the opportunity to talk through his rationale. "Think about it. The volunteers asked every neighbor within that private boat dock and no one remembers seeing this guy's truck in the parking area. Not so unusual but… They simply repeat what they told the cops. They're used to seeing Stockman come and go on occasion, like when he throws a party or two, or when he has guests stay overnight. That means whenever he entertains on the water, the neighbors expect to see the guests stay around to watch a sunrise. It wouldn't be out of the ordinary or draw attention. They're probably used to the place sitting vacant for long stretches of time, especially in winter."

"So what are you saying? Stockman admitted to us he rented the place out sometimes." The tenacious look on Josh's face said it all. He wasn't willing to budge off his notion. But thinking it through turned on the light bulb for Skye. "Ah. Then we should really bug Stockman for his guest list. If he gave dozens of parties over several years, or had renters come and go, he could potentially hold the key to checking out a lot of people who might otherwise slip through the net."

"I'm glad you're such a confident cynic because instead of looking for holes in Stockman's story we should…"

"Lean on him to give us that list, appeal to the fact that he's a long-time businessman with a certain standing in the community. He'd be doing his duty, the side that says…"

"Use the good citizen angle. That might do the trick."

Emmett stretched back on the counter, clearly fascinated at the way the two finished each other's sentences. "I'll say it again, you guys work well together."

Josh looked at Emmett now. "Hard not to when we share a spirit guide. It's a powerful link."

"Kiya seems to have gone silent the last couple days." She contemplated that while slugging down the coffee from the mug she held in her hand. "Any chance her absence has anything to do with your illness?"

"The timing is certainly curious," Josh noted. "However if you remember, Kiya's gone MIA before. If she doesn't show up tonight, we'll do our own ritual to bring her back. This spell business, did you delve into its origins with Travis?"

"Not really. There hasn't been time. If the hex, or whatever it is, our killer used also included getting rid of Kiya then it shows some knowledge about spirit guides. Travis thought it sounded like one of the fifty-five ancient katares, originating somewhere in the Mediterranean."

"You didn't mention that before. Why am I just hearing about this now?" Josh noted.

"As I recall, at the time, you were struggling to get through a migraine from hell and stand upright," Skye reminded him. "Before we get too far into this, I want to go on record, again, as resisting the notion that our subject is Native."

She pointed a finger at Josh. "Having said that, it seems to me that both you and Kiya should have been affected by this black magic spell or curse, whatever you want to call it. Logic dictates if he wanted to go for the spirit guide angle, it should have taken both of you down at the same time. Right?"

"You'd think."

"And yet, this guy's curse doesn't seem to have touched Kiya at the same time it hit you. Maybe that means it was aimed strictly at you. Maybe the symbolism in the backyard with the white wolf wasn't meant for Kiya at all, but rather meant for you. You're the white wolf."

Frown lines formed above Josh's brow. "Why target me?"

"He's afraid of you. The wolf inside you scares him. At least that's what I think."

Emmett spoke up. "That isn't entirely out of the realm of possibility. It's likely this particular unsub could have major issues with both males and females."

Josh tapped the keys on the nearest laptop. "Okay, if this guy does practice a black magic type of mojo, it would benefit us to know its origin, almost like a footprint to what he's into. If Travis suspected the curse came from the Mediterranean region that would take in places like Mesopotamia, Egypt, Greece, and Tunisia. All those cultures practiced a belief system that included supernatural powers, the occult, and voodoo— everything from protection to putting a curse on the enemy. I'd say he intended to bring me down. And he came damned close, too. If it hadn't been for the elders showing up, I might not be standing here right now. So whatever he used, it's safe to say, it packed a powerful punch."

"Let's not forget he hit you with a truck," Skye tossed out.

"So what's the plan?" Emmett asked.

"We narrow down what it is he used on me and we check the shops around town that cater to that specialty."

"Now I'm impressed," Skye stated with a grin.

"Who's to say he won't try to weave another spell, this time with more teeth to it?" Josh suggested.

"I don't want to think about anything stronger than a cargo van or what he used to make you sick."

A sudden flashback had Josh replaying the scene where he hit the pavement with his head. "Me either. But since Kiya's missing, maybe he already has." When he noticed Skye seemed distracted and was no longer paying attention, he added, "What are you thinking?"

"I've been kicking around an idea. Is Leo here?"

"Leo's in the middle of a project for Todd. And Reggie was so blown away at being asked to play Santa, he went out to hunt down a red suit. He plans to wear it to surprise the Fieldings. Uh, we might want to warn Hank and Melina before Reggie shows up at the front door with his Christmas agenda."

The joke cracked her up and served its purpose. It cut through some of the pressure hanging in the room. "I think it's adorable if Reggie follows through with that."

Josh stuck his head into the outer office. "Hey, Winston, got a minute?"

"Sure. What's up?"

When Winston came into the room, Skye laid out her request in one abrupt statement. "Is there any way you could get me into a chat room as a buyer?"

"What kind of chat room?"

"The kind that sells kids."

Winston sucked in a breath. "Sure. Once I get you in, what is it you're looking for exactly?"

"I'm hoping you'll be able to hijack a dormant buyer account. After that, I'm looking for a steady seller with an IP address somewhere near Lake Union or at least within a five-mile range of that area. If that comes up blank, we look for an alternate IP with a similar account history located farther out, using the lake as the epicenter."

"Okay. But what if I could do better than that? What if I could give you a phony history that a seller would trust right upfront? A user ID with multiple buys, multiple transactions that went off without a hitch."

"I love the way you think. That would be fantastic if you could pull it off. Thanks."

Winston scratched his head. "As my gran would say, it's more like looking for a needle in a haystack but I'll give it my best shot."

"I know you will. And Winston? Remember, I'm looking for that one seller in particular who advertises a local delivery so the buyer has to be within a reasonable driving distance."

By the look on Winston's face, the reality of human trafficking was never more real or disgusting. "No problem. Give me fifteen minutes."

"While Winston's performing a minor miracle, I'll go lean on Stockman," Josh offered. He punched a finger in the air at Emmett. "New strategy. What about contacting the cops back in Pocatello from right here on the phone first before making the trip." He thumbed a motion toward the outer office. "We have plenty of long distance at your disposal."

"Why the different tactic?"

"Because if this thing heats up, we may need you right here in Seattle."

With a half laugh, Emmett cut the tension with a joke. "Then I'll start by getting what I can out of them while sitting here on my butt. It won't be the first time I've done my best investigative work sitting at a desk."

Laughter erupted and made for a good way to end the meeting. Because they each had their assignments, they promised to triangulate their efforts.

Emmett got to work on the phone, dialing up the authorities out of state.

Josh headed out to wheedle more info out of Stockman.

And with Winston's help, Skye spent her Friday afternoon entering the online world of sex trafficking. The young hacker had located an inactive account with the kind of history they were looking for, one she could use to pose as a buyer named Reinhold Tannenbaum.

Peering over his shoulder, she gaped at the ID. "Tannenbaum? You're kidding?"

"In honor of Christmas. Appropriate, don't you think?"

"You're a wonder, Winston, a pure wonder."

Pleased, the young man lapped up the praise like a sponge. "Looks like it's an account north of here in British Columbia. It would still work. The drive from Vancouver to Seattle for a local pick up is only three hours at most. The ID was created two years ago in the hopes of buying a twelve-year-old girl in the Seattle area."

A sickening feeling settled in Skye's stomach. "A horrible thought but one I need to take advantage of at the moment. You're coming to our Christmas party on the twenty-fourth, right?" Her fingers flew over the keyboard as she started a new thread in the forum, determined to engage the other members in a wordy dialogue using as many catch phrases as she could think to type.

"I'm not much of a party-goer."

"Come on. Everyone else is coming. You could bring a date."

"Girls don't exactly find me all that attractive," Winston admitted from a few feet away. Sitting in front of his own screen monitoring the chat, he added, "It's hard to believe these guys could be this vile with children."

"I've seen worse but not by much. This is the dark side of the web no one wants to talk about much."

"I'm pretty sure I could write a program to track these trafficking rings starting with this particular website."

Skye's fingers stopped in mid-composing. "Winston, have I told you lately that you're my hero?"

He grinned and adjusted his glasses. "I've never been anyone's hero before."

"You are now." She wiggled her eyebrows up and down. "You track this website for other buyers and I'll see to it that a certain cute tester named Rhonda Braddock shows up at the party solo. What do you say?"

"Really? You could do that?"

"You bet. But after I get her there, it's up to you to wow Rhonda."

Chapter Twenty-Three

While Skye and Josh coordinated their energies ramping up assignments for the contingent of volunteers, the workweek came to a close for Dillard Barstow.

Friday afternoon found him drifting further into crisis mode. He found it difficult to function without Oreias.

Without the panther at his side, who would be left to take on the white wolf when it came to that?

He'd had almost a week to dwell on the fact that he'd boggled the whole baby thing. Failure had never sat well with him. He also had to admit he'd underestimated Skye Cree's dogged persistence. Aside from the botched abduction, his magic had failed to stop the white wolf. The spell had slowed Ander down somewhat, zapped his strength, but had done little to end him. He feared his second attempt had been just as ineffective. Destroying Kiya hadn't been the main objective. Killing the dog and bringing it to his enemy's door was supposed to weaken an adversary.

His grandmother would not have approved.

To be outdone by members of a Nez Perce tribe, savages really, left him feeling disappointed and humiliated.

On top of knowing Skye's people had managed to somehow counter the ancient curse, Josh Ander's release from the hospital had sent Dillard crashing into a minefield of past disasters. The combination of all those things had sent him reeling. The idea of failing at anything had always made him angry.

To boost his spirits, he pawed through his trophies—an assortment of earrings, bracelets, driver's licenses, wallets, handbags, and datebooks. Unlike before, even those failed to make him feel any better.

That left only one place to find solace. He opened his computer.

As he so often did on bad days, Dillard rallied people online in the chat rooms he frequented. Logging into his favorite website as a seller, using the ID King Oreias, he encountered a few hostile buyers. Stalling the ones he'd left dangling since Thanksgiving.

Putting them off wasn't something that gave him the slightest tugs of guilt. He had to remind himself he couldn't always be everything to everyone. But since he was good at coming up with a string of excuses faster than a used car salesman, he'd withstand the complaints.

Someone named Reinhold Tannenbaum wanted a Christmas delivery. Since Tannenbaum's request wasn't something Dillard could fulfill in the near future, he replied with a polite apology.

But turning down the business had a profound negative effect. No doubt, he'd miss the money. The extra cash always made him feel like a winner.

As he sat there, the walls kept closing in, which signaled that it was time to replace the failure of the botched kidnapping with action, an action that would garner a win in the victory column.

He went into the bedroom, took out his makeup case. With a great deal of care he applied the foundation to his face and neck, taking extra time around the eyes. This had always been his favorite part. Being able to decorate and highlight his best feature had always given him a rush.

He applied light blue eye shadow first, followed by eyeliner and then black mascara. When it came time to do his hair, he brushed his latest weave, donned the memory cap he'd paid extra for and adjusted the high-quality wig onto his head.

Inside his closet, he pulled out a white buttoned-down shirt and his best red jacket to wear over it. The bold fabric might stray from the traditional tan or black, but then a girl couldn't be expected to wear the same boring colors over and over again. Besides, just because he had to look the part didn't mean he couldn't dress with a little pop and sizzle. And with his olive skin tone, he looked good in red.

Pulling on a pair of tan, hip-hugging jodhpurs and the black riding boots he'd stopped to purchase yesterday completed the desired look.

Checking his image in the mirror he decided the costume made him look like a stunning, wealthy woman in her late twenties who rode horses regularly and loved competing in the sport.

"Today I'm Justine," Dillard said with a toss of his long hair and twirled in girlish fashion. "How do I look?"

The voice inside his head answered as Justine. "You look mah-velous, as always. See, you don't need that stupid panther to get the job done. You never did. Oreias was never your strength. Thinking like that gave you a false sense of power. All this time it was Tiffany and me looking out for you. Tiffany and Justine will take care of you. You'll see."

In an imitation female tone, Dillard fawned, "I like it when you're nice to me."

"You do a good job today and you'll be rewarded," Justine promised. "Remember there's no need for a hunt today. That means no need for one of your silly childish ceremonies."

"But I miss the ritual," Dillard admitted.

"There's no need for it," Justine repeated. "Without any effort at all you already know exactly where to find your quarry."

And with that, Dillard/Justine prepared to bring home a win.

Chenoa Starr's horse farm sat on twelve acres located down a winding road that led to a charming little cottage. By the looks of the place, the owner obviously spent more coin on the state-of-the-art equestrian facilities that came with the property than upkeep for her personal quarters. The house could've used a new shingle or two on the roof and a coat of fresh paint.

But the barn was in prime condition along with all the other outbuildings. Dillard recognized the new tack room, a testament that his first impression had been correct. With Chenoa, the horses came first.

As Dillard drove his Yukon Denali past the corral, he took note of the four magnificent mares in the covered paddock. The animals strutted around the arena, spirited and looking well fed.

A pity she'd never get to ride them again, he thought as he brought the vehicle to a stop. Scanning the rolling countryside that made up Chenoa's backdrop, he decided she had the place all to herself.

The woman who stood inside the pen waved at him in greeting. She was dressed much like he'd dressed, in riding boots and breeches. He could see her warm exotic eyes, high cheekbones and raven black hair. Those features reminded him so much of Skye Cree it was eerie, which of course, made today all the more thrilling.

Dillard waved back before getting out of the SUV. "I take it I have the right place. You're the one who has the mare for sale, right?" Dillard said in a raised, raspy voice.

By this time the striking woman known as Chenoa Starr had closed the distance and made her way over the pebbled walkway to the Yukon. "Indeed I do. And you must be Justine Barstow."

"That's me. My mama and daddy always said I had a knack with animals, especially horses." But at the words "mama and daddy," a memory flashed from childhood. The whip came down hard on Dillard's back. Pain seared him like a torch burning his skin. Like a beaten animal he cowered trying to avoid the blows.

Justine lowered her lashes—or was he supposed to be Tiffany today. Confused, his female counterparts dissolved and all but disappeared as Dillard resurfaced with a harder, meaner mindset than before.

From the handbag he carried, Dillard pulled out a small, handheld stun gun. He quickly held it up to Chenoa's neck even as she tried to back away from what she now realized was a man and not the female she'd believed wanted to buy one of her horses.

But Chenoa's recognition came too late. Before she could get away, Dillard discharged the voltage into her body with enough force to stop her from running. The energy from the gun might not have the power to take her down all the way, but it would give him the seconds he needed to gain control. And the fist to the woman's face took care of the doubt.

Dillard dragged Chenoa to the back of the SUV, picked her up like a rag doll and tossed her into the back. He took out a syringe full of the muscle relaxant, pipecuronium bromide, and plunged the needle into her shoulder.

Once he settled behind the wheel, he gunned the engine and did a sharp left turn to get as far away from the ranch as he could. Because he needed to whisk Chenoa out of the area before the drug wore off, he headed for the marina and his boat.

As soon as he reached the highway, he started shedding his disguise. The wig came off first. Next, he grabbed the box of tissues to wipe off the makeup he'd so carefully applied only ninety minutes earlier.

A sense of accomplishment had him feeling smug. He'd show Justine and Tiffany he wasn't as inept as they'd always thought. Exhilarated, he made the mistake of glancing at his reflection in the rearview mirror—and caught sight of the broken boy he'd been at fourteen. Sudden rage engulfed him, followed by a strong sense of teenage doubt.

"You fool," Tiffany called out. "It's too early to get rid of your disguise."

"Shut up," Dillard screamed into the car. "Shut up! I'm doing the best I can."

But his alter egos were having none of his excuses. Justine and Tiffany joined together in censure. The two females echoed back, "When has your best ever been good enough? Don't you know by now you're an idiot?"

Chapter Twenty-Four

The moment Josh walked into Dandelion Eatery he could tell John Stockman was in the middle of preparing for a hectic Friday night dinner crowd. But getting the brushoff from the busy manager wasn't in the cards. Not tonight anyway.

After several obvious dodges to avoid him, Josh had to corner Stockman behind the serving counter to get his attention.

"I need that list we talked about," Josh demanded.

"Can't you see I'm swamped here? It's the dinner rush for chrissakes. My line chef got here twenty minutes late and we're already behind."

"That's too bad. You've had time enough to come up with those names we need. Surely you could take thirty minutes and tell me who was on your guest list, maybe who's rented the place during the last year." Getting a blank stare from Stockman, Josh added, "Do I need to remind you the man who broke into your home is violent and dangerous? If we hadn't thwarted his efforts who knows what might've happened to the baby and mother."

"Okay, fine. I did work up a first attempt. It isn't complete but…"

"A first draft is a start. I need it now."

Stockman began to head to the rear of the eatery. "It's in the office. Something told me you'd be back."

Josh followed him to a small room off the hallway near the restrooms. He picked up on an underlying current. "What is it that you're holding back?"

"I don't want to get sued or anything."

"What? Why?" Josh held up both hands. "Look, I'm not expecting you to break a confidence but something tells me you hold the key to why that guy was there that night."

Stockman let out a deep sigh, ran a hand through his hair. "Okay. I get it. There's only so much guilt you can lay on me." He opened a desk drawer, brought out a piece of paper with the computer-generated index of names. "All right, this is what I came up with. As I began compiling the names my memory snapped back to one particular incident that happened last spring. That weekend I'd invited a bunch of people on the boat from the restaurant biz, people I come in contact with on a weekly basis. Anyone who had anything to do with the restaurant got an invite."

"You mean, like your vendors, your suppliers, food and liquor distributors?"

"Exactly. I decided on having this big buffet outside on the deck under the stars to take advantage of the beautiful evening. I grilled salmon and tilapia, served fresh asparagus tips, prepared all kinds of salads, and fixed a double chocolate mousse for dessert. It was going pretty well, too. Everyone seemed to be having a great time."

"But…"

"That's when one of my beer distributors tapped me on the shoulder and told me about Theron King. Theron was making everyone around him feel uncomfortable."

"Who's Theron King?"

"King's an organic grower. He's the owner of Tiffany Produce."

"Catchy name."

Stockman bobbed his head in agreement. "Oh, it is, for a reason. His products were the cream of the crop. Still are for that matter. At one time I was one of his best customers."

"But not anymore?"

"No, I had to let him go. And it was a shame, too, because Theron supplied the finest bagged lettuce in Washington State. Man, that guy grew the best tasting Bibb, kale, arugula, red endive and baby spinach that I ever served on a plate. In fact, the night of the gathering I'd used Theron's whole line of produce to make my lemon basil shrimp salad and the spinach and strawberry salad that were the centerpieces on the table."

"That's a glowing recommendation for a bunch of greens. So what was this Theron King doing that made the beer distributor so nervous?"

"It was the damnedest thing. King was standing at the rail looking out over the lake, having a conversation with himself. It looked like some sort of meltdown or schizophrenic episode. I once had an uncle who used to act the same way. That's what freaked me out. I recognized the indicators of a personality disorder. When I started thinking back to other times Theron had behaved in a weird kind of way, I put two and two together. But that night it was such a disturbing scene that I decided then and there to end my business association I'd had with him for good."

"How'd he take it?"

"There were no repercussions, if that's what you mean, maybe because I waited a couple of weeks before sending Theron an email laying it all out. But I never heard a word back from him in rebuttal."

"You didn't think it strange that he didn't try to get you to change your mind and get your business back?"

"I was a little afraid of him but there was no retaliation of any kind. That I know of anyway."

"Hmm, interesting. Which means King might've had a reason to get back at you the only way he thought best and that was to drag you into this whole mess now."

"Yeah, I considered that when I started thinking back to the parties. There are lots of people on this list but Theron King I put at the top."

Josh took the paper, perused the names. "I noticed that. We'll keep him at the top until he's eliminated as a suspect."

As he headed back to the car, he didn't wait to do a background check on Theron King. He used his phone to pull up the grower's Washington State driver's license. The picture ID showed a man with a thin face, deep-set eyes, and olive-colored skin. Even though King's records came back clean, Josh got a strong vibe from the photo. The vibe lodged in his gut, mainly because of the blank look that stared back at him from King's dark sunken eyes.

By the time Josh walked back into the foundation, Skye was still sitting at her laptop—online and chatting her way into gaining the trust of the other users at a website touted as a place to unite buyer and seller.

She looked up and spotted Josh. "I've caught the attention of a seller called King Oreias."

"King? I doubt that's a coincidence," Josh announced from the doorway. "Stockman gave me a name. Theron King."

"You're kidding? Could it be?" Skye looked back down at the screen. "Damn it. King Oreias went offline."

"That's okay. We'll find him. King owns a produce company and lives up on the hill near Lake Union. I even did a background check on the way over here and got his home address." Josh went into a replay of everything Stockman had told him. He tapped the screen on his phone. "This is our guy. I'm certain of it."

Catching the last bit of the conversation, Travis hung up the call he'd been on to a father in Pershing, Oregon. As Josh finished up his narration Travis butted in, "Did I hear you say something about Theron King?"

Skye eyed her father from behind her laptop before getting to her feet. "That's our suspect's name and the owner of Tiffany Produce. You know this King guy?" Skye rocked back on her heels. "Of course you do, you own a restaurant *and* a diner. Your paths would've crossed many times."

"I've done business with Theron for probably seven years. He's one of the best local distributors that I've ever bought produce from, specializes in growing greenhouse organics, best tasting kale of all the growers around for miles. You can't beat the man's prices either, most reasonable in the state. Theron knows what he's doing. That's why he provides most of the edible greens to some of Seattle's finest food establishments. Although he's sometimes…"

"A strange guy?" Josh finished. "Stockman thought so too."

Travis rubbed his chin. "Theron's always been a bit of an odd duck."

"How so?" Skye prompted.

"I once caught him talking to himself. I'd stopped by his company one day to straighten out a billing problem. His admin sent me back to his office. I walked in, and there he was, sitting at his desk, having a conversation with the air. I stood there at the doorway and watched as he had his hand up in the air like he was stroking an animal. You know, like you might a dog." Travis gave a demo of what he meant by waving his hand along the air. "I have to tell you that at the time, the entire scene gave me the willies."

Josh handed Travis his cell phone with the picture of King's driver's license he'd pulled. "Look familiar?"

"That's him. Thin, gangly, about six feet."

"Any chance you noticed if Theron King exhibited any feminine traits? Did you ever see him in a social setting, similar to the party Stockman described to Josh?"

Travis furrowed his brow in thought. "I never took the guy out to dinner if that's what you mean. Feminine traits?

Like what? That's a new one. You mean like a cross-dresser, wearing women's clothing?"

"To tell you the truth, I have no idea," Skye replied, looking at Emmett for help.

Emmett had parked himself in front of a desktop computer typing up his notes on the Idaho disappearances.

Skye rolled on, "But that would certainly be something a female personality might do, correct? He would dress the part, right? It might explain the woman Ashley saw that night who grabbed her."

Emmett sat back in his chair, intrigued. "It's fascinating to think a serial starts out as a man and then fractures into the opposite gender. But it could explain how he manages to gain access to the victims, especially at night. By putting them at ease dressed as a female, he wouldn't encounter a struggle until it was on his terms."

"And in the dark, the girls might not be able to distinguish him from the real thing," Skye noted. "I mean who really pays attention to that kind of detail when you least expect it?"

From across the room Winston had been listening. The hacker walked over to where Travis stood holding Josh's cell and stared at the official photo ID.

Skye took in the look on Winston's face. "If you have something to add, now would be an excellent time to do it."

Winston adjusted his glasses. "Well, I was thinking. According to the description of the delivery van from the night Josh was hit, I'd say this guy's vehicle is a fairly late model."

Skye grunted assent. "Yeah, more like a 2014. Why?"

Before going into his monologue Winston drew in a deep breath. "What a lot people don't understand is that automakers these days build cars with all kinds of wireless technology. Any newer, late model car has several dozen electronic control units on board, efficient little mini computers."

Skye looked at Josh with a puzzled look hoping she'd get a sign as to where Winston was going with this.

A realization hit Josh. Caught up in Winston's thought process, Josh slapped him on the back. "That's brilliant."

"If it's so brilliant maybe you two would like to share with the rest of us peons what you're talking about."

"Standard operating procedure from car manufacturers uses third parties to create these mini computer chips. What Winston is pointing out is that any chip can be back-doored or hacked, correct?"

A bit nervous, Winston adjusted his horn rims again. "Absolutely. With this guy's name we could easily take advantage of all the bells and whistles the carmakers have added—keyless entry, remote start up, wireless technology, Internet access, navigational systems, anti-theft devices and cellular-telematics—it's little wonder the automakers haven't been able to come up with a way to protect consumers from hackers like me."

Josh all but wrapped up the guy in his arms. "You've given this some thought. All those features are right there, right there for the hacking. A simple computer chip away from cracking into the system."

Skye stared at Winston. "Are you saying there's a real possibility you could 'interfere' with one of these 'features' to the point of hacking into a Theron King's…"

Winston sent her a wide grin and didn't let her finish. "Late model vehicle? You bet. Stealing personal data would be a snap. Better than that though, to suit our purposes, I could hack into the controls and cause the vehicle to do any number of things the driver didn't want it to do."

Riveted at the idea of that, Skye asked, "Like what?"

"Like accelerate, or stop or turn when the driver least expects it. I could even cause the headlights to blink off and on in a crazy, Stephen King *Christine*, devil car, kind of way. I could modify the speed, or change the gas-gauge readings to make it look like the driver needs to pull over for gas because he believes he's run out of fuel."

Skye's mouth dropped open. "You could do all that? I mean, you could make his vehicle come to a dead stop at the side of the road in the middle of nowhere? You guys better not be punking me."

"It's a fact," Josh stated. "And another tool we use to catch this guy because anything in the control panel is fair game."

Winston agreed. "As long as I know the vehicle type and manufacturer, if the feature's main function is to act like a mini computer, I hack the chip. That includes almost any of the security firewalls, or I should say the lack of firewalls. If you think this Theron King is our guy, then someone should do a vehicle search to see if he owns a van like the one that hit you."

"Do it," Josh ordered. "I have his address from the motor vehicle report. But I suspect he has an alternate property somewhere he takes his victims. He wouldn't want the neighbors to see him bringing in girls he's kidnapped."

While one programmer went to work, Josh whirled on the other. To Reggie, he suggested, "Skye started an online chat. See if you can keep the dialogue going. Run through the website's stats scouring their database for any IP addresses that link back to Theron King. Look for any beyond his primary residence, look for any other property he owns. Think outside the box. I want any property connected to his business."

Josh turned his attention to Emmett. "What did you find out from Pocatello?"

"Not much, other than Leo's data was spot on. After five young girls disappeared between ten and fifteen years ago authorities felt they were dealing with a serial killer. Keep in mind this is in a town with a population of about fifty thousand. But because no bodies ever turned up, it was just a theory at the time that went nowhere. They feel that if it was a serial at work, their guy moved on out of the area, eventually. The local cops had very few leads and the little they had never panned out. Even after doing ground searches, to this day they have no idea if the girls ran away or foul play was involved."

"So we have a name and an address but not much other evidence to take to Harry," Skye grumbled. "It's time to decide what we do about it. You know what my vote is. I say we hunt down this Theron King."

Josh bobbed his head. "So we snoop around the guy's house." He turned to Winston. "Any luck yet on that vehicle match?"

"Tiffany Produce owns not one, but two brand new Ford cargo vans registered to the business. Strangely enough neither vehicle displays a logo on the side like you'd think a normal business owner would do to advertise his product. In addition to the delivery trucks, each one of King's vehicles is technically owned by his produce business—a Chevy Malibu, a GMC Yukon, a Subaru station wagon, and an older model pickup."

"Geez, he has more vehicles than a used car lot. Let's hope he's using one of the newer cars and not the older truck."

Josh rubbed the back of his neck and began to pace. "So many choices at his disposal means a better chance at keeping law enforcement guessing if someone spots him nabbing a girl. That way, he could always change out rides. Talk to me, Winston. What else were you able to glean about King from the Internet?"

"King's primary address is less than a quarter mile from the houseboat. Here's the satellite image." Winston turned his laptop around so that everyone could get a look. "See how the house sits up on the hill above Lake Union in what could only be described as a stately mansion. It takes in acres and acres of gardens. King also owns a dozen or so properties all over the Washington State area and keeps a boat docked at Elliot Bay Marina."

Skye shoved out a sigh. "I'm betting he isn't anywhere near the mansion, which means he could be at any one of his other residences and move around for a month before we happened upon his nest."

She took out her phone. "I'm calling Harry. For us this is like looking for a needle in a haystack the size of the Pacific Northwest. But using Seattle PD we might narrow it down to a few."

"Suggest Harry start with Tiffany Produce and the estate. We'll fan out, take each location and eliminate them, one by one."

Winston had waited long enough before showing off a bit with the prize nuggets he'd uncovered. "But the real news is that I discovered Theron King was born Dillard Barstow, born and raised in Pocatello, Idaho. Once he got to Oregon State he went to a judge in Corvallis and changed his name."

Skye bobbled the phone. "Okay, so Corvallis is another link to the string of victims here. That's where Lindsey Claypool lived and went to school. This is definitely pointing to King or rather Barstow. It's all beginning to come together. So how do we play this?"

"We storm the castle," Josh declared.

"Uh, guys, there's more," Winston said. "If you go after this guy, you may have a lot of territory to cover. In addition to Theron King's organic growing business, he teaches horticulture classes at the Southside Community College three days a week, Mondays, Wednesdays and Fridays."

"And this is Friday. Damn. When did his classes let out?"

But before Winston could come up with an answer, Travis's cell went off. He snuck into the kitchen to take the call and came back a couple minutes later. "That was Chenoa's sister Jada. She hasn't heard from Chenoa since this afternoon at two o'clock. When Jada couldn't reach her by cell and Chenoa wouldn't return her text messages, she headed to Chenoa's place. Jada found her SUV parked in the driveway, the horses still outside in the corral instead of in the barn. But there was no sign of Chenoa anywhere. Jada had no idea that we'd broken up so she naturally headed over to my place. Then when I wasn't home, she made the call to me. I told her to go ahead and contact the cops."

"Maybe Chenoa went shopping." Skye held her hands up when Travis gave her one of his stern fatherly glares. "I don't mean anything by it. Maybe there's a reasonable explanation. That's all I'm saying."

"Look, Skye, I need to go see if I can help find Chenoa. I don't have a choice. I promised Jada I'd meet up with her and the cops at Chenoa's place. "

"Then go. Let us know if you need help. In the meantime we'll check out this Theron King guy."

"Wait. Just wait a sec," Josh urged. "Slow down a minute. You don't think it's strange that all of a sudden Chenoa is unaccounted for? She didn't strike me as a woman who has a habit of leaving her horses unattended. Could she have gone missing because Theron King found his way to her ranch and nabbed her?"

Skye bristled at the suggestion. "That's reaching. Let's just take a step back. We're all over-reacting here. She probably ran to the store."

Travis put his hands on his hips. "Her car was still there."

"Okay, so maybe she went somewhere with a friend. Besides, Chenoa doesn't fit this guy's profile…at all. Why would he bother with Chenoa?"

Emmett interrupted. "Ashley Kendrow didn't fit the profile either, not with a baby on board. Chenoa's connection is right here in the room."

"I'm the connection to Skye and Josh," Travis pointed out. "Look, we don't really have time to be standing around debating this. Chenoa's gone and we need to find her."

Before Travis could charge out the door on his own, Skye needed to put aside her dislike for the woman. Didn't she have a foundation that helped locate people who'd gone missing?

"Josh is right," Skye finally said. "Do me a favor though. Just wait fifteen minutes for us to regroup. Let's narrow down which car we think King might be driving. That'll go a long way in the hunt. It'll probably mean a trip out to his villa on the hill to find out which vehicles he has left parked in his garage—process of elimination. Meanwhile, we'll send the cops by Tiffany Lettuce to check out the trucks there."

She grabbed her father's arm. "Do you trust me?"

"Sure."

"Then give me a little time to do what I do best. That's all I'm asking."

"Fine," Travis groused. "But then what?"

"From there, we call Winston with the info, let him use his hacking skills on whatever car the man's driving." She turned to the programmer. "Sound like a plan?"

Winston nodded. "I'll start work on improving my virus and malware bugs so they'll be ready to go."

"Come on, guys. What are we waiting for? Let's meet Harry at the King residence and find out what's there."

Chapter Twenty-Five

While Harry Drummond and Seattle PD descended on Theron King's estate with a warrant in hand, Josh and Skye scanned the man's massive gardens.

The well-kept grounds included several cordoned-off areas for tree orchards, a mass of greenery entwined with lush berry vines, enough blossoming flowers to supply most of the florists in the immediate area, and the kind of vegetation that would surely whet the appetite of every salad lover from here to Canada.

Water flowed from half a dozen fountains. The soothing sound of it caused the eyes to follow the path as it met up in a triangular pattern. In the middle of the triad was a large rectangular pond, complete with giant flowering water lilies floating on top.

Benches, made from both stone and wood, were positioned along the walkways at various gaps. Replicas of the famous Greek statues, from Athena to Zeus, were mixed in with the scenery. It was obvious to anyone who walked through the footpaths that someone had done their research on Greek mythology. The place looked like a public arboretum.

"It looks like Theron is quite the gardener. Stockman said he was good at growing things," Josh observed. "He was certainly a fan of the Greeks."

"That's an understatement. How could a person who put together this kind of beauty do the kinds of things we think Theron King has done?"

"Attribute it to one of his personalities. I can't wait to meet this guy face to face."

"Daniel Cree would've loved this place. It's a gardener's dream and a vegetarian's paradise. Now I see how he's been able to supply produce for most of Seattle."

"My guess is he has separate fields dedicated to his commercial enterprises. This place is personal."

"His personal garden," Skye repeated, beginning to understand the symmetry of the layout. Hedges of evergreen mingled with cherry laurel. Common beech had been planted among practical hazelnut and colorful dogwood. "You don't suppose there are bodies buried somewhere around here, like near that spot that looks like a cemetery. The one with all the sculptures." It gave Skye chills just to say it out loud.

Josh's eyes darted to the archway of flowers at the entrance and beyond that to the collection of stone and marble statues. "Funny, I was thinking the same thing. We should have brought Atka along."

"Definitely. Atka would've been an asset here. But cadaver dogs will work just as well. Better still, ground penetrating radar."

Harry overheard that last part. "This is definitely our guy. We found five different wigs in an alcove off the master bedroom and enough women's clothing to fill a small boutique."

Skye crouched down to get a better lay of the land, picked up a twig from one of the eucalyptus trees and snapped it at the center. She did her best to understand how anyone could have so many different sides to them. "King's girlfriend maybe?"

"My gut says no. Those articles of clothing are for a large woman," Harry replied. "Maybe because the dresses are sized to fit a very tall female about six feet and the same height as King."

"Aren't you the fashion expert," Josh deadpanned.

Harry ignored the comment with a cop's glare. "Not to mention the stuff was strewn all over the closet along with rows and rows of size eleven men's shoes and women's heels. That shoe print left at the Lisa Williams crime scene turned out to be a man's size eleven."

Skye arched a brow in her own cynical display of humor. "Do men's size elevens equate to the same size elevens in stilettos?"

Bothered by the levity, Harry barked, "How should I know? This is new territory for me. Where's that profiler of yours when we need him anyway? He'd be the one to ask."

"Emmett? He's standing over by the mansion gate trying to keep Travis calm."

"Okay, but I think the profiler should know we found a professional makeup kit. I mean the real deal, theatrical stage quality stuff. It tells me this guy was very much into the whole appearance thing, making the illusion look as real as he could get."

Harry scratched his head. "Just when I think I've seen it all my last case turns out to be one of the strangest of my career."

"We aim to please," Skye noted as she stood up, shifted her feet, beginning to get antsy. "This entire place is creeping me out. I'm chilled to the bone and I don't think it's the chilly north wind blowing in my face, either."

She glanced at Josh, then Harry. "I hate to remind both of you that just because we found the guy's main lair, we haven't nailed this bastard yet."

"And he may have a hostage." Josh looked up at the sky as the clouds began to spit rain. "It's time we check out the garage. If there's no sign of Chenoa it means Travis will be busting a gut to get moving."

The garage turned out to be a dead end even though they found the delivery van that had hit Josh—its front fender smashed—and the older model pickup truck parked inside. But they were unable to locate the Malibu or the

Yukon. Neither vehicle had been stashed in any of the other buildings on the property.

Which prompted Josh to share the details of Winston's plan with Harry. "We have year, makes, and models from state records. And if they have On Star technology it'll be that much easier. We need to know which cars the uniforms found at the school and at Tiffany Produce."

The detective took out his cell phone. After several long minutes he ended the call. "Southside Community College was a dead end. The vehicles in question weren't parked in any of the lots. Tiffany Produce has a Malibu parked behind the warehouse. So if I were you I'd get your friend to work his magic on the Yukon."

Josh sent a text to Winston. *Do you have the manufacturer's third party data ready?*

Got it.

What about the malware?

Ready to go anytime you give the word.

Locate the data for the Yukon. Let me know when you have Theron King's On Star info.

Roger that. I'll come in through the navigation system.

Let me know when you get results.

It took Winston eighteen minutes.

As soon as the text came in Josh announced, "Winston says it looks like King's Yukon is headed for his thirty foot boat moored at Elliot Bay."

Skye frowned. "That's a very crowded area. It's jammed with restaurants and people. He must be losing it to head to such a public place on a Friday afternoon."

"Then we take advantage of his unraveling."

Another five minutes went by before Winston flooded the controls of the Yukon with bogus information and then enough virus commands to stop the vehicle in its tracks.

Two words were all Winston texted back. *Mission accomplished.*

What's King's exact location? Josh asked via text.

1.75 miles from Elliot Bay Marina. SUV stalled on side street, Essex Place.

"What do you think Chenoa's chances are?" Travis wanted to know.

Skye rubbed his arm. "King hasn't stopped moving, which means she's still alive. There's hope and where there's hope, we work harder at getting her home in one piece."

Chapter Twenty-Six

As Dillard headed toward the marina and his boat, he took a shortcut to save time. While the SUV hummed along Essex Place lined with towering western hemlock and cedar trees, things were going well in his head. He'd calmed down from the adrenaline rush of abducting Chenoa. He'd managed to make it this far without freaking out.

The landscape changed from the gentle roll of hill to the pancake-flat, coastal marshland at sea level. Recognizing the familiar terrain, the anticipation made him step on the gas to get to his destination faster. As he grew closer to Pier Sixty-Six, where he could sneak his victim on board his boat, he tried to accelerate even more. But the Yukon stalled. It suddenly came to a complete stop in the roadway.

He checked the gas gauge. He had plenty of fuel. Desperate, he turned the key, trying to engage the starter again. But all he got for his trouble was a terrible grinding noise.

In his madness the alter ego he'd used to gain Chenoa's trust—the female named Justine—snapped out her disapproval of the situation. "What the fuck have you done now? We have to make it to Elliot Bay Marina and get out of the area while this bitch is still out cold. Because of you the boat is our only way out."

His other persona, the equally tall female, but always grumbling Tiffany, chided him in unison, "Dillard's incompetent. Surely you know that by now, Justine. He's going to get us all caught."

"Did you forget to fill the tank?" Justine needled. "How could you have forgotten to get gas?"

"We're out of gas? You idiot!" Tiffany grumbled. "Why is it Justine and I always have to do the thinking for you? Why?"

"We're not out of gas," Dillard claimed. "There must be something wrong with the engine."

"It's a brand-new car," Justine insisted. "Brand-new cars don't just quit."

He did his best to argue back, but as usual the voices inside his head didn't listen. The two women did what they always did. They exploded in condemnation.

Dillard blamed them because things were coming undone, and fast. If the women would just shut up for one damn minute and give him time to think clearly maybe he'd be able to fix the problem and get out of this mess.

He put his hands up over his ears trying to shut out the racket. But it did little good. "Don't you two start in on me, just don't! Both of you need to stop yelling at me. Now!"

The December afternoon began to darken and turn into a gloomy, drizzly evening.

"Well, we can't just sit here and wait for the cops to show up," Tiffany offered. "We'll have to walk the rest of the way."

"And do what? Drag Chenoa along behind us?" Justine pointed out. "No way. We'll leave her here. Another kidnapping Dillard's botched. At this point we have to save ourselves."

Dillard took the suggestion to heart and took out a flashlight from the glove box. He popped the latch for the hood release, got out of the SUV to see if he could locate what was wrong.

"What are you doing?" Tiffany wanted to know. "You don't know anything about fixing cars. You're useless when it comes to fixing anything."

Unfazed, Dillard stuck his head under the cover, jiggled a few wires. That was really all he could do before giving up. Tiffany was right. He didn't know squat about how to get the SUV going again. That left only one thing to do.

"A change in plans," he decided. "We'll attract too much attention on foot. We'll have to get to an alternate site."

"Don't do anything stupid," Justine warned. "You leave that woman in the car. She'll slow us down if you don't."

Dillard refused to leave his prize behind so he ignored the voice. After opening the back of the SUV, he slapped the unconscious Chenoa awake so she could stand on her own.

The woman was still groggy and disoriented, but despite her condition, he shoved her to her feet then dragged her across the road muttering to himself the entire way. With Chenoa in tow, he took off through soaring conifers and low scrubs, fighting his way past bright-red Fraser Photinia, deep green holly and stubborn Irish yew. His goal was to reach the summit, and beyond that, to his cabin on the north side of the peak.

Dillard knew Tiffany and Justine believed he was stupid. They always had, just as his parents had. But he'd show them all just how smart he could be. He wasn't lost. He knew exactly where he needed to go and he had a great sense of direction.

When his produce business had taken off, he'd bought a little A-frame cabin on five acres tucked away less than three miles north of Seattle's busiest regions with a perfect view of Puget Sound.

Isolated, the property sat on an inaccessible slope. Tonight, the side of the mountain would act as the perfect cover. He doubted anyone would try to make the climb in rainy weather to come after him.

Drenched, Dillard dragged Chenoa up one more hillside and down through a muddy bog. They were surrounded by timberland. The rain came down so hard, he could barely see ten feet in front of him. When Chenoa lost her footing, he pulled her up and shoved her to get going again.

"Where are you taking me? Don't hurt me. Please," Chenoa pleaded. "I have money."

"Shut up!" Dillard shouted and slapped her in the face. "I'm tired of your criticism. All the fucking time, that's all you do is tell me what I've done wrong. So, shut up and do what I tell you. Now move!"

Fearing this deranged man, Chenoa did as she was told. They slogged toward a clearing in the distance, every step an effort as the mud clung to their boots like paste.

"We're almost there," Dillard uttered under his breath shoving Chenoa forward.

To reach the gate they had to walk another hundred yards or so. It wasn't easy tugging the woman over the rutted terrain, but soon he managed to reach a cedar fence with stone pillars.

Once they stopped moving, he let go of Chenoa long enough to remove the key from the pocket of his jodhpurs. He unlocked the padlock and let the chain clank against the fence in an annoying clatter.

The fierce wind caused it to dangle there while he pulled Chenoa into his arena, a muddy front yard. Once inside the compound he didn't bother to secure the gate. There was no need. With darkness and the rural seclusion, he felt safe here. No one had ever bothered him here before and he doubted they would tonight.

Before the two could reach the front door, though, Chenoa broke free from his grasp and bolted. She ran into the rain and the darkness, stumbling but doing her best to get away.

It didn't take long for Chenoa's breeches to get soaked from running over wet ground. She fell down three times but managed to get back up each time. She had trouble seeing her way over the rough terrain. Navigating became impossible and she ended up spending too much time bumping into cedar stumps and crawling up and down the rocky slopes.

Her riding boots were muddied up to the calf as she tried to make her way through the minefield of rock and mud only to get stuck. Without a coat or jacket, the freezing rain made her shiver in the lightweight clothes she had on. She had to keep moving. But keeping on the move didn't do anything to help her footing.

With her next step, she fell into a hole and went down.

Out of nowhere a big hand reached to pull her up out of the ditch. But when she glanced up she saw it was the crazy guy who'd taken her. He had makeup streaming down his face.

That's when Chenoa let out a scream as loud as her lungs would let her.

Ten minutes after Winston sent the malware to the Yukon, Skye and Josh led the group—Harry, Travis, and Emmett—to where the stalled vehicle had been left in the middle of a two-lane road off Alaskan Way. The SUV blocked what little traffic Essex Place offered up. The side street was generally used as a cut-through to reach the sights along Magnolia Boulevard like Smith Cove or Fourmile Rock—that scenic stretch before the landscape opened up to acres and acres of wooded rocky slopes.

"King's headed north. We need the GPS coordinates for his other properties in that area," Skye voiced. "I'll text Winston for a list."

"I know where he's going," Josh stated without hesitation.

Skye looked past Josh's shoulder and spotted Kiya in the distance, the wolf's nose to the ground. "Who needs coordinates when we have our own tracking device."

Josh leaned in, gave her a quick smack on the lips before spinning around to Harry and an anxious Travis. "Get helicopters in the air with heat-seeking equipment. There's a local search company that uses drones. Call them. Rally everyone at the foundation to meet us at the summit on Magnolia Bluff. Tell them to wear something suitable for hiking because they may need to fan out to cover the area. In the meantime, we follow the sloppy trail he's left for us."

After texting Winston, Skye took out her phone to use the map app. "You're right, this guy must be losing it to try and make it up to the peak with the light fading and the weather like it is."

Her cell phone dinged with a text back from Winston. She read it out loud. "One of King's string of real estate purchases includes a cabin near the old lighthouse, on the north side of Magnolia Bluff."

"So he's making a beeline for one of his other homes. It makes me wonder if King didn't want us to follow him."

"Maybe. He should be easy enough to track now. The ground there is soft, nothing but silt and sand. Back in 1996 there was a landslide in that same area."

Travis glanced up at the sky, noted a line of dark rain clouds hovering on the horizon and drifting slowly inland from the northwest. "If it keeps raining like this, chances are, there'll be another."

"How soon before we get the choppers and drones?" Josh asked Harry.

Harry finished the call he'd been on and said, "Bad news, guys. The weather has worsened. Heavy thunderstorms are moving in, headed straight for us. The choppers and drones have to wait until the weather clears. I think we should, too."

"That could take hours." Skye walked around to the trunk of the Subaru, started pulling out essentials—bottles of water, power bars, flashlights—and stuffing them down into a backpack. She turned to Travis. "Chenoa's out there somewhere. Her safety won't wait for the storm to pass. Don't worry, we'll find her and bring her back."

Josh pulled out his cell phone to bring up a satellite image of the targeted area. "We'd better get moving. We have rugged terrain ahead. If it's at all possible, send the chopper and the drones out at the first break in the clouds."

Travis wrapped up Skye. "Maybe you should listen to Harry. Wait until the storm moves through the area. I mean, I want to find Chenoa as much as you guys do, but sending you two out in this downpour doesn't make any sense."

"We'll be okay," Josh assured his father-in-law. "There's two of us and one of him."

But Travis wasn't appeased that easily. "Yeah, and this particular *him* is a crazed serial killer who probably has the strength of six people. You know, like they say meth heads have."

Skye cracked a smile at the concern, tossed an arm around her dad's shoulder. "Stop being such a worrywart. You stay here and hold down the fort. Get ready to board that chopper as soon as the word comes in that it's safe to fly. By that time, I'm sure we'll probably need a ride out of King's hellhole."

Travis grabbed Josh's arm and whispered, "I have a bad feeling about this. Don't leave her alone for any reason, no matter what."

"Don't worry. There'll be no more splitting our forces like the last time."

Chapter Twenty-Seven

Skye and Josh found the trailhead muddy, slick, and rough going. On the hike to the top of the bluff, their path took them past scenic drop-offs and a forest chock full of lush greenery. They passed through hedgerows tangled with winter-blooming camellias. The dark red petals tipped with raindrops. Josh bent to snap off a bud, handed it to Skye.

She breathed in the fragrant scarlet blossom, looked up at him, saw the big smile on his face. It occurred to her that even as they climbed toward unknown danger to confront a serial killer, Josh took the time to make this kind of romantic gesture. Unable to toss it away, she tucked the flower into her vest, keeping it close to her heart.

"What are you doing?"

"I'm saving it for later."

Their first look at the region as a whole wasn't nearly as isolated as the satellite image had led them to believe. Dotted among the surrounding hillsides were houses that sprang up in random fashion without warning, hidden behind a vast woodland full of gigantic evergreens. Sprinkled among rustic cabins were million-dollar homes.

"Maybe we should've waited for a ride with one of the choppers," Josh grunted as he scaled up another rocky slope behind Kiya.

"Where's the fun in that?" Skye joked as she slipped on a rock. "The easy way up is for Harry and Travis to board that helicopter."

They did their best to cross over the wooded topography as quickly as possible, covering as much ground as they could even though their boots were laden down with heavy blocks of mud.

From somewhere in the vast thickness of forest, they heard a woman's bloodcurdling scream. The sound echoed around them making it difficult to pinpoint the exact location.

"It's coming from that way," Josh finally said, pointing to where Kiya took off toward the crags and bluffs directly ahead of them.

They followed the tracks through a thicket of tall Ponderosa pines mixed with Bhutan firs. When the forest thinned out, they spotted the gate that led to a small clearing. Beyond that stood an A-frame cabin on a parcel of land that looked as if hikers or campers had been there recently. Someone had formed a circle of stones in what passed as the front yard and used it as a makeshift fire pit.

Skye glanced down and studied the charred timber then realized the leftover kindling looked more like bones than firewood. She hit Josh's arm and motioned for him to check it out.

Without a word passing between them, they understood the full impact of what was in the campfire.

About that time a brutal wind whipped across the yard. It was so strong it knocked Skye back a step. But she stood her ground and stared at the cabin. As the gust swirled again she had trouble moving her feet. That hesitation caused her to get her first real look at the man born Dillard Barstow, now calling himself Theron King.

She elbowed Josh in the ribs, fought the urge not to stumble backward. Dillard appeared at the corner of the house carrying an unconscious Chenoa over his left shoulder like a sack of potatoes. All the while he held a Smith & Wesson semi-automatic in his right hand.

Skye watched Dillard's face when he spotted them. She wasn't surprised to see him raise the gun, aiming the barrel at his visitors.

Overhead the heavens rumbled with thunder as if a higher power had taken note of their discovery and realized they'd unearthed an evil entity.

The trio stared each other down.

Skye's eyes squinted from the rain and the force of the wind. As the gust eased off and she could make him out better, she recognized right away that sadistic look in Dillard's eyes—eyes as dark as the pit of hell, eyes that held so much malice it seemed to radiate out from the man's pupils.

She'd seen the look of cruelty before in other serial murderers, the look that signaled a non-connection to emotion of any kind, on any level. But if she wasn't mistaken, this time their suspect wore a heavy coat of makeup. He'd attempted to wipe off the pancake greasepaint but he'd left a swath of residue over the peach fuzz beginning to sprout on his chin. In the downpour the dark blue eye shadow and black eyeliner were dissolving, running down his face, making it a gooey mess. It gave Dillard a Goth look, or maybe more like Vampira in drag. Either way, the man made an imposing, frightening figure.

"I put a curse on you," Dillard claimed, turning the gun toward Josh.

"You tried," Josh returned with confidence. "But as you can plainly see it didn't work."

"It will now. You're on my land. My power is greater here than in the city. You can't come on my property like this without consequences." Dillard's voice quivered like a girl's, his tone rising almost to a soprano in growing irritation.

Trying to mask her surprise at the man's appearance as well as his bizarre demeanor, Skye blanked her face. She took a step closer to what she considered a dangerous creature in human form. "And you can't go around kidnapping innocent women."

That accusation caused Dillard to drop Chenoa like a bag of cement where he stood. Skye winced as Travis's former girlfriend hit the ground with a plop in the mud.

That's when she saw what Barstow held in his other hand, another weapon, this time a professional-looking stun gun. He held both so tightly in his fists that his knuckles were turning white.

Her eyes drifted briefly past him to get a glance at Chenoa's still form lying in a puddle of mud. Skye tried to ignore the bloody mass on the woman's head.

"If you think I'll let you get close enough to me to discharge that stun gun, think again. But you're probably gonna need the nine millimeter," Skye told him in challenge as she took out her nightstick. While she distracted Dillard with her insults, she watched Josh circle around behind their suspect.

"In case you haven't noticed I zapped your fucking wolf off the map. I have my own spirit guide, a fierce panther that's ready to go head to head with your stupid Kiya."

Skye hooted with laughter as she decided he sounded like a petulant first grader. "Haven't you heard? Hallucinations from a psycho don't count."

Dillard's eyes shot daggers at Skye. "My guide through life was never that. My panther is real just like your wolf. For most of my life he was my only friend."

Skye shook her head as she maneuvered into position. She needed to keep him talking until Josh was ready to make his move. "Oh, please, cry me a river. I don't believe how you're willing to stand there and give me your sob story right about now when there's a woman lying on the ground at your feet, injured, hurting, probably dying because of what you did to her."

Skye spread her arms out wide. "Besides, if your panther is such a friend to you, where is he now when you really need him? In case you haven't noticed, you've reached the end of the line."

Dillard's eyes darted wildly around the plot of land, looking toward the woods then back at the house as if expecting to see help coming from behind one of the evergreen trees. When Dillard realized he'd been abandoned, Skye saw the fire flaring inside him, the anger building up.

"Big talk for a fucking female."

"Yeah? This female plans to kick your ass. What's the matter, Dillard? Are you beginning to realize it's time to give up? Drop the weapon and get out of the rain. Look at yourself. You're a mess. There's nowhere to go."

Their eyes locked. Foe-to-foe, they sized each other up. Skye saw the rage, the determination to win this round despite his skittish, erratic behavior. Since he seemed to be focusing on her and not Josh, she needed to take advantage of that.

"I've studied the way you move. I've prepared for this. There's no way in hell you'll take me down," Dillard boasted.

"Then you're in for one helluva fight, aren't you? I doubt you're able to take the both of us."

Just as she'd hoped Dillard fixated on her voice, on her bravado.

It allowed Josh time to advance from the rear. Timing and opportunity gave him the chance to get close enough to kick the handgun out of Dillard's fist. When it went sailing into the cedar trees, Josh tackled Dillard and took him to the ground.

Skye rushed toward both men and stomped her boot down on Dillard's arm—the one holding the stun gun—grinding her weight into his palm. But she underestimated Dillard's strength. The man rolled over in pain and grabbed hold of Skye's leg bringing the electrical device up to her calf. It made brief contact with her muscle, long enough to send a jolt of voltage through her body. The combination of the current plus Dillard's grip caused her to lose her balance. She tumbled over both men as they locked together in a tussle for control.

Dillard kicked Josh in the head and crawled a few feet away before getting to his feet.

Josh caught up with him and rammed his fist into Dillard's face. He pushed Dillard up against the cabin, but the guy used it as leverage to shove out of Josh's grasp. From somewhere on his body, Dillard pulled a knife, jabbing it toward Josh. But Josh managed to dodge the tip of the blade.

By this time Skye had picked herself up out of the mud. She snuck up on Dillard's blindside, attacking him by swinging her metal stick across the man's skull.

In a sweeping move, Josh elbowed the guy in the gut, which gave Skye another opportunity to crack the metal rod hard over the man's head.

He went down but he didn't stay down. Dillard fought like a crazy man high on PCP. Refusing to quit, he lashed out, hurling himself toward Skye in a body block. Skye darted out of the way, but the bastard snagged her ankles again in a last ditch effort.

But this time Skye was quicker. She batted his arms and head with her stick again and again while Josh rained down blow after blow to Dillard's torso. Josh used brute force to shove Dillard away from Skye.

Reeling from the onslaught, Dillard tried to head-butt Josh. But Skye pivoted, brought the stick down across his shoulder blades with a whack.

Dillard reached back, bent down, swung his arm out to snatch something that looked like a fireplace poker from the stone fire pit.

Josh ducked in time to prevent the metal from making contact. Skye kicked her leg up and out tripping the bastard. Dillard landed face first into the mucky earth, hitting his head on one of the large stones.

Josh pounced. He aimed for under the chin for full effect, landed a blow to his mouth about the same time Skye found the sweet spot for a solid crack to his jaw, drawing blood.

She latched onto Dillard's wrist, used her strength for leverage, and bent his arm all the way back until Josh could subdue him.

Skye narrowed her eyes and finished him off with a one-two, left-right punch.

This time, Dillard Barstow stayed down for the count. Kiya made sure of it.

High above Lake Union at Theron King's stately mansion the rain kept coming down. Each drop of water added up, accumulating in ponds, saturating the massive gardens located around the estate until the soggy earth could hold no more. The torrential downpour caused the already waterlogged ground to shake loose debris and rock. The manicured lawns began a slow slide down the hillside.

Sometime during the night, the earth grudgingly gave up hints of Theron King's very private personal habits. It revealed a good deal about how he'd started life out as Dillard Barstow.

Maybe in the spirit of Christmas, Mother Nature had given the ultimate gift, solving pieces of the puzzle that others might never have noticed. Since the mystery of Dillard's life unraveled—his special garden of bones would be a secret no more.

Chapter Twenty-Eight

The hours between midnight and six a.m. had been spent lurking outside a conference room at the Seattle PD. Skye sipped a cup of vending machine coffee from a Styrofoam cup trying to stay awake. No one had been to bed yet—not Josh or Emmett or Harry or Travis, certainly not Dillard Barstow.

Emmett and Harry had been crammed into an interview room for hours trying to get their suspect to give up information. Josh had even taken a turn, attempting to get the guy to open up to him. But so far Dillard had said very little to anyone.

No one was giving up hope, though.

She and Josh had cleaned up somewhat from their fight in the woods. They'd used a restroom down the hall to scrape off several layers of caked mud. But despite their efforts, their clothes were still damp and dirty.

Her pants and top had become stiff. Even her jacket and vest felt as if they'd never wear quite the same way again. Sitting with any level of comfort in clothes she'd had on for more than twenty-four hours was damned near impossible.

She needed a hot shower and a bed. But then, so did everyone else.

Travis paced in front of the large bank of windows on one side of the room, his own coffee steaming in his hand. "Jada called. She says Chenoa has a concussion but should be fine in a day or two."

"That's good news," Skye said knowing she had to get something off her chest. "Look, if you want to be with Chenoa, I completely understand. I know you still care for her. I promise I won't give you a hard time about it. Just because you two broke up, doesn't mean you couldn't pick up where you…"

Travis sent his daughter an amused look. "So, I have your blessing to get back together with her?"

Skye swallowed hard, but managed to toss out the word that wanted to catch in her throat. "Sure."

"That's good to know. There's just one problem. Chenoa and I aren't right for each other. You were right about that. Sure, I care about her but at this stage of our lives we have vastly different priorities, too many to overcome to go beyond anything but friendship between ranchers. Our relationship would be a constant battle of wills, an endless conflict. I know that now."

Elation washed over Skye but she tried not to show it. Her face though must have beamed with pleasure at the news because Travis flashed a wide smile.

"Don't worry. I already have my eye on someone," her father said with a wink.

Her eyes lit up. "Lena?"

Before she could get an answer, Josh stepped into the doorway and motioned for them to follow him. "You guys have to see this. Dillard is finally beginning to open up. But it isn't what you might think."

"What is it then?" Skye wanted to know. "Is he describing his crimes in detail yet?"

"Not exactly. Emmett's a ways off from getting him to do that. At least not the way you'd expect." Josh stopped in front of a window with a view into the interrogation room where Emmett and Harry sat across from the man still dressed in his riding outfit, dirty from the fight. With three people stuffed in there it made the small space seem very closed-in.

The one-way mirror effect and microphone allowed them a glimpse into the Q & A firsthand along with witnessing the man's splintering transformation into several other personalities.

They listened as Emmett picked up the questioning with a firm but patient tone, his voice dripping with understanding instead of a direct verbal assault. "Tell us why you ducked into the Stockman houseboat to hide? We know you'd been to a party there last spring long before the kidnapping took place."

It wasn't Dillard who answered, but Justine who took the stage to introduce herself and explain Dillard's actions. With a coy smile on his face, complete with feminine mannerisms and voice, Dillard morphed into Justine. "It's simple really. Dillard panicked. That boy always tended to choke under pressure no matter what he did. No pun intended," she added with a heartless laugh.

Tiffany wasn't about to let Justine hog the entire spotlight, so she chimed in—Dillard's voice changing slightly in tone and cattiness to take on Tiffany's more assertive persona. "What else were you expecting? A brilliant enlightening moment when you finally get it that Dillard had help, because he isn't bright enough to have acted alone." Tiffany snickered with delight at her own clever words. "You see, Dillard couldn't have done anything by himself. Like Justine said he was always panicking when the deed had to be done. It's time you understand that Justine and I were the driving force. That's because we have more balls than Dillard and Theron ever had put together. They never made a whole man in their younger days, let alone now."

"So you and Justine talked Dillard into committing murder all these years?"

Tiffany pursed her lips, put a hand up to her mouth, and motioned like she turned a lock. "I've promised not to say a word about that."

Undeterred Emmett changed tactics. "I'm curious about something. Why keep your victims' bodies hidden and buried, your activities off the radar? Then all of a sudden start leaving them in plain sight where they could be found? Why remove the breast implants, like you did with Lisa Williams, Carrie Montague, and Taylor Dinsmore?"

It was Justine's turn to speak up. "So those were their names? All this time I had no idea who they were," she said with a shrug.

But Tiffany held the key to this part, addressing the issue with an air of cool certainty. "Remember we're speaking about Dillard, right? Those women you mentioned were his rejects. The buyers he dealt with on a regular basis had altered the women's appearances. With their bigger breasts, Dillard no longer found them attractive, so he got rid of them. The girls had tattoos, belly rings, and tongue studs." Tiffany scrunched up her face in revulsion. "After those kinds of alterations, the women simply weren't good enough to put in his garden. He couldn't bury them on the grounds. He had to do something to get rid of them."

"I see. So Dillard Barstow was a major dealer in the sex trafficking business? And he allowed returns?"

"Of course," Tiffany said with a casual air, as if the sex trade was no big deal.

"That's unheard of. Sex traffickers don't usually take back the girls."

"Dillard did. It was his way of keeping the customers coming back, again and again. He found the best way to customer satisfaction was to take back what he considered damaged goods."

Because Tiffany seemed determined to keep talking, Emmett knew she was, most likely, the gatekeeper. It seemed to him that she didn't just want to talk, she *needed* to talk, not out of a sense of responsibility or remorse, but because she'd acted as the vault, the place where Dillard had stored most, if not all, the information about his crimes. The Tiffany personality seemed to be the strongest of the lot, the most cognizant, and the most perceptive. That's the reason she held the knowledge that would help unlock the puzzle.

So Emmett let Tiffany talk.

"What people don't understand about Dillard is that as Theron, he might be able to grow a decent patch of lettuce, but the man was a horrible businessman. Overall, he let his buyers walk all over him."

Emmett exchanged looks with Harry, who had turned over the interview to the profiler an hour earlier. Both Emmett and Harry understood that patience would be their greatest asset. Harry bobbed his head toward Emmett, indicating he wanted him to keep at it.

"How did Dillard let the customers walk all over him?"

"They'd often place orders, but then when Dillard would fill them, they wouldn't pay full price. Dillard let them off the hook every time."

"Something you wouldn't have done?"

"Never." She tapped the side of her head, leaned in to share a secret. "You're looking at the person in charge. Dillard was simply the brawn. But he'd often mess everything up in spite of all I did to keep control of the situation."

"I see. What was Dillard's motive? I mean, explain it to me. If you and Justine are Dillard's feminine side then why abduct women? Did Dillard have sex with them?"

For the first time, the question made Tiffany visibly uncomfortable. "You just don't get it do you? Dillard had all this rage and anger inside him. It was all geared at women. Killing them was a way to get back at them for being mean to him, for rejecting him, like his mother did. His mother hated him. You know she castrated him at twelve. Just got angry with him one day and cut off his…" Tiffany stopped talking long enough to spell out the word. "P-E-N-I-S."

That statement caught both Harry, the seasoned detective, and Emmett, the long-time profiler, off guard. It took several long seconds before Emmett was able to continue. "What on earth could Dillard have possibly done to his mother to make her that angry to do such a thing?"

Now, Tiffany whispered in hush tones. "He disobeyed her. No one ever bucked up against Hester Barstow, not even her husband, Harold. Hester ruled the roost, if you know what I mean. She thought Dillard was too much of a sissy. That made Harold beat the living daylights out of Dillard, more than once."

"I see. When did the abuse begin? When did you come on the scene?"

"Hmm, let me see. Dillard was about six when I popped out one day after school, to help him deal with his mother. But I seemed to make her angrier. So you see, my presence couldn't help Dillard much. Neither could Justine's."

"How many other victims do we have out there, Tiffany?"

"You mean Dillard. How many victims does Dillard have out there?"

"Okay. So how many?"

Tiffany threw out a number.

Emmett scoffed at that, knowing she'd take his disbelief as an insult. "No way, do I believe Dillard killed thirty-eight women."

Tiffany held up a right hand. "Absolutely he did. There are at least twenty on his property right now. If you don't believe me, check it out for yourself. There's another ten or so down in Oregon, eight more in Idaho."

Emmett shot a look at the detective.

Picking up his cue, Harry turned up the heat. "This is nothing more than bragging. There's no way you'll be able to convince me that you're smart enough to get that many women to go with you."

Tiffany fluffed her hair as if the wig were still attached to her head. "It was easy when they trusted another woman."

"Is that why you kidnapped a mother with a baby? What do you have to say about that?" Harry snapped.

Tiffany rolled her eyes. "That was Justine's ridiculous notion. She wanted to try motherhood. I knew it wouldn't work, especially not with Dillard trying to pull it off."

With that declaration an argument ensued between Justine and Tiffany—Dillard's speech changing slightly for each woman's voice pattern as he went rapidly back and forth from one persona to the other.

Harry took the moment to take a break, excusing himself from the room.

Out in the hallway, Skye watched with a jumble of fascination, confusion, and a major dose of implausible skepticism. When Harry rushed past her, she called out after him, "Do you believe this guy?"

But all Harry gave her was a wave of his hand and muttered, "We're about to find out. I'm headed now to contact the authorities in Idaho and Oregon. Maybe they'll be able to search the places where Dillard Barstow used to live."

Skye turned back to the window where the man in question sat, ramrod straight, his posture perfect in the uncomfortable plastic chair, acting like several other people. "It's amazing how calm and confident he is, how arrogant. How he comes off as so much smarter than everyone else in the room. We're all idiots hanging on every word that comes out of his mouth. Watch his soulless eyes light up each time he divulges a detail."

"So you don't buy the multiple personalities?" Josh asked.

"Buy his act? Not for a minute do I believe that inside that man's body, that brain, Dillard is harboring four unique personalities. Do you? I think it's a clever attempt to set up an insanity plea down the road."

Josh twisted his mouth in thought, the nerd surfacing as he tried to make sense of it all. "Dillard's no dummy. You have only to look at his successful business to see that. As Theron King he built one of the best well-run, organic produce farms in the state. Winston and I did some research back and forth via text this morning trying to find out as much as we could about Barstow's childhood. After much digging and calling around, I finally found an aunt in rural Idaho who says that as a boy Dillard voiced early on, probably around six or seven that he would rather live life as a girl. But that freaked out his parents. They were old school and appalled at the idea that their son might even consider living his life as the opposite gender. So together, they both punished him severely and often. The aunt says they beat him regularly, trying to get him to act more like a boy than a girl."

"I see. They wanted the son they thought they had. I get it." Skye chewed her bottom lip, thinking, considering. "And do we know what happened to his parents?"

"Neighbors say Hester and Harold Barstow loaded up the car one Friday afternoon to go to a church retreat in Helena, Montana, for the weekend. It was a three and a half hour trip straight up I-15. But for some reason they veered off course. They were killed in a one-car accident on a rain-slick back road. Dillard was a freshman in college at the time, living out of state."

"Interesting. Let me guess. Dillard was their only heir and despite the friction between them, he inherited everything they owned."

Josh nodded. "The Barstows died intestate, without a will. The probate judge gave their son the bulk of their wealth and property. It totaled in the neighborhood of half a million."

"Figures. What about this aunt? No doubt she sat on the sidelines all that time remaining silent through it all," Skye said with disgust. "Watching Dillard's bruises build up. Did the boy attend school? Where were his teachers? His counselors? The school nurse? Someone should have asked them how they'd like the idea of getting a beating."

After another two hours of batting the issue around in the hallway, Emmett finally emerged from the interview room looking like the life had been drained right out of him.

Skye put a hand on his shoulder. "You okay? Harry's looking as exhausted as you are."

"We've all had a long night. This is one of the most disturbing cases I've ever encountered in all my years in law enforcement," Emmett admitted. "If Tiffany is accurate, there are far more victims than we first thought. In addition to the number on Leo's list we should look in surrounding states as far south as California and as far north as Canada."

"That's what we were afraid of," Josh said, slapping Emmett on the back. "Which means we have a lot of calls to make, a lot of law enforcement agencies to contact."

"And families," Skye added. "Someone has to let the families know."

"How many personalities have appeared so far?"

"So far, just the four, the ones you know about, two men, two women. Dillard is the youngest. Emotionally, that is. In his head, Dillard Barstow is still in his early teens. Theron King, however, is the adult male, not just a name he pulled out of a hat to put on some line for a court document either. At eighteen, around the time Dillard went off to college, the boy took on another personality that would allow him to successfully navigate dorm life and interact with his peers. Theron became the prosperous, laid-back gardener, the pensive thoughtful man who likes to read and teaches others how to grow plants at the community college three days a week."

"We have victims in and around Oregon State. Theron had to help him kill and dispose of bodies if he appeared to Dillard during his college days." Skye's patience ran to the thin side. "Listen to me, I sound like I'm buying this crap."

"Make no mistake Theron had a part in all of it, as did Tiffany and Justine. They all played their independent roles to help Dillard gain the most success in the murders. The females, however, are another fascinating aspect of Dillard's life. Those two women are already taking over for him. There's no doubt about that."

"Protecting him? How convenient," Skye asserted, reverting back to her cynical side.

Emmett shook his head. "No. Dillard hasn't had a protector since he was a small boy, if ever. It's also interesting that Dillard hasn't uttered a word since four o'clock this morning. He's either surrendering the boy entirely, or he's letting Justine and Tiffany take point. The women have been planning a total mutiny for years now so it isn't that much of a stretch."

Skye sent a furious glare toward Emmett. "Seriously? You're buying this guy's act? So if you are right, and I'm not saying you are, what happened to his Theron King personality? What did it do, go poof as soon as Harry slapped the cuffs on Dillard? Uh-uh. Not buying into this at all."

"Just hear me out," Emmett said, appealing to Skye's logic. "Unfortunately, Theron King wasn't around as long as the two females, certainly not as long as Tiffany and Justine. I'd say Theron existed for no more than ten to twelve years at most. Like I said before, Theron probably emerged during Dillard's college years because the freshman likely needed help to make his way through the stress of college life. That's about the time he got the idea to go to court to legally become Theron King. On the other hand, Justine and Tiffany have been around since he was a kid. They know all about Dillard's childhood. Those two hold his humiliations, his secrets, and all his failures."

Emmett shoved his hands in his pockets and faced Skye. "I hate to break it to you, but not all of this is an act. There's no doubt in my mind that, at this point, the male personalities, Dillard and Theron, are losing out to the stronger females, Justine and Tiffany."

"For a reason," Skye argued. "Dillard's ass is about to fry and he needs a buffer."

"I don't think so. After all these years, the women are finally moving toward total control. And they will eventually get it. A good psychiatrist could probably get the females to merge at some point and become one. That's who Dillard will eventually become."

For Skye, it all began to tumble into place. But she didn't go down that road without a fight. "So you don't think the female mannerisms are fake or the attempt at sounding like a woman is a ruse?"

"I truly don't. Theron King's already been abandoned and Dillard's on the way out. It's actually fairly typical when a child fractures into other pieces. They often do it as a coping mechanism trying to deal with a difficult home life, or in cases of severe child abuse that occurs over many years, on many levels, the child seeks an escape for the pain. It's too great for one personality to bear so they splinter into others."

"And you're convinced that's what's happening here?"

"I am. I did get some important answers to our questions. One of the reasons the coroner didn't find ID numbers on the breast implants is because Lisa, Carrie, and Taylor were all shipped to foreign buyers within a week of their abductions, Lisa to Bulgaria, Carrie to Venezuela, Taylor to Syria. Each girl was given implants at the behest of their buyers."

A sick look washed over Skye's face. "And the surgeon didn't bother using reputable equipment, let alone manufacturers."

"I'm afraid not. The upside to all this, if there is one, is that Harry seized King's work computers and his laptop at home, we should be able to track most, if not all, of his trafficking transactions."

"Just let us know how we can help," Skye said.

Emmett turned to Josh. "Did you tell her the rest? Did you mention what you came up with on your own?"

"We were just getting to it when you came out. After Dillard's booking, I heard him keep mumbling something about Oreias. Knowing that was the tag he used at the website, I looked it up on my phone. Turns out, it means 'from the mountain.' Apparently it's the name he gave to what he saw as his spirit guide."

"The panther he mentioned, his only friend. That's what he said last night. But he isn't Native American," Skye pointed out. "So where does he get off claiming he has a spirit guide?"

"No, he isn't Native. In fact, Winston discovered Barstow's maternal grandmother was Greek. She died about two years ago. Her birth name was Athena Verdalos. The ancient Greeks were known to believe in mythological figures, gods and goddesses. They passed down powerful storytelling from generation to generation, much like Native Americans. In the Greek culture the panther was considered all-powerful. My guess is that as a child Dillard simply manufactured or rather imagined a protector of sorts, his panther, Oreias."

"Okay, I have a measure of empathy for what the child endured. The castration was horrific and inexcusable. If I could I'd…" She shook her head. "I'm not sure what. But it's no excuse for becoming a serial killer."

"Agreed," Josh went on. "I also found out that in Greek, Theron means hunter. It stands to reason that as a serial killer, Dillard changed his name combining two of the most powerful things he very much wanted to become. Theron, the hunter of women, and King, the king of… Something, his own domain maybe."

"Fascinating. I'm impressed you came up with all that," Skye admitted. After much thought, she added, "That might explain the origin of the spell that afflicted you. You said it yesterday. Greeks were big believers in curses, especially against their enemies. Going all the way back to ancient civilization, they practiced their own brand of sorcery."

"Archaeologists have dug up artifacts with inscriptions proving the Greeks targeted certain people back in the day with spells and incantations. The Verdalos family came from a small town called Tyrnavos. The town's claim to fame is that Homer mentioned the area in his epic, *Odyssey*, referring to the city as Aeolia. So if the family can trace their roots back that long ago, I'd say it seems logical the grandmother might've passed down a list of centuries-old spells to her only grandson to use. And here's another interesting tidbit. Dillard Barstow's grandmother came to this country in 1945 as a young war bride after she met and married an Italian officer named Marcello Tesslo. He was stationed on Crete during the war."

"So Dillard's grandfather, this Tesslo guy, fought with the Germans?"

"Apparently the entire Verdalos clan did. Winston came across documents, declassified now, that showed the Verdalos family were huge followers of Mussolini. Somehow, despite that fact, the couple made it into the U.S. without detection and settled down in rural Idaho."

"That's where we should start, back at the beginning to try and find out where Dillard put all his Idaho victims? Has anyone tapped into that well of information yet and convinced one of his alter egos to step up and tell us that?"

Emmett was well aware by now that Skye had the patience of a raccoon about ready to tear into a sack of trash. "I'll eventually get one of them to tell me where the bodies are back in Idaho. That's where Dillard, Tiffany, and Justine started out and that's where we'll find our answers to this whole disturbing odyssey."

Josh traded glances with Emmett. "Here in Seattle we had help from Mother Nature on that score. We've been preoccupied enough that we missed the other big news story of the day." He told them about the mudslide at Lake Union and described the aftermath.

Skye's reaction was typical. "Damn. So instead of heading home for a shower and a bed like normal people, we have one more stop to make first."

Josh grinned at his wife. "I was hoping you'd say that."

The rain had stopped sometime around dawn but not before making a mess of Seattle's streets and parks. Flooding had halted traffic in downtown and the surrounding suburbs. Because of that it took them twice as long to make a trip that should've taken twenty minutes.

Once they reached Theron King's place, Skye and Josh looked on as the crime scene techs donned their protective suits to collect evidence—exposed skulls and vertebrae from various graves.

The grounds hummed with activity as the teams worked like archaeologists digging for artifacts. What they'd discovered so far was an expansive area Dillard had used for a cemetery. The tidy gardens she'd so admired the day before were now in shambles. The heavy rain had taken its toll. Mud-laden topography had opened up crevices and uncovered what Dillard had hoped to keep hidden. Mass graves.

The lack of tattered clothing near the interment sites meant that some bodies had been buried naked while other graves still held various pairs of threadbare jeans, frayed shirts and blouses, even bras and panties—the clothing still clinging to skeletal bones.

It appeared that Dillard, the serial killer, had varied his methods, depending on the victim and circumstance.

"He most likely strangled his victims with his hands or used a knife, stabbing into soft tissue," Bayliss said without being asked. "I feel comfortable saying that after eyeballing some of the remains. I'm not seeing any apparent bullet wounds on the skulls or the rest of the bones."

"This is the reason we got such a creepy feeling while we were standing here," Skye said scanning the landscape. Looking out over the grounds another thought occurred to her. "I know he owned a lucrative business and the sex trade provided ample additional income. But when you look at this place, it took a great deal of cash to continue upkeep and maintenance. I mean look at the money he poured into his gardens."

Josh scratched his head. "I'm sure Dillard always fell back on his marijuana business for extra cash."

"What?"

"You heard me. While I waited outside the interview room to talk to Harry and Emmett, I studied the satellite images of all the outlying properties Dillard owned, or rather Theron King owned." He took out his iPad to show her what he was talking about. "I captured screen shots of the ones in question." He pointed to the display. "Those are marijuana plants, massive in numbers."

Skye took the device, studied the photos. "I'll be damned. I don't know much about the drug trade but I'd say those are prime plants. Maybe I could get a few tips from Dillard, the grower. You know, for my own garden. This guy definitely has a green thumb." The words had no sooner left her lips than the shocking truth dawned on her. "Oh. My. God. You don't suppose it's because of the human remains scattered in all these places do you?"

Josh got a sick look on his face. "That's disturbing. But it might explain a few things. Who mentions that to Bayliss?"

"That there are possibly other burial sites? Not me. I don't want the medical examiner to get his panties in a wad. That guy doesn't like me as it is." Her eyes darted around the property, checking out all the places where the most thriving flowers had existed yesterday before the landslide. From memory she counted twelve spots that had seemed to flourish more than the rest. "How many bodies do you think are out there?"

"Too many. Dillard spent years using his personal landmass to bury his victims. He counted on the bodies staying put where they were. But he forgot one thing."

"Yeah. You don't mess with Mother Nature."

Epilogue

Three days later, Christmas Eve
Bainbridge Island, Washington

People could see the farmhouse lit up once they turned the corner at the end of the block. It was hard to miss. For the past couple of days, Skye and Josh had gone crazy putting up decorations—everywhere. Out on the front lawn a lighted Mr. and Mrs. Claus display, complete with reindeer, waved to neighbors. They'd strung hundreds of lights that dangled from the roofline and eaves. They'd wrapped another hundred or so around the posts on the porch. A real lush wreath, laden with berries and pinecones, set off the red front door.

By the time they'd gotten around to hunting down a tree, the selections had been dismal at best. So they'd settled for a slightly lopsided, irregularly shaped, but no less beautiful, locally grown Fraser fir. The fifteen-foot tree dominated the corner of the living room.

Santa, otherwise known as Reggie Bechtol, was a hit with the kids. Skye had arranged for him to have his own big chair next to the tree where he sat handing out candy.

Even though there was no snow in sight, *Frosty the Snowman* played in the background while guests continued to stream through the door.

Phyllis and Doug Ander walked in, immediately oohing and aahing over the festive decor. "You've done such a wonderful job on the outside. And look at that tree, Doug."

"I see it, hard not to." Doug sent a sidelong glance toward his son. "Your mother's always been a sucker for a glittery tree. You know she still insists on putting it up the day after Thanksgiving."

Josh put his arm around Skye. "Some people hit the stores on Black Friday. Not Mom. She gets up at five a.m., spends all morning dragging out the decorations from the attic, and then recruits Dad to hang the lights around the house. She makes it an exhausting, all-day event."

Phyllis cuffed her son's arm. "It's not that bad. Sue me because I get into the Christmas mood early on. You've done an amazing job here, Skye."

"Thanks. It was sort of a last-minute rush to the finish line."

Josh directed his mom and dad to the bar. "It's set up in the dining room, wine, beer, cocktails. Mom, I'm pretty sure there's a martini with your name on it in there."

Phyllis waved a hand in the air. "I haven't had anything to eat since lunch, so I'll hold off on the martini until I get something on my stomach."

Skye picked up a tray filled with appetizers. "Try one of these mini shrimp cocktails, or a cranberry meatball, or maybe the cherry-pecan Brie with these little crackers. I'm told it's tasty. And we have non-alcoholic Christmas punch to drink for the kids made with cranberry juice, lemonade, and pineapple juice. Try a glass."

"Oh, that's sounds good. I'll start with that."

Once his parents had moved on to the dining room, Josh greeted Lena and Travis with the same directive as Zoe tagged along behind.

"Do I get a beer? Maybe a rum and Coke?" Zoe piped up.

"Yeah, in about ten years," Travis shot back. "Dream on."

"Hey, I'd be an old woman by then," Zoe argued. "And it's Christmas Eve."

"Try again in another seven years," Lena said to the teen.

Zoe shrugged off the joking around and immediately launched into something else. "Lena said I might be getting some work babysitting in the future. Where's the couple with the baby?"

Skye momentarily bungled her hold on the hors d'oeuvres tray. Josh noticed, reached over and took it out of her hands before she dropped it.

"Zoe's talking about Hank and Melina and little Alec," Josh gauged. "They're standing over by the tree. Go introduce yourself."

"Where's Atka?" Again Zoe had changed topics almost in mid-sentence.

"We put her in the upstairs bedroom. Maybe in an hour or so you could free her from confinement and take her out to pee," Skye suggested.

"Sure thing."

When the trio drifted to the other room, Skye leaned in and wanted to know, "Did those three just happen to show up at the same time or did they come together?"

Josh sent her a sly grin. "They got out of Travis's truck. So…"

"Ah."

Velma overheard the exchange and raised a brow. "You two better stop gossiping. The boss it seems has a new girlfriend. Who'd have thought, he and Lena, huh? What do you think?"

"That he's finally coming to his senses," Skye joked.

Skye fixed her gaze on Harry walking through the doorway with his wife, Elizabeth. Skye offered up a wave. "What do you think about Harry retiring?"

"He'll drive me crazy," Elizabeth retorted. "All kidding aside though, it's time. After so many years the job's getting to him. And the cases just keep piling up."

"And getting weirder all the time," Josh added.

"That's the truth of it," Elizabeth agreed. "This one kept him up nights walking the floor. It's a good time for me to thank both of you for how much you've helped Harry these past few years. You've taken so much of the pressure off him that I really appreciate the job you guys do."

Skye patted Elizabeth's hand. "You forget how much Harry helped me. In those early days when I first came back to Seattle, Harry was the one who looked me up, determined to become a friend. Maybe that's because he knew I needed one."

"It's good of you to remember that," Harry finally chimed in.

Before the conversation turned overly emotional, Skye wanted to know, "So how will you spend your time? If you find yourself bored, there's always private work you could do for the foundation." She leaned in to Elizabeth. "That goes for you, too."

Harry rocked back on his heels. "We'll keep that in mind. Right now, though, the plan is to take some time off to travel. Elizabeth and I have always talked about seeing a little bit of the world other than our own boring backyard."

"We're starting with Hawaii," Elizabeth offered. "I want to see Maui before the kids decide to ship us off to a nursing home. We have reservations for March to stay in Kahului."

"Good for you," Skye said. "Be sure to send us a postcard."

The background music changed to something a tad more adult. Leon Redbone's distinctive baritone sang out with his rendition of *Let it Snow* about the time Rhonda Braddock glided into the entryway. True to her word Skye had made sure Rhonda showed up without a date.

Skye spotted Winston the moment he caught sight of his heart's desire. Rhonda had managed to squeeze herself into a low-cut, tight-fitting red dress. It would be darn near impossible for any male in the room not to notice her. Which, of course, Skye supposed was the point.

Before the programmer's eyes bugged out for real, Skye decided to dish out some advice. "Hey Winston, dig deep, find your courage to approach her. Go for what you want." When Winston stood planted in one spot, Skye took his arm. "Come on, I'll break the ice for you. But after initial contact, the rest is all up to you. And it seems you're in luck. From the looks of that outfit Rhonda's wearing, she's in a party mood."

Winston's only comment was, "She's gorgeous."

"That's a given." Skye gave him a little push toward the target. "Now shoo, go impress her with your brain." She watched Winston walk away and could only hope that Rhonda saw the intelligent side to the shy man.

"What are you thinking?" Josh wanted to know.

"That if Rhonda dares to break Winston's heart, I'll do something vile to her."

Josh grinned just as Lena circled back around sipping a vodka and tonic.

Lena glanced out into the darkness of the backyard and teased her friend, "I thought you wanted to plant a vegetable garden out back. Why haven't you done that already in your spare time?"

Skye burst out laughing. "You're kidding, right? Maybe if serial killers would take a break for a few months, I might be able to turn that patch around the pond into a decent garden. After admiring Theron King's massive gardens, minus the bones of course..." She shuddered remembering all the graves unearthed there, twenty at last count. But she refused to let evil touch the festivities tonight. "Josh even agreed to help me build raised beds to keep Atka from digging up the seeds."

"She's waiting until spring when the weather warms up. Right now she's drawing up plans to plot the ground using the 'Three Sisters' approach," Josh explained.

"I've heard of that," Lena said to Skye. "Actually, your father explained it to me yesterday when he talked about what steps he might have to take to replace Theron King's produce. He was exaggerating of course, but the system, as I understand it, is Native American and goes back centuries."

Travis came up, looped an arm around Lena's waist. "The Three Sisters concept involved planting beans, corn, and squash as an interdependent crop in a way that best served the village. Since Natives believe the bounty of the harvest was a gift from the Great Spirit, they held ceremonies before planting and when it was time to bring in the crops. They passed the knowledge down from generation to generation. There are Native people who farm in the Pacific Northwest that still use this concept today."

Skye took up the story adding her own take on what she'd learned. "Because the corn depletes the soil of nitrogen, and the beans add nitrogen to it, the combination makes for an all-around balance. They'd begin by planting the corn in the center, then move out from there to plant the beans around the base of the corn because the stalk acted like the perfect climbing pole, allowing the beans to wrap and grow up. The cornstalk trunk also acted as a shield in harsh weather, protecting the squash growing below and closer to the ground, in between the rows. In turn, the squash acted as a buffer, keeping the garden soil sufficiently moist but weed free. When you stop and think about it, the system was incredibly savvy and offered up a near perfect diet. Corn is a great carbohydrate, beans offer protein, and squash is considered a fruit with a ton of vitamins. No wonder they took time out to thank the Great Spirit with songs and legends for what generally yielded a fairly nutritious meal."

Zoe had been listening. Impressed with just about anything that came out of Skye's mouth, the teenager wanted to know, "ever think of giving up the pursuit of bad guys to be a stay-at-home mom? 'Cause it sounds like you want to go domestic."

Zoe took in the faces in the crowd and realized she might've opened her big mouth only to stick her foot in it. "Not that it's a bad thing."

Skye slung her arm over the girl's shoulder to show she wasn't upset by the question. "I've given some serious thought to it lately. Should we tell them our news, Josh?"

"Now's as good a time as any." Josh drew Skye close, raised his glass. "If you guys could give us your attention for a minute, we have an announcement."

A hush fell over the crowd as everyone gathered in a circle around the couple.

"We're happy to tell you all that we're having a baby," Skye said, clasping hands with Josh.

"What? You're adopting?" Travis asked as he pushed a few people aside in the throng to get to his daughter's side.

Skye smiled. "Not exactly, although we were prepared to do that. But it seems the Great Spirit has other plans, giving us our very own Christmas present. I'm pregnant, due next August."

Travis wrapped her up in a hug even though he had to wait to take his turn. After Phyllis and Doug let go, Travis latched on. "I thought…there was no chance of that," he whispered in his daughter's ear.

"So did we. So I phoned my doctor this morning after I took the test for the fifth time and he couldn't explain how it happened either."

Josh squeezed her a little tighter, nibbled her mouth. "However it happened, we're over the moon. We'd already discussed making an appointment with an adoption agency after the first of the year."

Lena took her turn bundling Skye up. Curiosity got the better of her though. "I'm wondering, how long have you known?"

Josh fielded this one. "A couple days. Skye hasn't been feeling well for the past week. We thought it might be stress. That business with Dillard Barstow took its toll. We decided she might be suffering from exhaustion or maybe coming down with the flu."

Skye patted his chest. "What he isn't telling you is that as the date of the party grew closer, I started freaking out a little. There were so many things I hadn't done—shopping, ordering food, getting the tree, seeing to every detail. The very last thing either one of us thought about was that I might be pregnant."

She spread her arms out wide. "Just look around though, it all came together. Josh and I discussed not telling anyone until a few months had passed but… Right before the party, we both had a change of heart. Caught up in the spirit of the holiday, I guess. Anyway, we're so happy it wouldn't be right to keep the news to ourselves. We're sharing it with the people we love. Everyone in this room at one time or another has come through for us when we needed you the most, whether it was at the foundation or something more personal. So to all of you, thanks for coming. There's plenty to eat and drink. And know that Josh and I wish you all a very merry Christmas."

Hank Fielding stepped forward holding little Alec in his arms, his other hand gripping Melina's. "My wife and son wouldn't even have a place to live if it weren't for these two. I wouldn't have a job either. I'm pretty sure everyone in the room feels the same way we do. You gave us a second chance. We're grateful for it, more than you'll ever know."

No longer shy, or introverted, Judy Howe did the same. "This time last Christmas I wouldn't have been able to leave my apartment. Tonight I'm standing in the middle of a party among people like a normal person. Because Skye and Josh caught the guy who tried to kill me, I have a chance at leading a normal life now. I've come this far because of what these two people did for me, what they do each and every day for the people of Seattle. I'm one of the success stories. The thing is, I'm not the only one."

Skye sent the woman a wide smile before extending it to the others standing around the room. "And that's one reason Josh and I intend to keep up the work. The foundation gets new volunteers who step up all the time. In the spirit of Christmas, I have to say from the heart, you're all heroes in my book."

Dear Reader:

If you enjoyed *His Garden of Bones*, please take the time to leave a review.
A review shows others how you feel about my work.
By recommending it to your friends and family it helps spread the word.
If you have the time let me know via Facebook or my website.
I'd love to hear from you!

For a complete list of my other books visit my website.
www.vickiemckeehan.com

Want to connect with me to leave a comment?
Go to Facebook
www.facebook.com/VickieMcKeehan

Don't miss these other exciting titles by bestselling author

Vickie McKeehan

The Pelican Pointe Series
PROMISE COVE
HIDDEN MOON BAY
DANCING TIDES
LIGHTHOUSE REEF
STARLIGHT DUNES
LAST CHANCE HARBOR
SEA GLASS COTTAGE
LAVENDER BEACH
SANDCASTLES UNDER THE CHRISTMAS MOON
BENEATH WINTER SAND
KEEPING CAPE SUMMER (2018)

The Evil Secrets Trilogy
JUST EVIL Book One
DEEPER EVIL Book Two
ENDING EVIL Book Three
EVIL SECRETS TRILOGY BOXED SET

The Skye Cree Novels
THE BONES OF OTHERS
THE BONES WILL TELL
THE BOX OF BONES
HIS GARDEN OF BONES
TRUTH IN THE BONES
SEA OF BONES (2018)

The Indigo Brothers Trilogy
INDIGO FIRE
INDIGO HEAT
INDIGO JUSTICE
INDIGO BROTHERS TRILOGY BOXED SET

Coyote Wells Mysteries
MYSTIC FALLS
SHADOW CANYON
SPIRIT LAKE (2018)

ABOUT THE AUTHOR

Vickie McKeehan has twenty-two novels to her credit and counting. Vickie's novels have consistently appeared on Amazon's Top 100 lists in Contemporary Romance, Romantic Suspense and Mystery / Thriller. She writes what she loves to read—heartwarming romance laced with suspense, heart-pounding thrillers, and riveting mysteries. Vickie loves to write about compelling and down-to-earth characters in settings that stay with her readers long after they've finished her books. She makes her home in Southern California.

You can visit the author at:
www.vickiemckeehan.com
www.facebook.com/VickieMcKeehan
http://vickiemckeehan.wordpress.com/
www.twitter.com/VickieMcKeehan